Losing Time

Knights in Time Series

Book 5

Chris Karlsen

Excerpt from Losing Time

"How do we get to your home from here?" Harry asked.

"This way, it's not far," Felicia told him.

It didn't take long at a fast trot to reach the stretch of road and spot where her home should've been.

"No! This can't be." She twisted in the saddle searching for any familiar sight. She kicked her mount into a gallop the direction of the Lancaster's stable.

Harry and Cedric's large destriers with their huge strides quickly caught up with her. "Where do you think to dash off to? You were warned," Harry said in a raised voice to be heard over the galloping horses.

"The stable. I'm not running off." A moment later she was there but the stable wasn't. She wheeled her mount in a circle unable to make sense of the empty countryside in front of her.

Look for Chris Karlsen's Other Titles

The Bloodstone Series
Snifter of Death
Silk
Choosing Heart or Home
Knights in Time Series
Heroes Live Forever
Journey in Time
Knight Blindness
In Time for You
Dangerous Waters Series
Golden Chariot
Byzantine Gold

Visit Chris at her website

www.chriskarlsen.com

BOOKS AVAILABLE IN EBOOK, PAPERBACK, AUDIOBOOK, and FOREIGN LANGUAGE EDITIONS

ISBN:9781728834351

:

Chapter One

Gloucestershire, England

Late morning, April-current time

Voices carried from the clearing. A woman spoke but Felicia couldn't make out what was said nor could she identify her. This area of the woods didn't get many strangers hiking through. A scientist and his team had been using almost exclusively.

The scientists played it close to the vest when asked about their project. They gave vague answers about studying the universe and often switched the conversation to more famous scientists like Neil de Grasse Tyson and Stephen Hawking. Like all villages, rumors ran rampant. The most repeated gossip had the team seeking someplace in space that could support life in case our planet became uninhabitable. No one, Felicia included, knew for certain. But if true, she couldn't care less. As far as she was concerned, she didn't want to relocate to another planet. She'd prefer for the powers that be to stop hurting this one and keep it habitable.

"Chloe, come," she ordered. Her little dachshund, true to her burrowing breed, had been furiously digging at the base of a leafy shrub. Also true to her breed, the stubborn doxie ignored the order and kept digging.

Felicia patted her thigh. "Enough digging. Let's see who's in the glade."

As Felicia came into the clearing, the makeup of the group struck her as odd, very odd. Electra and Esme, the Crippen sisters, their husbands, Roger and Stephen, and the mysterious scientists Dr. Gordon and his son, Leland, hovered around a black box the size of a car motor. The sisters had been her friends since their school days. Funny they never mentioned having business with the secretive Gordons.

The group put earphones on just as Felicia was about to call out hello. *What the devil were they up to?* As she started their way, intending to ask them what they were doing, a rabbit darted out from the undergrowth. Chloe bolted after it.

"Chloe, come back here." Felicia chased after her. The dog ran past the group and between the black box and a granite outcropping with Felicia behind several steps.

A sudden chorus of male and female voices shouted, "No!"

Started, she glanced in that direction but immediately turned back toward Chloe.

"St—"

The rest was drowned out by a an explosive crack, like lightning overhead. The ground beneath her feet rolled in a hard wavelike motion. Felicia lurched forward and landed roughly on her stomach. She hadn't time to raise her hands to break her fall. Somehow she'd managed to turn her head and her knees and forearms took the brunt of the fall. Light-headed and dizzy, she fell onto her side when she tried to rise.

"What the hell?"

She closed her eyes and took several deep, steady breaths to relieve the unsteadiness. But when she opened her eyes everything remained fuzzy. She closed her eyes again, gave them a gentle rub and then opened them. The effort worked. Where the surroundings were initially blurry a moment earlier, they were clear now. Her mouth watered as though she'd been sucking lemons. She spit and spit again, not caring if it was unladylike.

"Can someone give me a hand, please?"

No one answered or came to her aid. She looked around. Gone were the sisters and their husbands along with the Gordons and the machine.

How could everyone disappear that fast? And why? What tripped her? There was nothing out of the ordinary on the ground. Crazy. She'd ask them later. Right now, she had to find Chloe. In the area of the woods they normally walked, the clever doxie could find her way home, if she ever got away from Felicia but this area was unfamiliar to Chloe. Using the outcropping for support, Felicia scrambled to her feet.

"Chloe..." she called out and started walking the direction the dog ran, brushing herself off as she did.

She couldn't shake off the mystery of the group's disappearance. She stopped and stared back at the spot where the machine and her friends had stood. Maybe she'd been knocked out. She looked up. The sun was still directly overhead. Plus, if she'd been unconscious for any length of time, she'd feel groggier. It didn't make sense that no one came over to help her or that they'd managed to move a large piece of equipment. Once she found Chloe, she intended to find out.

"Chloe..."

Felicia climbed up the path to the old Roman road. Fortunately it saw little vehicle traffic, mostly farmers on tractors taking a shortcut from one field to another. Chloe wouldn't be in terrible danger. The road gave Felicia a better view and Chloe stood a better chance of hearing her call out.

"Chloe..." she called louder.

Hoof beats sounded behind her. Three seasons of the year the woods were a lovely sight with leafy mature oaks and alders and flowering shrubs. Locals on horseback were a common sight on the old Roman road. The nearby ruins of Elysian Fields, a medieval Norman castle, was a popular spot for riders to stop and enjoy a snack.

As she turned to ask if the riders had seen the dog, a man said, "Hold where you are." He and two riders with him eyed her up and down. They all wore medieval armor but the visors of their helms were up. The frowns on each of them deepened as they scrutinized her.

"What in our Lord's name are you?" the one who told her to hold asked.

"I could ask the same of you, but I'm not really interested. Just tell me if you've seen a small black and tan wiener dog."

"It's dressed like a man but it has butterbags," the man on the left said.

The knight in the middle nudged his horse closer. "Are you a man or woman?"

"I'll ignore the insult, as I assume butterbags refers to my breasts. Did you or did you not see a dog?"

"I've no idea what a wiener dog is but we saw no dog of any kind."

"Thanks." She turned and over her shoulder snapped, "Speaking of boobs, you Renaissance Fair buffoons might try looking up chivalry."

The lead knight wheeled his horse to block her and

the other two flanked her. "You're going with us."

"Don't be ridiculous. I'm not going anywhere with you."

He tipped his head and the third knight jumped to the ground and wrapped a powerful arm around her waist. Felicia screamed for help and fought his hold, trying to brace against it, knowing a sharp elbow would do no good against a metal breastplate. She stomped down on the top of his foot. He swore and there was a slight lessening of his hold but not enough for her to break free. She spun as best she could and punched him in the nose. He reeled and with his other hand grabbed her ponytail and pulled back hard so his face was out of reach. The second flanking knight had joined the battle and took hold of her from the other side. She kicked at them and continued to scream. Again, no one came. Together the two knights tossed her across the lead knight's saddle.

She hit the curve of the pommel below her belly button with bruising force. "Ow. Let me go. I'll have the police on you."

She searched for an unprotected part of his leg to claw at but found nothing useful. All she could do was try to wiggle and fight her way to the ground and take off running.

"Tie her up," the lead knight ordered. One of the other knights took her hands and one her feet and bound her with leather thongs.

After they mounted, the three turned toward the castle ruins. "Where are you taking me? This is insane. You can't just kidnap people. I'm a doctor. People know me. They'll report me missing."

"You're trespassing on the Baron's land. You're in the Baron's custody now. We serve him."

Baron? These guys were tinfoil-hat-wearing-super-flakes. There hadn't been a baron ruling in this area since Cromwell's time. So, where were they taking her? And, what was up with the costumes? She wasn't a litigious person by nature, but she'd sue them all for roughing her up and detaining her and delaying her search for Chloe. Whoever these guys were, they needed to go to jail and pay a heavy fine.

"Who is this Baron you allegedly serve?" She had to yell to be heard over the horses.

"Baron Guiscard's nephew Geoffrey de Sable but you will answer to his steward Richard Armstrong."

"Never heard of any of them." She decided to try a different tack other than threats. "Let me go now and I'll never speak a word of this. You go your way and I'll go mine. I need to find my dog."

"Be quiet. Your blather is annoying. I told you we didn't see a dog. I doubt there is a pup. Nor are you from this area. That is a lie. We know all who live or serve on the Baron's lands."

There weren't any noble families nearby. She couldn't imagine who the devil they were talking about. "Where does this Baron live?"

"Elysian Fields."

Elysian Fields? The old castle was rubble. Obviously, these freaks didn't know that. Fine. They were headed the direction of Elysian Fields. If they were forcibly taking her where they believed the castle existed, good. A ruin was easier to escape from than a functioning castle with its numerous servants, locking doors, and different levels. Maybe she'd catch a break and be able to slip from their grasp.

A short time later they cantered over a drawbridge. Nowhere in the immediate vicinity did a drawbridge exist. Felicia raised her head as best she could to see where the devil they were. Next they passed through a torchlit stone archway. Above, set in the stone was a grilled metal gate sharp-spiked at the bottom. *Had they gone through a portcullis?*

As they entered an open area where wooden booths lined the side, a young woman waved to the knight carrying Felicia. "Good afternoon, Harry. Will I see you after you've dropped off your prisoner?"

"Perhaps. Depends on what Richard wants to do with her...," he patted Felicia's head. "At least it claims to be a her."

The three knights stopped. The one called Harry dismounted, untied her feet, and dragged her down from the saddle. He and the others handed their reins to young men. The other two knights walked off.

Felicia froze. It didn't matter that he'd untied her feet. She was stunned, frozen by the vision in front of her. She stood in the bailey of a full blown Norman castle, the courtyard a hive of activity. The castle was an impressive medieval fortress of blonde Cotswold stone with a round keep similar to the one at Windsor. A crenellated curtain wall three stories high with towers in each corner surrounded the bailey. The castle was also three stories high with wings coming from each side of the keep. It likely had one or more levels below the main floor as well. What baffled and astonished her was the very existence of such a structure. She grew up in the area, lived and worked here. If it existed, she'd have known.

"Where...where is this place?" she asked Harry.

"Elysian Fields. I told you that's where you were being taken."

"It can't be. Cromwell's army destroyed Elysian Fields during the Civil War."

Even in the shadow of his raised visor, she saw his expression harden, a deep frown line drawing all her attention to icy green eyes. "I've never heard of any Cromwell or this Civil War you speak of. I don't know what you're playing at but I mislike it."

Felicia retreated a step. Whoever these nutbars were, reality wasn't setting well. Panic at what they fantasized to do with her consumed her for several long seconds. Harry moved toward closer. A tiny cry of protest came out, so pathetic and small it took her a second to realize it was hers. She prided herself on never being pitiful or pathetic.

"Why do you whimper? No one has hurt you," Harry said.

The comment shook her from her terrorized state. Something was wrong, very, very wrong. She had no idea what yet but she was at their mercy and figured it best for the moment to cooperate. She mustered enough strength to consider a plan. She had to find an avenue of escape other than the way they came. Too many people and guards passed through or stood around the entry. She couldn't be obvious as she searched for another way out. Feigned interest might fool crazy Harry.

"What a fine stable. It's quite large," she said, pointing to the building where the boys were leading the horses. She used the observation to try for a quick look around the stable for an opening or gate. No luck there.

"The Baron has a good contingent of knights. We

all have destriers. A large stable is necessary."

"Yes, of course," she mumbled and turned her attention to a girl leading a small herd of goats through a gate several meters past the portcullis. The girl didn't bother to close the gate behind her. The goat gate might serve as an escape. She would have to run like the wind but it was her only shot.

Felicia eyed Harry. As far as she could tell, he only carried a sword, no gun. To the best of her recollection from history class, a combination of armor and mail weighed approximately fifty pounds. She couldn't outrun a bullet but a man wearing fifty pounds of extra weight, maybe, she might as long as no one else got in her way.

She glanced to make certain the gate was still open, raised on her toes and burst forward. Two steps, that's as far as she got, two paltry steps.

Harry quickly grabbed her upper arm so hard and fast, he lifted her off her feet.

"Oh come on, Harry. Let me go before anyone gets hurt while it's still no harm, no foul."

"That's Sir Harold to you." He hustled her forward. "Come along, you mad cow. Enough of your nonsense."

****

Gloucester-current day

Leland Gordon had seen pictures of Simon, Emily's powerfully built husband that she had taken on the solar phone and sent through on the memory box. Prior to her being caught in the time tear, he'd known Emily in passing from the village.

Simon picked up his crutch and using the outcropping for support struggled to his feet. Resting a hand on his knee, Simon remained bent as he shook his head then spit a couple of times before he straightened completely. "Emily, are you and Kendrick all right?" He extended his hand and helped her to her feet. She held their toddler, Kendrick, tight to her chest as she stood.

"I think so, yes." She also spit but once on her feet, swayed. "Simon...help."

His crutch propped against his side, he wrapped his arms around her and the child. The cloth of his tunic bunched where she clutched it to keep her balance. He looked around wide-eyed. "You're home." His awed gaze landed on Esme's husband. Simon broke into a huge grin. "Stephen!"

Esme and Electra ran to the couple. "Emily let go of Simon for a sisterly group embrace. Roger led Stephen to where Simon hurried to greet his long lost friend.

A miniature black and tan dachshund came bounding out of the woods, a wildflower stuck in her collar. The dog stopped between the two groups and looked around. She trotted to the outcropping, sniffed and then began to bark and paw at the base of the rock.

"Oh, please no, that's Felicia Wycliff's dog. She plays with our boy Sammy every once in a while," Esme said. She and Leland hurried over. Esme picked the dog up and stroked her to help quiet her down. "Shh little one, it's me, Esme, Sammy's mom."

Leland turned toward the direction the dog came from. "It's the doctor's dog but she's nowhere in sight." His father, Oliver, rushed over. "I have a bad feeling," Leland told him.

"You don't have to say it, I had the same terrible thought cross my mind when we didn't see or hear the doctor appear beyond the outcropping."

The others were excitedly talking and hadn't heard Oliver or Leland's concern. "I hate to interrupt this joyous reunion but we need to ask Simon and Emily something important. Did either of you see a woman as you crossed through the passage?" Oliver asked.

Emily shook her head. "I closed my eyes and just kept my cheek plastered to Kenrick."

"I saw a flash of yellow and white but it was so fast I can't say for certain what I saw. Why?" Simon asked.

Leland exchanged a concerned look with his father. "We fear we've lost a local doctor into the time tear. Just as we powered the lightning source into the outcropping, she ran past and disappeared."

Simon spread his hands in a gesture meant to offer some relief. "I cannot say I saw a woman. I saw only a streak of white generated by I don't know what."

"The good doctor was wearing a white blouse," Oliver said with a troubled sigh.

Leland, the color drained from his face, turned back to his father. "My Lord, what have we done?"

Chris Karlsen

Chapter Two

Elysian Fields-1359

"Stop pushing me...*Harry*." Felicia attempted to wrench her arm from his grasp.

Stepping inside the great hall, Harry stopped and spun her around taking hold of her other arm too. He proceeded to shake her twice. He didn't hurt her but it did startle her enough to ramp up her fear factor.

"Stop fighting me." He gave her another small shake then his grip on her arm lightened but he continued holding onto her. "I've no desire to be overly harsh with you. I won't hesitate to force you to cooperate, should you put me in a position. I repeat. One more time, you will explain to the castle steward why you trespass on the Baron's land. If he's satisfied you pose no danger, then you will be free, *eventually*. But know this, I will argue in favor of keeping you under our watchful eye, at least for a while."

"Why? You saw I wasn't doing anything wrong. I was searching for my dog. Lord knows where she's gotten to now. If he says to let me go, please allow it. My little dog isn't use to being out on her own, please."

"Again, this mystery dog that my friends and I never saw."

"She's going to get hurt. Raccoons or foxes will attack her if she doesn't come home."

"Are you going to cry? You sound it."

No, not yet. The one thing in the world that could always make her cry was for something bad to happen to a beloved pet. "I'm afraid for her, is all."

"The creature giving you trouble?" A bald knight said and came over from a side corridor. He was one of the three who kidnapped her.

"No Cedric. But she is being a thorn in my paw about her dog. I suspect it is a ruse to gain freedom."

"It's not a ruse," Felicia insisted. "She's only ten pounds. She can't defend herself. You didn't see her because she's tiny. Oh bloody hell, talking to you two is like talking to a couple of tins of tuna." This time when she jerked to free her arm, Harry let go.

"Do you know where Richard is?" Harry asked Cedric.

"His chamber. You up for a game of Hazards? They're getting a game together in the barracks."

"I can't. I don't know what Richard will want to do with our troublesome trespasser. I may be awhile."

"Well, if you get done in a timely manner. I'm sure we'll still be at it."

"See you at the evening meal," Harry told Cedric. "Come along," Harry ordered, taking her arm in a firm hand. "And no more twaddle about your dog."

Harry rushed her through the hall where long dining tables were propped against the wall toward a rear staircase. As they quickly passed, Felicia tried to note the placement of doors and if any weapons were stashed in corners or anywhere in sight. She tried to commit to memory what she could of the room. In case this Richard fellow released her, she wanted to tell the police as much detail as possible.

The hall had numerous rectangular leaded glass windows on the eastern and western walls, positioned so that a good amount of natural light streamed into the room. Leaded glass windows during any period of time were expensive. This Baron Harry spoke of must've spent a fortune on the windows alone. A fireplace the height of a man was built into the eastern wall with an elegantly carved surround of battling knights. Tapestries covered the farthest wall. One had a Latin phrase but they went by too fast for her to read it. Not that she read Latin. She'd still like to have seen it. When or if she ever got free, she'd look up the meaning.

They climbed a spiral staircase with torches along the interior wall. Inset arrow loop windows along the exterior wall gave the castle's archers a strategic view of the bailey with no blind spots should the castle get attacked. It had been years since she'd studied the middle ages in school. She'd found the period fascinating. She remembered reading about medieval warfare strategies and how they were utilized defending various fortresses and castles.

"I'm going insane," she mumbled, realizing she'd allowed herself to forget she was a prisoner of lunatics, forget that whatever this place was, it was not the real and true Elysian Fields, medieval castle.

"What?"

"Nothing."

They stopped in front of a black oak door about eight feet tall with large iron studs and a heavy metal lock made for a skeleton key.

Harry knocked and a man inside said, "Enter."

They went inside and Harry closed the door behind them. A middle-aged man with salt and pepper hair and a well-trimmed beard seated at the desk looked up. On the corner of the desk sat a thick, white wax candle clock with the hours marked off in red wax. *A candle clock. Where does a person even buy those these days?* To Felicia's surprise, it appeared to keep fairly correct time. She didn't dare sneak a peek at her watch, fearing they might take it from her just out of nastiness. But based on her estimate on how much time passed since she lost sight of Chloe. The candle looked like it was right.

"What have you got here, Harold?"

"Good day, Richard. We found her trespassing near the woods by the old Roman Road. She claims to be looking for her dog. We never saw any dog. When we advised her she trespassed on the Baron's land, she insisted there was no Baron. Then, she even went on to tell a bizarre tale that Elysian Fields didn't exist anymore, that it was turned to rubble by someone named Cromwell during an alleged Civil War."

Richard shifted his attention from Harry to her. "You can see this building, can you not?"

"Of course."

"And us?"

"Again, of course."

"How can you claim the castle doesn't exist? Explain this Civil War and who is Cromwell?"

Harry let go of her and crossed his arms over his chest. "Yes, please explain."

"Have you never picked up a history book? Cromwell fought against King Charles, the First, in the 1600's. During the uprising he destroyed many castles belonging to nobles loyal to the king, Elysian Fields was one. There. Satisfied?"

Richard stared at her hard for a long moment. It occurred to Felicia that if they'd recreated an authentic castle in more than superficial ways, it had a dungeon. She couldn't be sure that the heat in Richard's eyes wasn't a send-her-to-the-dungeon look. The bottom line here was: if they were willing to kidnap her, what would stop them from throwing her in a dungeon? Nothing, to her way of thinking.

"Come here," Richard said at last.

She did and stood at the front of the desk.

"Give me your hand."

She reached over, and Richard took her hand and walked over to Harry. "Put your arms down and remove your breastplate." Harry did. Richard pressed her hand against Harry's chest. "Do you not feel a man's heartbeat?"

"Yes."

"He practically dragged her back to his desk and slammed her palm against the top. "Do you feel that?"

"Yes."

Still holding her hand, he pulled her with him and went over to the wall with the door and laid her hand on the stone. "Feel that?"

She nodded.

"Feel cold...hard...rough?"

"Yes."

"Like castle stone?"

"Yes."

"Then why do you tell this tale about the destruction of Elysian Fields?" His warm breath blew her bangs up, and she smelled the sweet wine he must've had earlier in the day.

Enough already. She'd had enough. "I don't know. Why do you kidnap innocent women?" She succeeded in yanking her hand from his. "I told Harry here my dog ran off. I chased after her. I was looking for her when he happened upon me. I know nothing of *this* castle, but I know what I studied about Elysian Fields. I know I grew up in this area and if this place were Elysian Fields, I'd have seen it long before this. I don't care why your lot is perpetuating this fiction. Just let me look for my dog."

Richard huffed. Defeated, Felicia's shoulders sagged. All the explaining and all she got for it was a mild huff. In the background, Harry grunted, which elevated the huff on the response rating scale.

Richard looked her up and down and up again. "What is this outfit you wear?" he asked, waggling his finger.

"What is wrong with my outfit? Never mind, don't answer. I'm sure your reason will be something lame. I was out walking my dog. What more do I need to wear other than jeans and a blouse?"

Richard walked in a circle around her and pulled once on her ponytail. He turned to Harry. "Emily and Electra wore similar clothes and their hair in a similar fashion when they first came here. Do you recall?"

"They did. I hadn't thought about it--but now that you mention it."

Emily and Electra? Emily Crippen had disappeared two years earlier after going on a picnic with Electra and Roger. He couldn't be talking about the sisters, could he? Felicia had to know. "What did this Emily and Electra look like? I might know them."

"Oh? Emily lives here with her husband, Simon. Richard went to the door and called out to a knight passing by in the corridor. "Norton, see if you can find Simon and

Emily. Bring them to me when you do," he instructed. "Let's see if you two know each other," he said, turning to Felicia.

What the hell was happening in this place? "Emily lives here?"

Richard nodded.

"For how long?"

"Going on two years. Why?"

What was this place? Nothing made sense. Had this band of crazies kidnapped Emily and been holding her? But thinking back on the day of her disappearance that didn't seem right. Felicia tried to remember what she'd read about the incident. According to the paper, Electra was with Emily the entire time. There was no mention of them being attacked. To the best of Felicia's recollection, the police also confirmed there wasn't any evidence that there'd been a struggle. Nor had anyone suggested either was abducted. Wicked gossip followed Electra and Roger when Emily disappeared. With no evidence of foul play, officially the case remained a mystery. But if she'd come here of her own free will, wouldn't Electra have said? Something was desperately wrong with this entire scenario.

Richard picked up a ewer from his desk and a goblet. "Wine?" he asked Harry.

"Please." Richard poured and handed him the goblet.

Felicia had no intention of accepting wine should he offer, which he didn't. Instead, Richard sat halfway on the corner of his desk, one butt cheek and thigh on and the other off, the way men do in offices the world over. Except instead of a shirt and tie and proper trousers, he wore a white tunic with a swan in red over a grey linen undershirt and dark grey knit hose. That and he was talking to a man dressed from a page of Ivanhoe or a book on the Crusades.

Ignoring her for the moment, Richard asked Harry, "Think the French will stay true to it?"

Harry took a swallow of wine before answering. "Hard to say. They're a cunning lot. I hope they see the wisdom of the treaty. After all, John is still Edward's unwilling guest."

From the few details mentioned, they were talking about the Treaty of London. What began as a knot of irritation in Felicia's stomach morphed into a hard ball of fear. These crazies were taking the medieval routine way too far. The Treaty of London was from the mid-1300's, for God's sake. Edward's unwilling guest, John, could only be King John of France, captured at the Battle of Poitiers.

Weird as that was, none of that insanity applied to the here and now. At this point, she'd rather not wait to see the missing Emily. She'd demand to leave, and once she was home safe and sound, she'd report what she heard to the police.

Ever so slowly, Felicia inched toward the door.

Harry's head snapped left. "Where do you think you're going?"

"Home. This is stupid. You're stupid." She jabbed the air with her finger wishing it was his chest. "This whole ridiculous business you people are up to is insane. I'm leaving. Don't you dare try to stop me." She spun and made for the door.

"Oh no you don't." Harry clamped a hand on her shoulder and forced her to turn around.

That was the last straw. She'd had enough of being manhandled by loons. As soon as she was halfway around, she punched Harry in the nose. She should've waited a fraction of a second longer and caught him square on the beezer. But in her haste, she got part nose, part cheek but it was enough to make him loosen his grip and stumble back a step.

"Witch!" He hadn't let go completely, so he tightened his grasp on her shoulder, then grabbed the other shoulder and shook her like a rag doll.

"Stop it, you brute." She kicked at his shin and had a painful run-in with metal. She bent her leg and aimed higher, hoping to hit crotch. "I'll kick you so hard, you'll squeal like a girl."

Richard broke them apart. "That will be enough of your threats and trying to escape." He slid his hand under her upper arm and ushered her to a chair across the room while Harry shot her a foul look and rubbed the sides of his nose.

"You made me shake you,' Harry said, sounding more nasal than before. "I've no desire to do such things. It's not a man's place to hurt a woman. So stop acting like a trapped badger."

"Let me go and I will." Felicia thought once she was out of there, the second thing she'd do after reporting them to the police was to take a self-defense course.

Richard poured another wine and handed it to her and then sat on the corner of the desk again. "You must reconcile yourself to the fact that you cannot run from this room or the keep for that matter without being stopped. We shall work for the truth. Who are you and how do you know Emily?"

"I am Dr. Felicia Wycliff. I've lived in this area all my life. Bring Emily here. She'll tell you who I am. I've known the Crippen family all my life. I went to school with the sisters.

Harry pulled a chair over and sat in front of Felicia.

"Now do I get to ask a question?" She held her agitation at bay as well as she could but her nerves were breaking through.

Harry sipped his wine and stared over the rim of the goblet. "No. If you know the sisters, why hasn't Emily ever spoken of you? For that matter, Electra never mentioned anyone by your name."

"I've no idea. I can't answer for them. I imagine they were as flabbergasted by you cheeseballs, to use an American term, as I am." Expressions of confusion chased the initial frowns from their faces at the term cheeseballs. "I'm positive I was one of the last people on their minds in their dealings with you."

"I know what a ball of cheese is. What is an American?" Richard asked.

"What do you mean you're a doctor?" Harry interjected, looking more confused.

"Forget the American expression. It's not important. But in spite of the period you two seem to want to be stuck in, I'm comparable to any male physician. For the record, I'm alarmed I have to explain."

This time Harry huffed. "I remind you we were supposed to be working from the truth. Physicians and doctors are not women. You might be a healer. That is the more sensible statement. We've one of those in the village. I don't see where all this loftiness on your part comes from."

"All right, playing along with your misogynistic game I'm not just any healer, Harry. I'm a healer extraordinaire."

"It's Sir Harold to you."

She stuck her tongue out and blew a raspberry his

way.

"Rude wench."

She blew a second raspberry.

A scowling Richard asked, "What is the meaning of that word you called us-mis something?"

"Misogynists."

His scowl deepened. "That sounds like an insult. Is it an insult?"

"Not to another misogynist," she said in a snippy tone, tiring of the insanity of the situation.

There was a knock on the door and Norton stepped inside. "Martin and I can't find Emily or Simon on the grounds anywhere. I sent Martin to see if they were sitting along the river with the baby."

"You checked the lists?"

"I did."

"Strange. I've never known Simon to not oversee practice. Odd. Well, send them to me as soon as they're found," Richard told him. "A healer extraordinaire eh? In what way?" he asked turning to Felicia again.

"Seems self-explanatory but I am able to cure illnesses and injuries that your village..." she almost said bumpkin but stopped herself. The healer, whoever she was, supposing their gender feminine, was probably sincere in her efforts and working with the best herbs and treatments she had available. She deserved respect and not a dismissive, snarky name. "I've learned many new means of treating injury and illness not commonly known here."

"Hah! There it is. The liar's slip of the tongue." It was Harry.

The accusation briefly knocked her for six. What had set him off? "What slip of the tongue are you on about?

Everything I said is true."

"You claimed to be from this shire. You said you grew up here and are known to all. Then, you said you have grand knowledge unknown to us. That means you've acquired it elsewhere and you must practice your healing powers elsewhere. Otherwise we'd have heard of you. You lied to us."

"I could say the same about you two and this castle. I hate to circle back to my original statement about Elysian Fields but the castle is a ruin now. I don't know what this pile of stone really is but it is not Elysian Fields. Wait until Emily sees me. She will confirm what I'm saying and who I am."

"She's never spoken such nonsense about Elysian Fields." Richard stood and gestured for Harry to join him several feet from where she sat. They whispered about her unaware of her excellent hearing. They were unsure what to do with her.

"Let me go. I'll be out of your hair in a blink," she said.

One of Harry's brows arced. "You heard us? Apparently, you did." The brow eased down as he answered his own question. "Your opinion is not required."

"I want her out of my chamber." Richard sat back down. "I've work to do and she's too much of a distraction with her silly nattering. Do something with her," he ordered with a dismissive wave of his hand.

Harry made no attempt to hide his objection to the order. "I'm no lady's maid. What if I lock her in one of the chambers until we find Emily?"

Richard gazed over at Felicia. He was working out what he wanted Harry to do, that much was clear from his hard scrutiny. Felicia guessed he might be gauging how much of a danger she presented. To her way of thinking, she obviously presented none but who knew what he imagined?

"I believe we can put an end to some of her foolish allegations while we seek Emily. It will save us time if we eliminate much of her drivel and focus on the core issue of her presence in the area," Richard told Harry.

Richard moved away from Harry to stand in front of Felicia. "You've seen your beliefs about Elysian Fields are wrong. What will you do if we show you that your cottage can't be near here or on the Baron's land either? Then will you tell us the truth about yourself, knowing that continuing with a false tale cannot benefit you?"

"How can I promise that without knowing what you intend to show me as proof?"

The two men turned their backs on her and after a bout of furious whispering, Harry said, "Get up. Can you ride?"

"It's Gloucestershire. Who doesn't ride?"

"Let's go."

"Where?"

Harry went to the door. "Your fantasy cottage."

"How do I know I'll be safe...that your intentions are honorable?"

"Either go with me or stay here locked in a chamber until Emily is brought to us. Your choice."

She only hesitated for less than a minute. If he or the other knights meant to do her harm, they had their chance when they came upon her. "I'll go with you."

Outside the castle walls she might have a small opportunity to escape. Small being a highly optimistic view of her chances but inside the walls gave her no opportunity.

They waited in the bailey while three squires brought out three saddled mounts. Two were immense warhorses, at least 17 hands high, the third was a hand shorter and had smaller bone structure. Its conformation was similar to a Thoroughbred's but with a narrower barrel and flank.

Cedric, the bald knight, joined them, taking the reins of a bay warhorse from one of the squires. "You called me away from the Hazards game for your thorn in the paw? I was winning."

"Sorry. Richard wants us to take her to the place she says she lives."

"Is it close by?"

"So she says, but..." Harry made a circular motion with his finger by his temple. "I believe, she's you know, soft in the head." He took the reins of a chestnut warhorse from another squire. Nodding to the young man holding the reins of a smaller bay, the squire held out the reins to Felicia. "Mount up," Harry ordered.

Cedric rode on her right and Harry on her left. As they approached the portcullis Harry halted and said, "If you are harboring a notion to dash off once we cross into the open, I advise you to disabuse yourself of the thought. Cedric and I will chase you down. The castle does have a dungeon. There's no guarantee you go from captive to a locked comfortable chamber. You could go to a locked, rat-infested cell. So, you best behave."

Outside the confines of the castle and across the drawbridge, at the edge of the woods, Harry stopped again. He turned to her. "When we come to the area you say you live and you see it is different than you claim, as different as your claim about Elysian Fields, I hope you are inspired to

30

be more forthcoming with the truth."

"You'll see the proof I live here. That won't affect what I know about the castle. I know what I know."

Harry turned to Cedric. "This is what I mean. She's daft. She thinks Elysian Fields is a ruin."

"She was there. She saw it wasn't."

Harry made a finger circle by his temple again. He turned back to Felicia. "Well healer, where's this cottage of yours? What village are you close to?"

"My practice is in Stroud. I live at Daffodil Cottage not far from here. It's close to the Lancaster's stable."

"What do you mean 'my practice'?" Cedric asked sharply, as though she'd deliberately tried to drop a confusing word on him.

Harry waved off the question. "Ignore it. It's more of her blather." He angled his horse across the front of hers. "I'm also interested in your reference to this Lancaster stable being close to here. This is all the Baron's land for miles and miles. There are no tenants by that name. If you know of some, they are squatting as are you."

No point in arguing with him. Let him see for himself and explain to her what he was all about, he and Richard and the rest of the costumed kidnappers. "Let's have a look, shall we?"

"We'll use the outcropping as our start point."

They rode in silence to the granite where Felicia's world turned topsy-turvy in the blink of an eye. One second she'd been running after Chloe, the next she was on the ground, disoriented and alone.

"How do we get to your home from here?" Harry asked.

"This way, it's not far. If either of you see a small,

red dog, let me know."

"Hmm, your imaginary wiener, whatever that is, of a dog," Harry commented.

It didn't take long at a fast trot to reach the stretch of road and spot where her home should've been.

"No! This can't be." She twisted in the saddle searching for any familiar sight. She kicked her mount into a gallop the direction of the Lancaster's stable.

Harry and Cedric's large destriers with their huge strides quickly caught up with her. "Where do you think to dash off to? You were warned," Harry said in a raised voice to be heard over the galloping horses.

"The stable. I'm not running off." A moment later she was there but the stable wasn't. She wheeled her mount in a circle unable to make sense of the empty countryside in front of her. "I must've taken a wrong turn somehow."

"I told you there was no family Lancaster on the Baron's land. Your cottage could not exist either or we'd have known." Harry's gaze dropped to her trembling hands. He sidled closer, close enough to reach over and place his hand on hers. "Calm yourself. You're shaking."

He was right, of course. She was a physician. She'd been trained not to panic, no matter what unexpected complication or dilemma arose. A doctor acting in panic was often more deadly than the problem.

"Let's return to the rock and ride out in a partial star formation. We'll eliminate the possibility of misdirection on her part," Cedric suggested.

"You've stopped shaking. Good." Harry removed his hand. "I think Cedric has a good idea. Once you see there is no cottage and that all you speak of is false, then we can work on the truth."

They kept going back and forth from the outcropping. Using the rock as a hub and riding out at various degrees and directions like the spokes of a bike. Nothing was where it should be. The trailers that housed the scientist's labs, the trailer Oliver Gordon lived in, her house, the Lancaster's stable and arenas, the groundskeeper's tithe cottage, the school down the road from her place, all were gone.

This cannot be. It just cannot. "Can we ride down the Old Roman road for a little way?" she asked Harry.

Harry glanced over at Cedric who gave him an I don't care shrug. "If you wish."

She was grasping at straws with the request. A kilometer away should be a signpost indicating the location of an old World War Two airfield. No one had bothered to take it down. Decades later, the sign remained with its faded spitfire painted in black and an arrow pointing to the field's site.

Deep down, she questioned the wisdom of making the side trip. Any sane person would've accepted that she'd entered the modern day version of the *Twilight Zone* just from her missing cottage and all the rest. Her world was one of scientific fact not supernatural theory or speculation. She didn't even care for movies about the supernatural. She needed to exhaust all examples of the world she knew. Until then, she couldn't begin to consider explanations for what was happening to her outside the realm of normal.

Please let the sign be there.

"This is the place," she said and brought her horse to a halt. She slid from the saddle and feeling nauseated pressed her forehead to the saddle's leather flap and closed her eyes, fearing she'd vomit. Behind her, Harry told Cedric to hold their reins.

"Felicia?" Harry stood next to her, his gauntleted hand on her back.

She opened her eyes and stared up at him. He'd never addressed her by her name. "You called me Felicia."

"Is that not your name?"

"Yes, but you never used it."

"Seemed like the right thing to do at the moment. Don't mistake kindness for weakness."

"No worries there. I don't. You surprised me. That's all."

"You're ghostly pale. Are you all right?"

"I don't know."

"What did you hope to find?"

"A sign, an old sign. Certainly not this farm." She gestured to the man ploughing a field with a large horse. Behind him, a woman planted seeds she carried in a folded apron. She wore the apron over an old-fashioned ankle length dress. It was a working farm but she'd had been down the road a thousand times and never seen the farm. It was undeveloped land owned by the Lancasters.

"Perhaps you are not in the right place. Can you have misjudged where you wanted to stop?"

"No. This is the right spot. See the cornerstone on the farmer's rock fence. The LXVI carved into it is Roman. The stone marker has been here all my life.

"I don't understand what is happening to me." Lightheaded and dizzy, she felt as though she'd risen too fast after giving blood. She took a stumbling step and grabbed onto Harry's arm but had trouble holding on because of his armor.

Harry caught her around the waist. "Hand me your

34

skin of water," Harry told Cedric.

Cedric untied the bag and gave it to Harry who pulled the cork out with his teeth. "Drink," he said, holding it to Felicia's mouth.

The water helped shake her from her shock enough to give her the courage to go back to Elysian Fields and face whatever they planned for her. Not that she'd have a choice whether to return or not.

"More?" Harry asked.

She shook her head. "No, thank you. I'd like to have a better look at the farm." She headed for the gate to the farmer's yard. She'd seen oodles of movies and knew how realistic a set designer could make a façade appear. The barn and house might be a façade. Again, deep down, she doubted it was but desperate people take hope where they can.

She entered the barn, which proved to be almost identical to modern barns with a hayloft, stalls, and basic equipment. It didn't have any power tools or equipment common to the barns she'd seen up to today.

"Do you wish to see the inside of the cottage?" Harry asked. "If so, I will get permission from the couple who live here. It wouldn't do for you to enter without permission."

Felicia shook her head. She had all the proof she needed. Sadly, this was no movie set. "I'm ready to return to Elysian Fields."

"Do you wish to speak of what is going through your head?" Harry asked as they rode the Old Roman road toward the castle.

"No." What could she say? *I don't know what the devil is happening to me. I don't have a clue who you and your friends really are. Tell them she might've sustained an* injury and was in a coma. This might be a coma induced hallucination. *I hope it is.* She'd talked to colleagues who had patients who'd come out of comas. They said the patients never remembered what went on with them mentally. She'd never done much reading on the topic. Maybe there were survivors who recalled odd dreams or hallucinations. If she came out of this, she'd definitely research the subject and write a paper for the medical journals based on her experience.

"Lady Felicia, since you claim to know many strange things, do you know what the Roman markings on the stone mean?" It was Cedric.

Lady Felicia, how grand it sounded to be greeted that way. "It's a number: sixty-six." She did a quick calculation in her head of how far a Gallic league was. "If I had to venture a guess to its meaning, I think they used it as a distance measurement to Londinium."

"Londinium? You mean London?" Cedric asked.

"Yes. That's what they called London. As I recall from reading *The Charge of the Light Brigade* and *Twenty-thousand Leagues Under the Sea,* a league equals around two-point-two kilometers. I had to look it up for classics class and London is around 145 kilometers or sixty-six leagues. I'm not sure how your group measures."

The professor was a former military man and demanded the class learn the distance so they'd appreciate how deep the Light Brigade rode into the volley of Russian cannons. She thought it weird to make them learn. The poem spoke to their courage. She didn't need to wallow in brutal detail.

Suspicion returned to Harry's eyes. "How is it you know the ancient Roman language?"

"I only know a tiny bit, some of their names for places in Britain like, London, Bath, and Chester, and numbers, and a bit of their history." She was tempted to ask how could an Englishman, like himself, not know? It was his history too, if he was indeed English. But there was no way to make that question sound anything but rude and she was still dependent on their mercy. Not to mention she couldn't be certain they were English just because they sounded it. The American actress Meryl Streep managed to sound like Margaret Thatcher.

"You speak of a light brigade and a charge. Are you referring to an army unit? We have no such brigade, no military unit by that designation." Before she could answer, Cedric continued and from the hard tone of his voice, he thought he'd trapped her in a lie about her origin. "Nor do the French have such a unit. I'm curious. Where is this brigade and tell us about this charge."

Harry shot a crooked, half smile her way. "Do tell."

"It's from a poem. You know of poets and poems, right?" They nodded. "I don't know what army the poet refers to or where the word brigade is from," she lied, telling them the poem is about a suicidal charge by the English army could only cause her trouble.

"I want to hear some of the brigade charge tale," Harry said. "Is it about cowards or brave men?"

"Very brave but most were slaughtered," she told them honestly.

"I'd still like to hear part of it."

"I can't remember it all but I can recall a stanza or two.

Half a league, half a league, half a league onward,
All in the valley of Death Rode the six hundred.

'Forward, the Light Brigade!
Charge for the guns!' he said.
Into the valley of Death
Rode the six hundred."

"What is meant by guns?" Cedric asked.

Felicia never considered if they didn't know what a brigade was, they might not know about guns. Who didn't know about guns? "It's another word the poet created," she explained, continuing with the lie. "I am not sure what he meant."

"If you don't know about a brigade or guns, how do you know the six hundred were brave and slaughtered?" Harry would ask a tough question. "While we're on the topic, what is a classics class?"

"Come on...you're having me on, now."

"Having you on? Rather ribald talk from a woman who presents herself as the opposite of willing or appealing even."

Harry's condescending tone rankled worse than the insult to her appearance. "How am I not appealing? There's nothing unattractive about me. I'll have you know loads of men find me appealing."

He eyed her up and down like he was eyeing a wet cat. "And these are Englishmen?"

"Yes."

"What do you think, Cedric," he asked his friend.

Cedric rolled his eyes. "Lady, you are dressed worse than a squire. I'll grant you're cleaner than most of our squires—,"

"Most...*most*?" she interrupted.

"Probably all, if it pleases you for me to say that. But you are far from womanly dressed. Other than a mild display of butter bags, you've not much else that stirs a man's thoughts to: ooh, I'd like to mount that."

"Stop calling my breasts butter bags. That's a disgusting expression. Can we talk about something else?"

The knights chuckled.

"You never answered my question. What is a classics class?" Harry persisted.

"It's a place I went to take lessons on literature."

"Sounds boring."

At times it was. While almost every minute of this conversation qualified as bizarre. It was turning into a day for *B words*. The thought brought her back to the possibility she'd been bonked on the head and this was, God willing, a hallucination.

When they first arrived at the castle, Harry had removed his helm. Like her hair when she wore a riding helmet, his hair was damp and stuck flat to his head. Now his dark brown hair hung loose, curling under at the shoulder. He must've run a towel over his head and combed his hair when he'd taken a few minutes to visit the privy. "Why aren't you wearing your helm?"

"I didn't feel like it, not when it's so warm out. This isn't like we're on patrol. This was a special jaunt to please you and prove a point."

She didn't need the reminder of the original purpose for the trip as it failed to prove she lived there. It stirred panicked thoughts without explanation of where her home had disappeared to. Not that she really cared but idle conversation offered a decent diversion from what might happen to her next. "You know where I'm from. Where are you two from?"

Harry answered first, "My family has a farm near

Painswick. Truth be told, I hated farming. I have two brothers and two brothers-in-law who have farms adjoining land to my father's. My dad had enough hands to help work the land that he could afford to let me leave. He asked the old Baron Guiscard if I might be allowed to serve as a squire and if I served well, become a knight in his service. The Baron agreed and I came to Elysian Fields when I was twelve summers old."

"What about you, Cedric?" Felicia asked.

"I was a foundling. I was left at the gate of Blackfriar's Monastery."

He was about 5'6, shorter than her by at least three inches. But based on the other men she saw in the bailey, Cedric was average height. What he lacked in height he made up for in mass with a broad chest, thick arms and legs, and hands like hockey gloves.

In those days, the church didn't let go of strong, young men easily. Curious as to what wicked deed got him ousted from the monastery, Felicia pressed him. "How did you wind up a knight? Why didn't the monks keep you? You look just the sort they want in their clutches."

"They'd have kept me except for my penchant for fighting, which began at an early age. In spite of innumerable thrashings from the largest of monks to whip the storminess out of me, my nature refused to change. So, they brought me to the old Baron and suggested with training I could turn my anger against the French. The Baron accepted me, and here I am."

The admission he'd had that anger in him since he was a boy sent a shiver down her spine. A deeply ingrained character flaw like that doesn't disappear with age, in her opinion. She worried he might be a wife beater. "Are you married, Cedric?"

He shook his head. "No."

"What about you, Harry. Are you married?" She asked out of simple curiosity.

"No." His gaze dropped to her hands. "You wear no ring. Are you not spoken for?"

"No."

He cocked his head to the side, then straightened and said, "Why has no man claimed you? Setting aside your odd manner of dress and less than womanish appearance, you're comely enough."

"I'll have you know, I've had several...many admirers. I haven't found any who generated special a spark."

Cedric snorted. "Special spark indeed! After a chinwag with her, they realized she was touched in the head and ran like foxes with the hounds on their heels."

"I can hear you, you know." Cedric shrugged, and Felicia turned to Harry. "Your old Baron sounds like a generous and good-hearted man."

"He was, although I didn't know him long before he died. I knew his son, Sir Guy, much better. Guy was a good man too. His wife, Shakira, was another woman who, like yourself, spoke of strange things. I never talked to her, but Stephen and Simon were her guards and they'd return to the barracks at night often baffled by her."

Shocked, Felicia inadvertently tightened her grasp on the reins. Her mount shook his head, rebelling against the action and she loosened her grip. "Sorry," she said and patted his neck. "You say Guy's wife's name was Shakira?"

"Yes. Why?"

Could it be? Was he talking about Shakira

Lancaster? What the hell? First they mention sisters named Emily and Electra. The odds of two sisters with the same names as the Crippen girls were slim to none and now a woman named Shakira was here. No, there was no way this Shakira wasn't Alex Lancaster's wife.

"You didn't speak to her but you saw her, right?"

"We both did, every day, when they weren't in London," Harry said.

"What did she look like?"

"Tall as you, straight hair black as a raven's wing, dark eyes—" He turned to Cedric. "I never did know her age, did you?"

"No." Cedric leaned forward in the saddle and scrutinized Felicia. "'Bout as old as her I'd say. What do you think?"

"Sounds right. How old are you?"

"Thirty-two."

To Felicia's chagrin, Harry and Cedric had a brief discussion whether Shakira could've been as old as that. Cedric leaned forward and gave Felicia another once over before he gave Harry a tiny shake of his head.

"We believe Lady Shakira was a few years younger than you," Harry said at last.

"I gathered as much." Felicia couldn't remember Shakira's age. They were close in age but younger by a couple of years was within the realm of reason. She pushed her vanity aside to contemplate the insanity surrounding these people and how it involved people she knew. Electra had never spoken of them nor had Shakira.

Why hadn't they mentioned their experience with this bizarre group? There were some big pieces of this puzzle missing and Felicia needed to uncover them. "When

Shakira was here was Elysian Fields the same as it is now? Did it look the same?"

"Yes."

"What did it look like when Electra was here?"

"The same," Harry said. "Why would it change? I don't understand your questions."

"I'm trying to understand a whole bunch of things. Why aren't they here anymore?"

"Electra left to live in France two years ago. Lady Shakira disappeared."

"Disappeared how?"

Harry tipped his head toward Cedric and said, "Neither of us saw the incident. Stephen and Simon witnessed the event. Guy was away and they followed her to the outcropping where we found you. Stephen said she stood there a few minutes when suddenly the earth took her and Eclipse, the horse Guy gave her. For a brief time there were whispers among some she was a witch. Rumors that the devil called her back to his lair. Guy put a swift end to them. I never heard an explanation for what really happened to her." He turned to Cedric. "Did you?"

"No. I didn't ask too many questions though. I never thought it wise considering how hard Guy took her disappearance."

"This occurred at the outcropping, you say. How odd." Felicia thought about the group hanging around the rock earlier that morning. Leland Gordon had been standing by a machine she didn't get a good look at. What were they doing?

Felicia stopped questioning the knights as far more unusual questions ran through her mind. After they rode into the bailey of Elysian Fields and dismounted, Harry instructed her to remain in the great hall. Cedric had gone off to the barracks. Minutes later Harry returned and led her to an upstairs chamber.

"Richard had wine, bread and cheese sent up to the chamber you're to rest while you await his call for you," Harry said, opening the door. "The garderobe is at the end of the corridor. I'll have the maid bring you a basin, linen, and ewer of water as well so you can wash the road dirt from your face and hands. Do not leave the room without permission. If you require anything else, there's a bell pull by the bed. A servant will attend to your needs. I will come for you when Richard is ready."

The chamber was once a woman's, that was certain. The huge bed had gold lace-covered velvet drapes on three sides with thick corded tiebacks. A plush comforter of the same gold velvet covered the bed. Pillows of embroidered silk and various tapestry patterns lay at the top. The food and wine were on a wooden table with lion's heads carved on the legs and the water basin rested in an iron stand. A wooden chest with a swan carved on the lid sat under the leaded window and two ladder-back chairs were placed in front of the table. She chided herself for assuming. *Foolish me. Nothing is certain here.*

Felicia nibbled on the cheese and bread. She hadn't realized how hungry she was until she smelled the fresh bread. The texture of it was different than any she'd had before—grainier but also richer and sweeter from using milk that wasn't homogenized.

She brought a hunk of bread and cheese with her, opened the window, and sat in the embrasure. She couldn't begin to guess what insanity the Crippens and Shakira had gotten involved in with these people. She couldn't begin to explain how everything that was part of her world hours ago had disappeared. What these folks had no control over were the skies. They couldn't tamper there without drawing government attention. The shire was on a flight pattern for Heathrow Airport. It wouldn't be long before she'd see planes overhead. As soon as she did, she'd have Harry and Richard outside looking up. Then they'd be doing the explaining.

She wasn't sure how much time passed while she sat in the embrasure. At least twenty to thirty minutes she guessed. Heathrow was one of the busiest airports in the world. In that length of time, a couple dozen planes would've passed over, yet none had. Why?

From her perch, Felicia had a panoramic view of the bailey's activities. She spent another twenty minutes or close to it watching for any slipup by one of the people below. She alternated her search between the tradesmen's booths and the people for a quick peek at a cellphone, a snippet of wristwatch edging out of a sleeve, even a bit of electrical cord hanging down.

Nothing.

She sat back, ignoring the hard, cold stone of the embrasure pressing against her spine. It's rough stone a confirmation of her new reality.

Unthinkable thoughts crept into her mind. Far-fetched and terrible thoughts that explained a world that had no explanation for the existence of a castle destroyed hundreds of years earlier. *What if the Gordons weren't working on finding a planet? What if they were working on time travel? It would explain why they were so mysterious about their work. Time travel has fascinated scientists ever since H.G. Wells wrote* The Time Machine. *Could they have discovered a means through time, a means she had mistakenly gotten caught in?*

The frightening possibility teased the edges of her mind and she pushed them away as much as she was capable. She needed to focus on the here and now. When she fell at the outcropping she knew exactly where she was. But where the hell had she landed?

Chapter Three

Gloucestershire-current time

Everyone turned to Leland and Oliver. "What are we going to do?" Electra asked.

The Gordons along with the sisters and their husbands stared at each other in breath stealing dread. Long seconds ticked by as each considered the question none could answer.

Leland and his father were the scientists. The others expected them to offer a suggestion to help Felicia, if not an answer. To his regret and shame as a man of science, Leland didn't even have a theory to offer. His two successes moving people through time involved their knowledge of the lightning machine and a ton of luck. Since Felicia had neither, he was as clueless as the others.

"I'm sorry. I don't have an idea off the top of my head. What about you, dad?"

Oliver shook his head. "Sorry."

Electra spoke again, "She'll be confused when she shakes off the dizziness of the exchange and doesn't see us. Her initial concern will take a backseat to searching for Chloe and confusion will turn to extreme distress when she can't find her. But it won't be long before she is in full panic mode as the world she knows is no longer."

"What's your point, darling?" Roger asked.

"I don't have a point. I thought it might help to talk

about what she'll go through step-by-step. Maybe an idea would come from that." Electra shrugged.

Kendrick squirmed in his mother's arms. "Down, Momma."

Emily lowered him to the ground and he ran over to Esme. He stood on his toes and lifted his arms, trying to touch Chloe. "Please, me now."

"No, son. Chloe's mommy is missing and she's scared. She might snap at you," Esme explained.

"Kendrick, come here." Emily pulled a small bunch of grapes from her pocket and gave them to him. "Stay by mummy and daddy. The effects of the exchange will be weird and unexpected, but you're right, she'll continue searching for Chloe for hours. Sooner or later, she'll go home. She's going to be out of her head scared when she discovers her home gone."

"I suspect it's worse than that," Simon said. "By this time, we've begun midday patrols."

"Armed patrols?" Leland asked.

"Naturally. It's a standard security check on the immediate area around Elysian Fields and on the tenant farmers."

The worry line between Leland's eyes deepened. "You think there's a chance she'll be found by a squad of knights?"

Simon nodded. "In all likelihood. They're bound to hear her calling to the dog. Or, they'll see her on the road. Or, as we discovered with Emily and Electra, a local farmer will detain her and send word to the castle. Knights will respond and take her prisoner."

"Will they hurt her?" Leland's expression shifted to alarm.

"Depends on how much she resists them. If she doesn't grab a pitchfork and try to run them through or do something equally foolish, they'll plunk her down in a saddle and return to Elysian Fields. Richard, the castle steward, will question her and what he decides is based on who and what he thinks she is. Normally, they'd have me report to Richard and listen to the interrogation," Simon told him, laying out the scenario.

"You didn't put us in a dungeon so I'd hope Richard would be as decent to Felicia," Emily said.

"We had time to concoct a story to explain our strange clothes and presence on Elysian Fields land." Electra smiled at Esme, who smile back at the memory of their shocking arrival. "Felicia's probably just going to get dropped into the soup. She won't think to dream up a story. She'll blurt the truth and stay with it until forced to lie."

Chloe began to wriggle and fuss. "Roger, would you happen to have anything in your car we can use as a leash?" Esme asked, struggling to keep hold of the dog. "Never mind, I'll put her in our car. Felicia takes her for rides all the time."

Oliver gestured for the others to move away from the outcropping toward the lightning machine. "We still haven't solved our problem," he said as they gathered around. "How do we get Felicia back? We need to brainstorm this and fast. We men should meet at my trailer in two hours, after Emily and Simon have gotten settled at her parent's house."

"I'll pick up Simon on the way," Roger said.

Emily raised her hands. "Hold it right there. What's this *men only* business? Why can't we come? I didn't leave one medieval world to join another where only men have valid opinions," she stressed, lowering her hands to her waist. "I'm sure my parents will be delighted to watch Kendrick, besides he's due for a nap. You're not having any discussions without we women."

"No offense meant." Roger gestured toward Simon and Stephen. "I thought we men would start on creating a plan. After all, the three of us are from that era."

"We might have useful suggestions. We want to be part of helping get our friend home."

"What do we want a part of?" Esme asked, rejoining the group.

Oliver opened his mouth to speak but Emily interrupted. "Oliver here thinks to isolate the three of us, you, me and Electra, from discussing any rescue operation. He wants it to be men only."

"She's misinterpreted my intent. I welcome you ladies. We're meeting at my trailer in two hours."

"Enough—both of you!" Leland told them. "If you want to come, then come. Dad's trailer isn't going to seat all of us comfortably. Come to my cottage. Roger you know where I live?"

"I do. I'll bring Emily and Simon. Esme can follow me with Stephen."

"Good, see you all in two hours," Leland said.

****

Oliver walked over from his trailer and helped himself to a pint of beer before sitting on one of the two chairs that faced the sofa.

Leland poured a glass of Bordeaux and took the other chair next to Oliver. "I've given this problem a lot of thought. I can't see a way for us to help Felicia unless someone goes back for her. If she knew about the memory box, we'd get a message to her or hope she'd remember and check the box. But without her knowing about the box, she has to be led out. And I've been giving that part a lot of thought as well."

"Me too," Oliver said.

Leland had left the front door open and the rest of the group walked in. "There's beer and wine on the counter. Serve yourselves. Dad and I were just discussing the fact that since Felicia doesn't know about the memory box, someone has to go back for her."

"The four of us came to that conclusion on the drive over here," Roger said.

"We did too," Stephen added.

"Process of elimination whittles the list down fast. Roger can't go, being French. They'll assume he's a spy. Stephen, for obvious reasons, no offense. The women, most certainly are all out," Leland said. "No offense to the ladies, but it's too dangerous."

The sisters didn't argue. "When whoever is going is ready, I can offer the names of one or two servants, if you're caught, that are kind. I wouldn't trust them with the truth but in general they'd not be apt to do anything wicked to you and might be able to help."

"Thank you," Leland said.

"Looks like it's Simon, Leland, and me," Oliver said as though no one could argue the decision.

"Not you, dad. You barely got out with your life last time."

Simon agreed, "That's a mad suggestion. You're too old, and you weren't a favorite of Prince Edward as it was. You'd be pressing your luck beyond measure if you were caught again."

"Steady on! I'm not *that* old."

"Dad, the point is you're older than all of us. Politics of your presence there aside, physically your age affects your ability. We also need you here to run the machine." Leland had him with the last point. Oliver had to remain behind.

"That leaves Leland and I," Simon said.

Emily bolted from the sofa down the cottage's narrow hall. She kept her head down but Leland suspected she fought tears. Her sisters must've suspected too. Esme and Electra followed her.

"Simon, as your oldest friend, I must speak honestly," Stephen said. "I don't think you should go while Emily is ill."

"I'm the best choice to help Leland. I know the lay of the land, the local people, and the dangers. I am most able to get this woman out and home again."

Oliver tapped Leland on the shoulder. "Switch seats with me."

Leland moved. Oliver took his chair and laid out reasons for Simon not to go. "All you say is true. That said, you haven't considered the arguments against your returning."

"Oliver—" Simon began to interrupt.

Leland stopped him. "Allow me to finish. Emily's illness, should it prove to be breast cancer, is serious. If so, there's a good chance it's curable but that is not an absolute. Treatment is not easy. She'll need your support. If it's not cancer, she'll still need you until she is on the mend from whatever she's suffering from."

Stephen leaned over. "Heed what Oliver tells you. You must stay for her sake. God forbid but if something happens to Emily, you'd never forgive yourself. Bear in mind, there's no guarantee Oliver can bring you back. Think of your son."

Simon listened and offered no counter to their reasons. Leland didn't want to bring up the obvious and come across as insensitive for mentioning the man's handicap. But Simon was missing his left leg from the knee down. Leland didn't doubt his skill in training knights or the man's knowledge of battlefield tactics. Both those advantages took a backseat if they found themselves in a position where they had to run from danger. Simon couldn't run with a crutch.

"Please listen to my dad and Stephen. Please stay."

Simon sighed long and hard, then said, "You're right. Emily needs me. Hopefully Kendrick won't need me in the way you suggest."

People can't *literally* feel their hair turning grey. Sitting and contemplating what he had to do, Leland swore he was an exception to the rule. He could swear he felt each of the hairs on his head going from dark to grey at the thought of executing a rescue operation using only his wits.

He wasn't like Roger or Simon or Stephen—before Stephen was blind. They were trained warriors. Leland's life from his teen years on had been filled with laboratories and white boards full of equations. He'd never been a fighter. The closest he'd gotten to being in a fight was several years earlier when he took a six-week self-defense course after he'd been robbed in London. He hated the course. Even though physical contact between instructors and students was controlled so no one was hurt, he still hated hitting people and hated being hit.

"Can you think of anyone you'd trust to tell what is

going on and who'd be a strong travel companion?" Roger asked.

"Not really. I'd have to give it some thought," Leland told him.

"Time is of the essence," Roger unnecessarily reminded him.

The sisters returned and sat down. If Emily had cried, she'd splashed water on her face so it didn't show.

Electra took a sip of wine. "Are you still talking about who should go?"

"I'm going," Leland said. An excited exchange between Simon and Roger began. "We're stuck on deciding who, if anyone, should go with me." Roger's French accent grew more pronounced with the rapid conversation that now had the women interjecting their views too.

Leland stood and stepped out onto his patio for fresh air and to clear his head. He hadn't bothered to close the slider. When he couldn't listen to the chatter anymore, he threw back the remaining wine in his glass and went inside again. He'd made a decision. He refilled his glass and standing his ground at the top of his sitting room, he said loud enough to be heard over the arguing, "Stop fighting. I'm going alone."

"No!" Ramrod straight in his chair, Oliver's face reddened and he challenged his son's decision. "I won't allow you to do that. You cannot. That is all there is to it."

"Dad, you can't stop me. I'm a grown man. It's my choice to make my own victories and my own mistakes."

"No Leland. Please, you risk too much. I will go with you," Roger said.

"Roger." Electra grabbed his arm. "You can't."

"She's right," Simon spoke up. "We're at war and

54

you are the enemy. You tempt fate to visit our soil again."

Resigned to facing the worst solo, Leland said, "None of you can come and you know I'm right. I understand the dangers. If someone trustworthy comes to mind over this evening that is approachable with the truth, I'll ask if they wish to go on an adventure-possible suicide mission. Otherwise, I'll go alone."

"What about Ian and Alex?" Roger asked Stephen. "They are men of that time originally and Alex has experience with the time portal, or whatever it is called."

"Ian is out of the country on a location shoot in Europe," Esme told him. "He'd have to go through a lot of red tape to stop production and that's time consuming."

"When Alex was thrown back in time, he was taken for Sir Guy, who the people there believe was later killed in battle. If he were to turn up now, back from the dead, I hate to think what a serious time travel can of worms that would open," Stephen said. "No way can he go."

"What's your timeframe?" Simon asked.

"I'd like to leave the day after tomorrow. I need input from you and Roger. Stephen, I'd appreciate it if you sit in too. The more information I have regarding the castle and security around Felicia, the better."

"Absolutely," Simon said. "I'll sketch out a detailed layout of the castle and grounds tonight."

"I'll bring weapons and..." Roger looked him over. "You're close to my height. I'll bring some of my old clothes so you stand a chance of blending in with the people."

Weapons. Leland hadn't given a thought to carrying weapons. In his mind, this was what Special Forces types in movies called *an extraction.* He and possibly a trusted friend would find their way into Elysian Fields, and sneak along corridors until they found the chamber where the doctor was kept. They'd wrap her in a dark cloak and return the way they came. A transfer time would be agreed upon through the memory box. In the meantime, the two or maybe three of them would hide out in the woods until the right hour. *That's* how it went in his mind.

"Weapons?" Leland repeated the word. "What sort of weapons? I've never fired a gun. I've never so much as touched one."

"Not a gun. No one mentioned a gun." Roger shot a sharp look Oliver's way. "What is it with you and your father that you're obsessed with guns?"

"You know my fondness for American gangster movies," Oliver claimed in self-defense.

"Gangster movies are neither here nor there for me. I just assumed you wanted to give me a gun because they seem to be everywhere these days," Leland said.

"I am talking about a sword and a knife, although I hate to give up my sword. My father gave it to me but..." Roger shrugged. "This cause is worth it."

Simon waved off the suggestion. He'd come through the time tear wearing his sword in case something went wrong and he needed to protect the family. "I'll give him mine. Mine is plain and carries no sentimental value to me other than it's served my purposes well."

Esme, who'd been the quietest of the group and most reticent to offer an opinion, spoke out, "A sword? Do you guys think to turn him into Jack Sparrow in a single day?"

"He needs some kind of weapon," Stephen told his wife. "If for no other reason than the sight of it might deter someone he encounters from challenging him. With no sword or knife, he's as defenseless as a kitten."

"My trip. My decision. I'll take a sword and whatever else you three think best. You're the experts," Leland said. If a sword deterred anyone from attacking him in some way, he'd carry it.

Simon rose and put his empty beer bottle on the counter. "Emily's mum is expecting all of us for dinner. We'd best be on our way."

Simon turned to Leland who'd walked them to the door. "You don't need to do this, Leland. No one will think less of you if you change your mind. We'll figure out another plan. Discuss it with your dad tonight. Roger, Stephen, and I will be back in the morning to see how you feel."

****

Leland and Oliver continued the discussion but failed to come up with an alternative plan. From a practical standpoint, in spite of lacking the advantages Simon and Roger had, Leland was still the best choice to go. What Oliver didn't know was after he left, Leland paid a visit to his best friend, Tony Halliday.

People often took Tony and Leland for brothers. Both were broad-shouldered and over six-feet in height, Tony an inch over and Leland two inches. Both had light brown straight hair. The differences came in small ways. One was coloring. Tony had an olive skin tone and dark eyes, while Leland was fair-skinned with blue eyes. Leland had a white scar across his right eyebrow where he fell from the monkey bars as a child. near-sighted, Tony wore black-framed glasses much of the time. Without them distant objects were a fuzzy blur. The farther out, the fuzzier they appeared. He had contact lenses, which he rarely wore.

Leland hadn't slept. He rose early, showered, made coffee, and waited for the others to arrive. Oliver came over. Tony showed up minutes later.

"Does this mean what I think?" Oliver asked Leland, who nodded and said, "He knows."

"All right, then. I'll make us some breakfast," Oliver said.

Leland ate a rasher of bacon. Before he dug into the scrambled eggs, a wave of nervous nausea passed over him and he was done with breakfast.

What was about to take place didn't affect Tony's appetite. He wolfed down everything Oliver made plus Leland's eggs and grilled tomatoes. When he finished, Tony took the liberty to pour all of them more coffee. "Since you did all the cooking, I'll do the dishes, Prof."

Oliver had been Tony's astrophysics professor while he worked on his PhD. He went from calling Oliver, Dr. Gordon to Prof, while he was his student and never stopped. After receiving his degree, Tony became part of Oliver's group studying time travel.

The other three arrived as Tony finished the dishes. Roger brought a duffle bag, Simon brought his sword sheathed in a leather scabbard, and Stephen came with whatever additional knowledge he had to offer.

"We were only expecting you and Oliver," Roger said. "Should we come back?"

"No. This is my friend Tony. He has been told of the situation. He is aware of the dangers involved and has volunteered to go with me." He introduced Tony to the three former knights.

Roger opened the duffle bag and retrieved two

knives and set them to the side. "Simon, you're the closest in size to Tony. Excuse the question but is your left trouser leg pinned up or cut at the knee?"

"It's loosely knotted. It can be let down."

"Good. I'm going to call Emily and have her wash the clothes you traveled in and bring them here. Stephen, can Tony use your sword?" Roger asked.

"Of course. Esme is home. Emily can stop and pick it up on her way."

Roger made the call and then came over to Leland. "Let's get your clothing situation out of the way first." He pulled out a linen undershirt from the duffle along with a plain brown tunic, knit hose, short leather boots, and a belt with two ring holders, one larger than the other that he draped over his arm. "The shirt and tunic will be loose and baggy. You're thinner in the torso than me but the length is good on the sleeves and leggings."

Leland took the clothes from him. "I'll put these on in the bedroom."

He came out a few minutes later. He'd tied the drawstring on the hose as tight as he could but it still felt like they were falling as he walked back into the sitting room.

Roger tipped his head side to side. "You look fine. Very medieval. I have to wonder tall as you are and with your shoulders, how is it that one of the weekend rugby teams haven't tried to recruit you?"

"A couple tried. I don't like sports. Most sports that is. Never have. I liked snow skiing the few times I went. I get my build from my Scottish grandfather. He's the athlete."

Stephen and Simon stood on each side of Roger quietly listening like a couple of mute bookends. Their expressions mirrored each other and made their feelings loud and clear. They wondered how a man as soft as Leland reached the age he had. Leland wouldn't disagree. From their medieval point of view the question made sense.

"What about you, Tony? How strong are you?" Simon asked then clarified, "I am...was that is, the Captain of the Guard. I train the knights at Elysian Fields and I've been a knight for many years. They are as strong and stalwart a group of men as you can imagine. That's not said to scare you but I want you to be certain of your choice."

"Leland explained the circumstances. The ability to travel through time is something I've dreamt about since I was a child. Then, I dreamt as little boys do and wished to ride dinosaurs. As I've grown older, the goal behind my dream changed but the desire remained," he said with a smile. "I can't let my best friend have all the fun or all the risk. We'll succeed or fail together."

"A noble sentiment but you didn't answer me. How strong are you?" Simon asked again.

"Suffice it to say, I'm sure if you tested me in the lists in any event you put your men through, you'd consider me a colossal disappointment. That said, I've been told none of you three can go. It's Leland and me or no one."

Stephen propped his white cane against a chair. He stepped closer to Tony and patted him down from shoulder to wrist, giving his arms an occasional squeeze. "You've a solid build. Is there no sport you are adept at?"

"Darts."

Stephen hung his head.

"God help us all." Simon sat at the dining table and spread out the drawings of the castle and its grounds he'd brought. He whispered to Roger, "What's a dinosaur?"

"Massive creatures that have been dead for sixty-five million years."

"Like dragons?"

"Kind of."

Tony helped Stephen to a chair across from Simon as everyone else came to the table.

"I'll make more coffee." Oliver went into the kitchen.

"Don't start yet. I want to change back into my own clothes before we go over everything," Leland said.

Simon laid out the map of the woods first. He began with the area of the outcropping and worked his way toward the castle. He didn't know what conditions existed today but explained the environment they'd find in 1359. Details of the castle grounds took longer and the interior the longest. Emily came and went with Simon's clothes and Stephen's sword. By the time he finished telling them about the patrols, and where and when they might run into the knights, and the best way to sneak into the bailey it was time for lunch.

After lunch Roger and Simon decided to go outside and show Leland and Tony a few defensive moves with the sword. They started with the basic maneuver of removing the sword from the scabbard in one action. The two faced each other. They demonstrated the smooth extraction and execution into a finish position to block a strike.

They did this several times before Roger asked, "Are you ready to try?"

Leland looked to Tony who nodded. "We are."

Three attempts into their efforts, Simon stopped them. "You don't have to wrench it out of the scabbard like the scabbard is on fire. Slow down. The movement will be smoother and you won't stagger off balance as the weapon is freed."

"I think we were both attempting to emulate your actions," Leland said.

"We've had years of experience. Just do it slow and right. Let's work one on one with them. Roger, you take Leland. I'll take Tony," Simon suggested.

A half-hour later Roger told them to stop. "I think the most expedient thing is to give them a ring holder for their sword. It will be less cumbersome for them than a scabbard."

"I agree," Simon said.

"Are they as bad as it sounds?" Stephen asked Oliver in a low voice but Leland still heard.

"Yes, sadly."

"You'll carry a knife mostly for eating but it's also a weapon if needed. Would you like to try some knife work?" Roger asked.

Leland looked over at Tony. Tony shrugged. Leland said, "We're game."

Oliver tied a paper target he'd drawn to a tree.

Simon demonstrated an underhanded knife throw. "Your turn." He handed the knife to Tony.

Tony hit everything but the target. On attempt number six he turned to Simon. "Can I throw overhand?"

"Sure."

He hit the target dead center. He threw several more times, hitting the center with every toss, and amazing the others judging from the wide-eyed look of surprise on their faces.

"How long have you been practicing knife throws?" the stunned Simon asked.

"Never. I threw it the way I throw darts. I'm the three-year darts champion at the Falcon's Nest pub."

"Well done, you." Roger patted him on the back and handed his knife to Leland. "Throw it anyway you prefer."

Oliver replaced the old target with a new one. Leland also threw overhand. He wasn't nearly as good as Tony but he did surprisingly better than Roger and Simon expected.

"I play at the pub too," Leland explained. "But I don't have the keen eye and wrist action Tony has. But I do get my fair share of free pints."

"That's enough for today. Speaking of a pub, shall we head over to the Falcon's Nest for a pint?" Stephen asked.

"I'll be along shortly," Oliver said and took the target down.

Leland noticed his father lingering by the tree, the target dangled from his hand, and his head was down as though he was fixated by something on the ground.

Tony stopped and called out, "You coming?"

"Go on ahead. I'll be right behind you." When the others were out of sight, Leland asked his father, "What's wrong, dad?"

"You're all I have in the world, Leland. I know what dangers you face. I'm afraid," his voice cracked. "I can live without a soul and that's what will happen if something happens to you. I'll breathe. I'll walk and talk but I will be a man whose soul is crushed." Oliver's shoulders began to shake as he spoke. The trembling increased with each declaration.

He'd never seen his father cry. Leland wouldn't let

on that he was as fearful of what he and Tony were about to do. It would only make his dad worry more. Instead, he wrapped him in a tight hug. "Don't cry, Dad. I'm going to be fine."

"You don't know that. Nobody knows that."

"I do know. In my heart, I know. I have a sixth sense for this sort of thing. You've seen it work for me. You're not going to lose me." He reassured his father hoping Oliver believed him. In truth, his heart was in his throat, and a knot the size of the outcropping had his stomach in a painful twist. He secretly swore if he got through this, he'd never gamble on anything again.

Leland let go of Oliver. "You have to see this through the right lens. Like Tony said, we've talked about this and dreamt of it for years." He gave his dad's shoulders a hard squeeze. "It's the ultimate adventure."

Chapter Four

Elysian Fields-1359

Someone knocked on the chamber door.

"Come in," Felicia called out.

Harry opened the door partway, peeked around the side, and seeing her came inside the rest of the way, leaving the door open. "Why do you not come to the door and ask who is there before granting entry?"

"What difference does it make?" she said with a shrug of one shoulder. "I figured it might be you or Richard telling me you want to talk more. Or one of the maids wishing to take the tray back or perform some other domestic duty. I didn't think it was someone intending to haul me away. If so, they'd not have bothered to knock. They'd have rushed in and dragged me off to the dungeon."

"You shouldn't assume you are safe even when behind the protective walls of the keep. For the time being you are under Richard's and my protection, Cedric's too. There are times none of us are on the grounds and you're still mostly safe, but it doesn't hurt to discern who's at the door before granting entry."

Harry had shed his armor and had donned a knee-length white tunic with an embroidered swan on a red field on the front. The tunic was worn over a white, long-sleeved shirt. Over-the-knee black boots covered his hose and were different from the boots he'd worn under his greaves. From the wear marks and creases at the ankle, these were his kicking around, everyday ones.

He walked over to the window embrasure where she still sat. He looked inside the ewer and then at the tray and saw she'd drunk two goblets of wine but hardly touched the food. "Is the fare not to your liking? Emily's sister, Electra showed our cook ways to make her dishes tastier with various spices. She's much improved."

There it was again! Proof the Crippen sisters had been here together. Electra was a sous chef at a Michelin star restaurant in Oxfordshire.

"I had some bread and cheese. I'm not very hungry at the moment. You mentioned Emily. I would still like to talk to her."

"We can't find her or her husband Simon. It's very strange. Simon missed the morning practice in the lists. He's never missed."

Harry used his arms for support and leaned over her to stick his head out the window. "Why do you sit here? There's nothing special to see," he said and straightened. "You look forlorn. Is it over the disappearance of your fantasy cottage?"

"It's not a fantasy! My world has been turned inside out and I don't know why or what to do about it." There was no point in arguing with him. "Why are you here? Am I dungeon bound after all?"

"Richard wishes to speak with you again but we have time before I take you in to see him." He moved her legs off the stone sill and sat next to her. "Tell me about your morning prior to our finding you."

"I don't see patients on the weekends so I sleep late. I didn't get out of bed until 8:30. My coffee maker is set to start brewing at 8:15, so coffee was ready. I poured a cup and let Chloe, my dog, out in the backyard. When she came back inside I gave her breakfast and made myself eggs and toast. I watched BBC News while I ate. I showered and spent the rest of the morning tidying up and doing laundry. A little before noon, I took Chloe and we went for a walk in the woods."

The puzzled look she was growing used to returned to Harry's face. "What are a coffee maker and a BBC? While you're explaining, what is a coffee?"

Would this medieval game of theirs ever end? If they thought she'd play along with all their silliness, they thought wrong. "None of that is important."

"If you say so, although I wonder why you bother to mention what is out of place then refuse to explain yourself," Harry said. His tone made his irritation clear.

"All this took place at the home you could not find and show to Cedric and me?"

"Yes."

"You saw nothing out of the ordinary in the woods? Or did something out of the ordinary happen to you? Did you fall and hit your head, perhaps?"

She started to say no but paused. The group gathered by the outcropping was a bit odd. That part of the woods is where the Oliver Gordon's group did their studies and probably conducted experiments as well. Why else have trailers that serve as labs? Why were Esme and Electra Crippen there with their husbands?

"I did fall. But I'm sure I didn't hit my head. Nothing hurt when I got up. Nothing felt bruised or banged. I was chasing Chloe but she wasn't running so fast that I had to turn on the afterburners."

"Afterburners? What is this?"

"Nothing. It's an expression. It's kind of weird because the ground around the outcropping is flat, as you know. It was like I tripped over air."

"Perhaps you are clumsier than you think."

"I'm not clumsy at all."

"Bend down."

What was he up to? She eyed him for a long moment. "Why?"

"Just do it."

"If you do anything weird, I'll bite you."

"Duly noted."

She bent only so far as to have her head level with his shoulders. If he tried anything, she was in a position to resist better. To her surprise, he gingerly ran his fingers over her head.

"I don't feel any bumps." Then, he wrapped his hands around her head. Startled, she sucked in a quick breath when he tightened his grasp. "Hurt?"

"No. Honestly, I didn't hit my head."

He moved his hands from the sides of her head to the front and back. "Now?"

"No."

He dropped his hands. "You saw nothing odd as you chased after your dog?"

She shook her head. She'd keep the sighting of Electra and the others to herself until she knew more about her status or she had a chance to talk to Emily.

"We should go see Richard now," Harry said and offered her his hand, which she took.

On the way, they ran into Cedric. "Have they found Simon and Emily yet?" Harry asked him.

"No. As a matter of fact, Richard sent out two parties of men to search for them. One to travel the river, the other to search the woods. No one has seen either since early this morning."

****

"Harry tells me your home and none of the places you spoke of exist," Richard said.

He hadn't given her permission to sit. He sat behind his carved oak desk, while Harry sat in a tall-back chair in front of the desk. She stood like a naughty schoolgirl facing the principal. Resentment bubbled up at the demeaning treatment. She had years of education in a highly respected profession. "My home exists. I don't know why it wasn't where it should've been but it exists."

"You've spoken with her the most. I trust your judgment. What is your opinion on her ravings?" Richard asked Harry.

"They're not ravings," she blurted, although perversely she had to admit to anyone but her it appeared that way.

Ignoring her outburst, Harry said, "I believe she believes what she's saying. I didn't doubt the sincerity of her dismay when she found no cottage where she claimed her home should stand."

They talked like she was third person invisible. "You two can see me, right? You do know I can hear you?"

Harry chuckled softly. "We know."

He stood and brought a matching chair to his over and set it in front of the desk. "Sit...if you wish, Milady of

Tender Feelings. There was further distress at the sight of the Yardley's farm," Harry added as she sat.

"Why would the sight of a farm trouble you? The shire is covered with them." Richard asked her, looking baffled.

No matter what she told him, he'd keep questioning her and she had reached the last of any reasonable answers to give him.

When she didn't respond right away, Richard turned to Harry. "Do you know?"

"She said no farm should exist at that spot and she expected to find a sign. She insisted on venturing into the barn to verify it was really a barn."

"What else would it be?" His expression shifted to—*you're bonkers.* "What sort of sign? Do you claim to speak to saints or see visions of them or the Lord even?"

A fresh spark of fear shot through her at the question. Whoever these people were or thought they were, they were rooted in the mindset of the middle ages when Joan of Arc claimed to hear celestial voices. It didn't work out well for Joan.

With that in mind, Felicia figured if they were going to think her mad no matter what she said; she might as well keep trudging ahead with the truth. First she'd disabuse them of any religious notions they might attach to her story. "No, I don't see or hear from saints or angels or whoever else is traipsing about heaven. I hoped to find an old airfield sign from World War Two."

"World War Two?" Richard's focus returned to Harry.

"I told you she says words without meaning and speaks of things no one has heard of. I suspect she has suffered an injury that's affected her..." Harry tapped his temple. "You know."

"Again, I can hear you and *see* you. We discussed this, Harry. I didn't hurt myself. You felt my head and didn't find any bumps and I don't have any bruises." What could she say or do to convince them something she couldn't explain had taken place? If she were in their position, she'd think she was bonkers or a liar up to no good, or worse, a witch.

"By World War Two, do you mean the Crusades? They involved many countries," Richard said.

"It's not a war I can explain to your satisfaction. Suffice it to say, I wanted to see a sign I was familiar with and it wasn't there. I know I sound weird to you both. I wish I had some logical explanation for my house disappearing and all the rest. I don't. I...I..." She couldn't stop the tears she prided herself on not shedding. They poured down her cheeks and off her chin. Fiercely wiping at them did nothing to slow the stream.

Harry grabbed a linen cloth that had been folded by Richard's wash basin and knelt in front of Felicia. He put the cloth in the palm of her hand. "I'd tell you not to cry but in my experience that order never works on a weeping woman," he said with the ghost of a smile.

She held the cloth to her eyes and struggled to take a deep breath as fear grew into a panic attack. Tightness in her chest forced her to take shallow puppy-panting breaths. "Can't breathe." A whisper was all she could manage.

"Bend down so your head is almost to your knees," Harry said. He laid a hand on her back. "Inhale a small breath as I count. Stop trying to fight for breath. Then, hold your breath while I count and at ten, let it out slowly. You need to slow your breathing down to get the air deep inside. Understand?"

She set aside the humiliation of a lay person talking her, a doctor, through her hyperventilating episode. She nodded and followed his count. On the second try, she still had to fight for a deep breath but not as badly. She did better than a moment earlier. He started over and this time it worked. Her breathing regulated.

"Sit up when you're ready," Harry said.

She straightened and wiped the damp from her face. The tears had stopped while she fought for breath. "Thank you, Sir Harold."

He laughed aloud this time. "Oh no. It's too late now for you to start calling me Sir Harold. Let us stay with Harry."

Richard had poured her a goblet filled with water and handed it to her. She hadn't realized how thirsty she was and drank all the water then set the goblet on the desk. Richard poured wine for Harry and himself and filled her goblet too. He slid the goblet over. "Wine to calm you."

"Thank you, Sir Richard. This is excellent. The wine in my chamber was too," she said after a sip. She half expected him to grant her permission to call him Richard and was disappointed when he didn't.

"The Prince brought it back from Bordeaux, our province in France.

"What do you plan to do with me?" she asked, unable to shy away from the inevitable question any longer.

"I haven't decided. Truth be told. I'm not sure what to do with you. I'll know more after I talk to Emily," Richard said. "Until then, you'll have to eat dinner tonight in your chamber. You're not dressed decently to eat in the hall."

Felicia raised her goblet. "Here's to finding Emily soon."

Harry and Richard raised their cups and drank to the wish.

****

Later that evening someone knocked again. This time Felicia asked who was at the door before she opened it.

"Come on in, Harry."

He entered and shut the door. "I see you finished most of your meal. Can I assume it was to your liking or was it simply hunger?" he asked as he passed the table.

"Both." She poured him a cup of wine without asking and another for herself.

He dragged one of the two chairs over close to the wooden chest under the window. He sat and propped his feet up on the chest. "How are you doing? No more tears?"

She shook her head. "No more tears. I'd like to assure you I am not a crier by nature but I imagine I killed my credibility in that area with this afternoon's display."

"Don't fret yourself."

"Am I correct in assuming you haven't found Emily yet since I haven't been called to Richard's chamber again?"

"You assume correctly. This is a major worry. Our search parties spoke to farmers and the villagers in the area. None have seen her or Simon. They also contacted the boatmen on the river and the fishermen. None have seen them on the river either. No strangers have been seen on the road or in the village, so we are ruling out attack by highwaymen, at least for the time being. Simon is an excellent swordsman. If attacked, he might lose to greater numbers but one of the search parties would've found a dead robber or two."

"When were they last seen?"

"The guards on the tower saw them leave shortly before midday. Not unusual. It's a lovely day for a family meal in a pretty wooded spot."

The coincidence that they were last seen around the time she found herself in this strange situation danced across her mind. She didn't give it much importance. The coincidence was so loose.

The fact Shakira disappeared in the exact place Felicia had fallen and recovered only to find herself in an unfamiliar world had to be more important.

"You said Shakira disappeared by the outcropping. Did Simon or Stephen notice anything else about the event? Anything at all."

"It happened a few years back. I have to think on what they said at the time." He took a few more swallows of wine as he quietly tried to recall the day. "The only other comment I remember, and I remember it only because it sounded odd, was Stephen said the event occurred in less than minute. He said his vision blurred. She became watery looking, like he was seeing her image through a glass pane in the rain."

Another coincidence. Dizzy and light-headed, Felicia had fought to regain her balance when she stood after the fall. Her vision had also been briefly blurred. "Huh."

She scrutinized the man in front of her. He spoke of people she knew. Two came home and one stayed. By choice? None of that information got her closer to answering what this place was exactly. Could Harry be acting a part to its extreme? If he handled a sword for most of his adult life, he'd have calloused hands.

"May I see your palms?" Felicia asked.

"Yes." He lowered his feet and scooted his chair nearer to hers. He extended his hands palms up.

She ran her fingers over his palms which were heavily calloused. She could see the rough ridges but she felt them anyway, wanting her eyes to be wrong.

"What were you looking for?" he asked when she finished.

"Callouses. If you were an actor and not a knight, you'd have soft palms."

"An actor? Like a minstrel or some such thing?"

"Sort of."

His sour expression rivaled that of a female contestant forced to eat a slug on a reality show she watched on the telly in an airport bar.

"I'm insulted. Do I look like a vagabond minstrel? Certainly not. I told you I've been in service to the Baron for twenty-two years, since I was a squire of twelve. I've never so much as wasted an hour of my time banging about on a tambourine or prancing around for coin."

Felicia gave his hand a light squeeze. She did the same with needle-phobes before she drew blood. "Don't get in a twist. I meant no offense."

"You'll be best served to refrain from calling any knight an actor. Disturbing twaddle."

"Again—sorry, Sir Harold."

"Stop the Sir Harold. I know it's insincere rubbish. I told you, stay with Harry. Before I forget, Richard said he'll send a maid with a couple of Emily's dresses tomorrow morning. He assumed she wouldn't mind if you do know each other," Harry said without removing his hand from

Felicia's.

Felicia let her hand rest on his for a moment longer before she pulled her hand back. "How kind. Emily is much shorter and fuller..." She wanted to hold her hands out to indicate more buxom but feared that would only lead to butter bag language again. "She's fuller in the middle. Her clothes may not fit well."

"Don't you sew? I can ask the maid to send along a sewing basket too and you can alter the dresses."

"If you cut yourself, I can sew you up like you've never seen. Hardly a scar. Trust me. But sew cloth? Not a chance. I'm all thumbs."

"That's right you're some kind of miracle healer. Hmmm. I'll have the maid measure you and do the alterations. I don't think Richard will send a cobbler as he hasn't heard what the Baron wishes to do with you. Cobblers are expensive and their work takes much longer than sewing dresses."

She didn't need the reminder her destiny was in the hands of a young boy Baron. "My loafers are fine."

"You call your shoes loafers? It sounds like you're wearing bread."

"A lot of what goes on here besides the language is weird to me," she said with a sigh. "Am I a prisoner? I mean, is that how Richard will describe me to the Baron?"

"He'll call you a trespasser but he will also tell the Baron that nothing you did indicated you meant to do harm to his property or people."

A trespasser. If he believed her a harmless trespasser, the Baron might decide to have Richard release her. Then what would she do? She'd already verified her home no longer existed. None of the people she knew as neighbors existed. If set free, she had no idea how to proceed. "What happens to me if the Baron says to release me?"

"Don't you wish to be free and to go about your business?"

"Not if everything and everyone I know is gone from my life. I have nothing. It's one of the reasons I'm worried about Emily's absence too. I need her counsel, desperately. How much influence did Emily's husband, Simon, have? If the Baron ordered her imprisoned or set free, could Simon plead for her?

"You said Simon oversees the knight's practice. If he was one of Shakira's guards, then isn't he a knight too? Why doesn't he participate more?"

"He lost his left leg below the knee when we fought at Poitiers. Sir Guy made provisions for Elysian Fields to serve as home to its wounded knights for the length of their life so they'd never be forced to beg. Simon's injury prevented him from performing normal duties. Richard, realizing he was too proud to not serve in some way made him Captain of the Guard."

"Very wise and kind of Richard." She smiled, struck by how matter-of-factly Harry spoke of the battle.

"You're smiling. It's the first I've seen from you. Dare I ask why?"

"I'm smiling at your description of Poitiers. You speak as though you were really there."

Harry flinched like she'd slapped him. She hadn't meant to hurt his feelings but come on. He needn't be the medieval knight every second of the day.

"I was there!"

He slid his chair so their knees touched and placing

his hand under her chin, lifted her face up a fraction. She had to look him in the eyes. "I've no reason to lie, Felicia, not about my service to the Barons of Elysian Fields. They've given me a good life and I owe them my complete loyalty. I also fought at Crecy thirteen years ago. I will continue to serve wherever the new Baron and King Edward wishes."

King Edward? He claimed Crecy was thirteen years earlier, which would make the current year 1359. She thought she'd return his warm gesture and maybe it would coax the truth from him. She lightly cupped his cheek with her palm. "Somewhere deep inside of you, you must know it isn't 1359."

A brow lifted. He ignored her comment and grinning asked, "Do you flirt with me?"

"No. I was returning your sweet gesture of touching my face." She yanked her hand away.

"Flirt if it pleases you. I've a goodly amount of lady admirers. I'm flattered to have you among them."

"Don't count me among them. It was an act of kindness, nothing more you conceited peacock."

He clasped his hand around hers. "I speak from my heart when I say I'll not challenge your protest although I believe it to be blather. As for the year, of course it's 1359. What year do *you* think it is?"

Why did this feel like a trick question? After a split second of hesitation, she said, "2018."

"No really. What year do you believe it is?"

She pulled her hand from his grasp. "2018. There's no king. Queen Elizabeth is the monarch."

Harry's expression turned serious. "I'm going to ask you a few questions. Do not take long to answer. If you do, I will know you cannot be honest about your alleged belief."

"All right. Fire away."

"Fire what?"

"Never mind. Ask what you wish."

"What is the year of your birth?"

"1986."

"You say you're a healer. Where did you learn this and how long have you been such?"

"I said I'm a doctor. I trained at Leicester Medical School and graduated in 2013. I've been a practicing doctor for four plus years."

"There is no such place." Harry pushed his chair back and stood. "I wish I understood why you cling to this tale of yours."

"While we're wishing, I wish I was home with Chloe watching reruns of *Grantchester.*"

"I assume you have been to Gloucester numerous times."

Felicia nodded. She'd been hundreds.

"You know what you think it should look like?"

"Yes."

"I'll tell the maids to work the night through and hurry and make the dress alteration for you. I want it ready by midmorning. We'll ride to Gloucester. See the town as it is. Perhaps that is the best way to convince you of the year."

New hope raised her spirit. Maybe the sight of the modern town would be the proof she needed. "We'll see it together. See who's right."

"Goodnight Felicia."

"Sleep well, Harry. Harry-" she called out as he was about to shut the door.

"Yes?"

"Since you're filling in as the Captain of the Guard, will you be sleeping in the keep or are you remaining in the barracks?"

"I'll stay in the barracks. Why do you ask?"

She didn't want to admit to him she hoped he'd be sleeping in a nearby chamber, that the possibility gave her some relief. What small measure of safety she felt in this bizarre place, she felt with him. "No reason, I was simply curious."

****

The dress was a lovely sapphire blue brocade with light blue slashes around the skirt. The color would've gone well with Emily's red hair and creamy skin tone. The length fit but the maid hadn't time to finish the bodice properly, which hung loose across Felicia's breasts and ribs.

If she read the candle clock correctly, it was near 10:00. Harry would come for her soon. She didn't know what to do with her hair so she put it in a ponytail. The same way she wore it the day before. She tried to braid it first so she drew less attention as many of the women in the bailey wore their hair in braids. Twice she attempted and twice the braid unwound and she gave up.

Someone knocked. Before she asked who it was, Harry announced himself. "May I enter?"

"Yes."

"I see you're ready and the dress suits," he said, eyeing her.

"Should I bring a skin of water or wine? I'm not sure what is normal," she asked and blew out the candle clock.

"Cedric and I have all you need. There's a tavern in Gloucester. We'll stop and have a meal when we arrive. Are you troubled by what you might find?" he asked as they walked.

"No. Yes. It's been the strangest twenty-four hours of my life. I don't know what to think or feel." As they reached the doors of the great hall, she found the courage to admit what weighed on her most of all. "Harry..."

He stopped. "Yes."

"This mystery I find myself engulfed in terrifies me. I'm afraid of what will happen next."

"Nothing bad will happen to you with Cedric and I protecting you."

"My terror goes beyond your protection," she whispered when they started walking again.

****

Felicia recognized the town they rode into as Gloucester. It was the same but different. Different in the way that nearly shattered her composure. The cathedral was as it should be and the docks located where she expected, except the boats looked nothing like the modern fishing fleet. Nor did the docks look anything like the Victorian ones of modern day Gloucester. This town wasn't as big and had no paved roads, all were dirt or cobblestones. There were no sidewalks or streetlights or traffic signals. Sheep now roamed where cars zipped around normally.

"We'll stop at the Boar's Head at the end of the street." Harry pointed to a wooden sign swinging in the breeze with a painted version of the animal's head on it.

When they reached the tavern's stable, he helped her dismount after her brief struggle with the long gown. "Well?" he asked.

Cedric stood by listening. He'd handed his reins over to a stable boy. She guessed Harry had told him what she said the year was.

"I know it's Gloucester. But it's not my Gloucester."

"Does it appear to fit the Gloucester of my time to you?"

"Yes."

Harry handed her reins and his to Cedric. "Take care of our horses too, if you will." Cedric tipped his head and left to hand them over to the stable boy.

"Still terrified?" Harry asked her.

"More than ever."

Chapter Five

Gloucestershire-current time

Roger and Oliver insisted Leland and Tony eat a hearty breakfast. "You don't know how long you'll be in the woods, waiting for the right opportunity to get to Felicia," Roger told them. "If all goes well, you'll execute a swift extraction. We'd love nothing more than to have you three back in time for dinner."

"I'd love nothing more myself," Leland replied as he carried his dishes to the sink. "I don't believe for a minute you think this will be a swift extraction." He'd tossed and turned all night but wasn't tired. Nor was he hungry but at his father's insistence, he forced breakfast down.

"You can't wear those." Oliver pointed to the glasses in Tony's shirt pocket. "You can't wear something they didn't know anything about. If you're caught, they'll turn you inside out wanting an explanation for how you got them. You have to wear contacts. I know you have a pair."

"I can't stand to wear them. I only have them in case my glasses break."

"Oliver's right," Roger said. "Wear your contacts."

Tony huffed then agreed. "I'll bring my contacts in case of a rare emergency need. I can manage not wearing my glasses. Thankfully, I don't have to wear them for everything. I've excellent close up vision."

"Tony, you can't have them on your person in any manner," Roger stressed. "If you're caught, they'll search your belongings and find the case. Don't be an idiot. Why are you fighting wearing contacts?"

"I'd rather not say."

Oliver employed the glare on Tony he developed over years of dealing with excruciatingly pompous university administrators.

Unable to endure the heat of that glare, Tony fixed his attention at a spot on the floor and mumbled, "I can't bear to stick them in my eyes."

"What?" Leland couldn't believe Tony never wore them. "Didn't you try them on at the optician's?"

Tony nodded. "Yes, and one other time when my regular glasses needed repair but not since. I can't help it. When my finger gets close, I automatically shy away." He mimicked reflexively pulling away as his finger with a contact nears.

"Get over it," Oliver said and stuck his hand out. "Give me your glasses."

Tony dug into his knapsack and handed them over.

"Did you even bring your contacts?" Leland asked. "Or are they still at your place?"

"Yes. I feared this would happen and brought them in case."

"Let me go through your knapsacks to verify what you're taking," Roger said and did. "Looks good." He turned to Oliver, "What time did you set for the transfer attempt?"

"Same as the other day, noon."

"Shall we start setting up?"

More than a little nervous, Oliver said, "Keeping busy would be a big help for me right now.

****

Elysian Fields-1359

The maid finished alterations on the second of Emily's dresses and left it on the bed Felicia's chamber. The plain wool dress with lace collar and cuffs was in a dark grey color that would flatter Emily. It would contrast nicely with her bright red hair and rosy complexion. Most grey tones washed Felicia out with her ivory complexion and blonde hair. She preferred jewel-toned colors that brightened her eyes and face and helped accentuate the highlights in her hair.

She chose to wear the grey dress, deciding to save the nicer sapphire blue one for that evening's dinner. Richard let her eat in the great hall, since she was out of the jeans she wore when they found her. Now she had a dress and was attired like a proper woman, according to Richard.

Felicia left her chamber door ajar. She expected Harry any minute. He agreed to take her wherever she wanted to go this morning. "If it will help convince you of the correct year, I'll take you to anyplace you desire within reason."

There was a knock and Harry stepped just inside. "Have you chosen a place?"

"I have. I'd told you when I arrived I had my office in Stroud. I'd like to see the town, if you don't mind."

"I'll have the horses readied."

He left before she could ask about the search for Emily and Simon. He and Richard sat next to each other at breakfast and spoke in low voices about the situation. She heard the names Emily and Simon mentioned and that more search parties were sent out. They'd been instructed to travel further than before. She couldn't hear all that was said but it was hard not to look too obvious while eavesdropping.

Yesterday, she'd spent time in the garden and walking around the bailey. People were whispering about the missing couple and speculating. One of the squires asked Cedric if he thought Simon was dead. Cedric told him no. They or someone would've found his body by now. The worry in his expression betrayed his confidence in that theory. Felicia also questioned the theory. There were a lot of ways to hide a body in the woods and a lot of animals to nibble on soft flesh. She shivered at the thought.

She joined Harry who waited in the bailey with his horse and the same one she'd been riding since arriving. "It's just us two?" she asked.

"It is. I assured Richard I thought you could be trusted not to do anything rash. Don't make a liar out of me."

"Like I said yesterday when we discussed the possibility of gaining of my freedom and why at this point I don't want it. I've nowhere to go unless there's a big, big wonderful surprise on tap in Stroud."

"I hear doubt in your voice."

She patted Harry's breastplate. "Oh Harry, doubt is an understatement."

****

On the way to Stroud, they passed two places where dual-carriageways existed, or should exist, but were farms now. Felicia said nothing to Harry and pressed on stubbornly needing to see the town for herself, afraid she already knew the depressing outcome ahead.

The acrid smell of urine and the moldy grass stench of animal fouling's assaulted her as they reached the edge of Stroud. Her vision blurred behind watery eyes before she adjusted to the odor. She recognized the other animal sharp smell for what it was: fear. She empathized.

"We are here." Harry continued along a rutted dirt road leading her first past animal holding pens. Confused lambs were separated from their mothers and the flock bleated nonstop. Sheep and goats taken from pasture bleated and paced knowing instinctually to be afraid. Felicia turned from the sight.

Once they were past the animals destined for market, the road changed to cobblestone. Booths and tradesmen's cottages lined the road. The lesser tradesmen like fletchers and tinsmiths had wooden booths attached to single room cob cottages. A handful lived in shabby huts behind their workspace. The better tradesmen, like stone masons, blacksmiths, and coopers had half-timbered black-and-white cottages, larger than their poor colleagues. The cooper displayed a row of his oak barrels in front of a home with a second story that looked to be living quarters and not a loft for winter animal feed. None of the houses had glass windows. The people weren't that prosperous. Black oak shutters covered the windows of the half-timbered homes and canvas covered most of the cob cottage windows.

They must freeze their butts in the winter, Felicia thought.

"This is the High Street," Harry said, which she assumed from the activity. "Where was your office?"

Felicia tipped her head toward the blacksmith working out of a three-sided shed on a draught horse. "There." Her office was once a Tudor guild hall converted to a medical building in the late 1970's. She shared the space with three other doctors.

"Do you wish to continue on?" Harry asked.

"For a short way more, if you don't mind." She

trotted on ahead without waiting for him to answer. She stopped about a block farther down in front of a rundown building. "What is this place?"

"The wool exchange. What did you want it to be?"

"A pub called the Drunken Puffin I used to stop in after work with friends. The owner's wife made the best bangers and mash."

"Bangers?"

"It's a type of sausage."

"By pub I take you to mean an inn?"

Distracted, not wanting to believe her own eyes, she didn't respond. There were no stockyards on the outskirts of her Stroud, none of these buildings or booths existed, and the streets were paved. Her Stroud had buildings mainly built from Cotswold stone and a few from the Victorian years in red brick. The remaining half-timbered Tudor buildings were concentrated on side streets and didn't dominate the heart of the town.

"Felicia? Did you hear me?"

"Yes, it's a kind of inn."

She took several deep breaths, trying to ease her anguish and not melt into a weeping heap. "I'd like to leave now."

They left by the same road they took into town but Harry changed directions on the way back. "I thought you might like to stop in the village near the castle and have a mug of wine before returning to Elysian Fields."

"That would be nice."

Chapter Six

Gloucester-current time

"Ready lads?" Oliver asked from behind the lightning machine.

"Ready as I'll ever be," Leland said.

Tony widened his stance and crossed his arms over his chest. "Do your worst."

Leland laughed at his friend's false bravado. Roger and Oliver just shook their heads.

"What are you playing at—the giant in Jack and the Beanstalk?" Leland asked Tony.

"Nothing wrong with looking fierce. Go on then, Prof."

"Idiot," Leland muttered.

****

The force of the charge knocked them to the ground as it had Felicia and everyone else who experienced it.

Leland's mouth watered like crazy. He spit and then rolled onto his knees but couldn't keep his balance and fell onto his side. There was a strange salty taste to the saliva as though his mouth was sweating from the heat. He spit again and again then rolled onto his knees. This time he pressed his hand to the granite outcropping for support. Too dizzy to attempt standing, he closed his eyes and counted to twenty. When he opened them again, the dizziness had passed.

Tony had managed to roll onto his knees and stay there but he leaned his whole upper body against the rock. Breathing hard and fast, he held a palm under one eye and worked to remove the contact and then repeated the same with the other eye. "My eyes. My eyes. They're on fire."

He closed his hand over the contacts. As he did his shoulders dropped, his breathing evened, he turned and swallowed several times.

Leland, still using the outcropping for support slowly stood. "Can you stand?" he asked Tony.

"Yes. I'm fine now. The heat from the machine made my eyes feel like the lightning shot straight through them," he said and stood. "I'm going put to put these away and give my eyes a rest for a bit. That should help."

"Can you see all right?"

"Well enough. I'm a tad fuzzy around the edges but if you're not asking me to read the fine print on a legal document, I'll be able to do whatever we need to."

"Let's start toward the castle. No point in delaying."

"Yeah, no point in putting off the inevitable," Tony said.

They just crossed out of the clearing with the outcropping when Leland and Tony both stopped.

"Did you hear voices?" Tony whispered.

Leland nodded. "We need to hide." He dashed for a patch of thick shrubs with Tony right behind. The shrubs were far too close to the source of the voices for Leland's comfort but they'd no time to find better concealment.

They got hunkered down as Felicia and a knight on horseback came into the clearing by the outcropping. Felicia brought her horse to a halt, looped the reins, laid them over the pommel and dismounted.

"What this? Get back on your horse," the knight ordered.

"In a minute. I just want to check out this outcropping."

"Why? What's to check out? And by that odd term I assume you mean examine it in some way."

"Yes." She ran her hands over the stone's surface, working her way from the outside in to the center.

The knight tossed his reins over his mount's neck and jumped down to the ground. He leaned against the horse's side with crossed arms. "Such interest in a rock—more madness. You caress it like the stone is a granite lover."

"What tommyrot I'm not *caressing the stone.* I'm *exploring.* There's a world of difference."

"Could've fooled me. I've been caressed by a bevy of lovelies and it looked just like your exploration." A playful wink accompanied the cheeky grin.

"You're a lusty one, Harry."

"True, I wear it well don't you think?"

"Hush up and come here. Feel this. Right here." She patted the rock. "Feel how warm it is. It's borderline hot."

"It's a sunny day. Of course the stone is warm." He huffed and pushed off from his horse. "And listen to you, Lady Lofty ordering me about."

"If you're done waffling on, feel this." She patted a spot in the center of the rock.

He removed his gauntlet and touched where she indicated. "So, the sun has warmed the stone more than usual."

"There's a noticeable difference. The top of the stone should be warmer than the center. The sun beats down on the top harder. Feel it and you'll see it isn't though."

He did.

"How do you explain that?" she asked.

"I can't. Why should I? I don't see why you feel this is of much importance."

"I don't know that it is. But I have what is...a grain of a theory and because I haven't any other ideas, I can't help feeling that someway, somehow, this outcropping is more than it appears."

"More than it appears how?"

She turned her face from him. A long moment went by where she didn't answer.

"Felicia, more than it appears how?"

Finally she turned back to look him in the eye. "Don't laugh but I wonder—" She held her thumb and forefinger close together—"a tiny bit if there isn't a force field or similar entity and that somehow caused me to wind up here, and caused Shakira to disappear."

"What's a force field?"

"An area, in this case a not too broad space surrounding this outcropping that contains an unusual form of energy. When I say energy I mean an unseen power. For whatever the reason, when I ran past and from what you said happened when Shakira disappeared, it changed where we existed. Oh, please don't look at me that way, like you believe me moon mad."

With his palm over his mouth Tony said softly to Leland, "She's going to figure it out."

Leland nodded. "Stop talking, Felicia," he whispered under his breath, willing her to sense his message.

The knight put a hand up to hush her. He cocked his head and looked their way scanning the area around the thicket where they lay. For what seemed an eternity, the knight's gaze fixed on their hiding spot.

Leland's held his breath afraid even an intake of air would bring discovery.

"Did you see something?" Felicia asked, breaking the knight's focus on their spot.

"I thought I heard someone whisper."

Leland's heart dropped from his throat to his chest again and he managed to take a quiet breath.

The knight removed his other gauntlet and tucked them into his baldric. He wrapped his arms around Felicia. "Sit with me." He guided her down so they sat at the base of the rock.

On the ground he released her but turned her face to his. "Listen to me and listen well. You must never, ever tell anyone what you just told me. Do you understand? I don't know yet what Richard plans for you. Since he is aware you have no means to support yourself or a home to return to, he'll likely let you stay at Elysian Fields. That said, if you go about telling folks this stone has this energy business, some odd field of power to send or bring people hither and thither, you will be thought mad or worse. If it is rumored you are a witch, you could die at the stake. Richard might not have the authority to override the church if the Abbot petitioned Rome and the Pope declared you a heretic witch."

She gave his chest a playful push. "Sir Harold, are you saying you'd miss me?"

"I've grown a certain fondness for you. I'd not want to see you harmed."

"I've grown a certain fondness for you, too, and

don't you dare say something utterly conceited like 'of course you would.'"

He opened his mouth to speak but kept quiet instead and simply grinned.

"Back to my thought on the stone. I didn't say the stone had the power for certain. I said, I had a grain of an idea it might, a meager trifling of a thought. You felt the center. There's no logical reason for the center to be so much warmer unless some internal force is powering through and out. Clearly, it can't be external as there's nothing visible to produce that reaction."

The knight put a finger to her lips. "You must listen to me. Do not give voice to this thought of yours again."

"There has to be an explanation for what's happened to me."

"What did you think of our village?"

Felicia smiled. "It was cute. Small, but nicer than I expected. The wine at the inn isn't nearly as good as at Elysian Fields."

"Never will be either, we bring in regular supplies from the Bordeaux. The Prince was a close friend of the late Baron's and has always been generous with us and wine from his province."

"Just for the record, I know what you're doing by changing the subject."

The knight shrugged.

"How worried are you about Emily and Simon?" Felicia asked.

"We'll continue to search but we're at a loss to explain their absence."

She looked over her shoulder at the outcropping.

"Don't say it," the knight warned.

"Fine, I'll keep my thoughts to myself. "Right now, I wish I had some chocolate. You're shaking your head. You don't know what chocolate is, do you?"

"No." He extended his hand. "Time to go, before your nonsense words overwhelm me."

Felicia and the knight mounted and rode up a path toward the Old Roman road, which Leland knew was the shortest way to the castle.

He and Tony had just crawled out from under the bushes when there was the sound of a horse coming back down the path.

"Split up," Leland said quick and low. "So we're both not caught."

The knight went straight to the shrubs where they'd been hiding. He dismounted, drew his sword and whacked the heaviest leafed branches away. He stared at the ground and then visually swept the immediate area.

It occurred to Leland he stood a good chance of being run through before their first medieval hour was up. He'd be buried in an unmarked grave. If his father arranged for a symbolic marker back home it should read: Here lies Leland Cyril Gordon, brilliant in mathematics, brilliant in science, tragic at survival.

The knight had begun poking thickets with his sword when Felicia returned. "I told you to remain on the road."

"I know. I didn't want to. I wondered what you were doing. Obviously, you thought there might be ne'er-do-wells here and you're doing your knightly duty. I figure since there's only one of you, you might need help in case you're outnumbered."

The knight laughed.

"You're laughing but I'm serious. You think, silly woman, I can't do anything, right?"

"Pray tell, milady, what is your weapon of choice?"

"My horse. I'd trample a scoundrel trying to kill you or I would've until you laughed at me."

The knight sheathed his sword and mounted his horse. "I commend your inventive and courageous spirit. You are mad." He smiled and tapped his temple. "You do know that, don't you?"

"You find me charming. I know you do," she said as she pulled at her skirt and shifted in the saddle.

"Perhaps a wee bit, when you're not giving into dangerous blather."

"That's part of my charm."

"Felicia, remember what I said."

"I know. Keep my ideas to myself."

Leland and Tony waited for several minutes after they left before they came out from hiding to make certain the knight didn't return again.

"When that knight started poking around with his sword, I thought we were finished," Tony said.

"Me too."

"At least we know they haven't hurt her, thank heavens."

"They haven't hurt her, yet," Leland said. "You heard the knight warn her about the energy field theory. She's studied enough science and her speculation is close enough for her to want to experiment with finding a way back. If she gets desperate, she'll disregard his warning. Then the church or superstitious village will demand her death."

Leland removed the map Simon drew for them. A

castle patrol would spot them on the road so they had to avoid it. The map displayed a pathway through the woods to the river. The path took longer but was safer.

"Once you reach the river," Simon had told them, "you can climb the cliff behind the castle and from there make your way to the rear gate. There's a wide path up the side but don't use it. That's for deliveries and is well monitored."

Leland had spent many pleasant family outings at the river with his parents when they were still happily married. The cliff offered no decent cover or concealment. "How will we not be seen by the fishing boats?" He'd asked. "They'll send someone to warn the castle guards of strangers approaching the rear."

"You're taking a watch?"

"Yes, a pocket watch." He showed Simon the watch.

"Wait until 3:30 to start up the cliff. The fishermen have taken their catch into market by then. The ones delivering to the castle have done so as well. That should take you about fifteen minutes. When you've reached the gate, wait until 7:00. That is the best time to try and enter the grounds. The changing of the guard occurs then and the activity at the tower posts distracts from watching the gates."

"It will still be light. Where can we hide?" Tony asked.

"The garden." Simon pointed it out on the drawing he made of Elysian Fields grounds. "The kitchen staff will have gathered what they're going to use for the evening meal by then. The storeroom is the best entry for the keep itself. With the activities of evening meal going on you should be able to slip inside. I cannot say where the doctor will be.

That information you'll have to gather on your own."

****

"What do you think?" Tony asked, eyeing the cliff from the Severn's beach. "Simon made it sound easy to scale."

"Maybe for someone like that knight fellow with Felicia but I haven't climbed, *as in climbed a bluff* since childhood."

Leland sighed. "No use whinging. This is the only way. It doesn't look so terrible. What is it? Maybe twenty feet, we can do that."

"I don't want to risk dirt in my eyes. I can't wear my contacts if I get dirt in my eyes and I might need them so I'll go first," Tony said.

Leland gave him an approximate six foot head start. At that distance, if he slipped Leland could give him an assist. As for himself, he just had to hope not to slip since there was no one to lend him a hand.

Tony placed a foot on a large dead branch but big enough to support his weight or at least it looked that way. The branch broke away from the cliff. Tony slid down within inches of Leland who reached out to help stop his slide. But Tony had managed to latch onto branch that did hold his weight.

He climbed another few feet and stuck his hand around a protruding rock to help lever himself up. A few feet from the top Kittiwakes surged from a hollow behind the rock. Protecting their nest, the birds dive bombed the climbers, pecking at their heads and screeching.

"Bloody hell," Leland cursed. He and Tony held on with one hand and batted at the birds with the other while continuing to climb.

"I can't believe we made it," Tony said when they reached the top. "I expected to fall and break something when that branch gave way."

What a nightmare scaling that beast. Fifteen minutes is all it will take you, Simon had said. Fifteen minutes my dying rear end. It didn't look *that* wicked standing on the beach." Leland ran his fingers over his head. "I'm going to get a scab I can tell. I had a bird dig its talons into my scalp, the evil creature."

They were crouched under an apple tree, one of many in the castle orchard. Leland picked one up from the ground and bit into it. "Sweet."

Tony did the same.

Leland kept checking his watch and at 6:55 they crept past the open kitchen door. As soon as they were a safe distance past the kitchen they stood and stepped toward the double doors of the storeroom.

"Where do you think to go?" A deep male voice behind them asked and the sharp point of a knife pressed into the base of Leland's spine.

Leland and Tony turned with their hands up. A bald knight held the knife against Leland. Another knight, blond and younger had his knife on Tony.

"Put your hands in front of you," the bald knight ordered and they did. "Tie them up," he told the blonde knight.

After they were tied, the knights brought them up what Leland knew was the rear staircase to the third floor. That was where the private chambers were according to the schematic Simon had drawn. He wondered why there and not to the dungeon right away but this wasn't a good time to question a stroke of luck, even if it was temporary.

The bald knight stopped in front of one of the chambers and knocked. The knight identified himself as Cedric and the other knight as Ben. He said they had two prisoners and the man inside bid them to enter.

*****

Felicia changed into the prettier sapphire dress for dinner. The maid who helped her with the million tiny buttons in the back offered to brush the days dust from the dress she'd worn earlier. Felicia gratefully accepted.

In the corridor as she headed down to dinner, she immediately stopped stunned by what she saw. Momentarily panicked, she dove into an alcove.

Leland Gordon and Tony Halliday.

Cedric and Ben were ushering Leland and Tony into Richard's chamber.

How could that be? What madness had taken over the world that they wound up here too? The heat of excitement warmed her cheeks. They'd come to rescue her. Why else were they here? Did they come to just help or did they have a certain means home?

The excitement died as fast as it hit her. Their attempt to help her might cost them their lives. What would Richard and company do to them? Richard would demand to know their purpose. What would the scientists say? If they admitted an acquaintanceship with her, however innocent, it could put her in worse danger.

Oh God, oh God, oh God.

So far Richard and by extension the Baron, had been kind to her, much in part due to Harry's influence she suspected. Her mind raced with possible outcomes of this new turn of events. She could only see two: The castle dungeon where they stood a good chance of being held and sooner or later be brought out for trial. Richard wouldn't hold them forever. He'd have no reason to think they weren't up to some nefarious deed when they were caught. In the absence of evidence to any specific wrongdoing, Richard might consider the imprisonment they've already endured enough punishment and release them. Or, in the second outcome there'd be no trial, they'd be condemned to death. Even if they never mentioned her, she'd have to step up and reveal she was acquainted with them. Either way, it wouldn't bode well for her.

She heard Richard's door close and peeked around the wall to verify the corridor was clear. On the way to the great hall, she tried and failed to think of a way to avoid the truth. Resigned, she decided her best option was to tell Harry about knowing Leland and Tony. Get ahead of the problem by giving him her version first.

Beulah, the cook, had made berry tarts for dessert. Harry dug into his and eyed another when Felicia finally mustered her courage. "Harry, I wanted to talk to you in private. Will you come to my chamber after you're finished here?"

He looked puzzled, then smiled. "Certainly."

"I'm off to my chamber. See you in a bit."

"That you will."

****

An hour passed and he hadn't shown. Felicia had never been stood up in her life. How humiliating. She poured a goblet of wine and plopped down on the bed. *How dare he?*

The knock at the door startled her. Harry cracked open the door before she asked who it was. He held a bunch of multi-colored wildflowers, probably an apology bouquet for being late.

"Hi, I thought you weren't coming," she said in a clipped, borderline snippy tone. She didn't mean to sound tense. She was but didn't want him to know it bothered her that he would stand her up.

She stood to move to one of the chairs. As he stepped close, a whiff of lavender reached her. "There's a touch of lavender about you."

He nodded. "Richard's wife loaned some of her special soap. I bathed before coming and didn't want to use the lye soap we have in the barracks."

"How thoughtful."

"I brought these for you." He handed her the flowers.

"They're lovely, thank you. I'll have the maid bring me something to put them in later." She set them on the table and turned ready to ask him to sit while she told him about Leland and Tony. As she turned, Harry enveloped her in a tight embrace complete with a deep and thorough and oh-so-well-done kiss. It took her far too long to even try to break off the kiss from the tempting knight.

When she finally did with some reluctance, truth be told, she retreated a step and said, "Harry, I...um..."

"Felicia, have I mistaken the intent of your invitation?"

"Yes." She shocked him. He looked at her with an expression of genuine surprise. Obviously he'd never been invited to a lady's chamber for a nightly visit to just talk. *Could I be more thick-witted? Had I the sense God gave a goose, I'd have thought about that when I extended the invite.* Even when he said he bathed for her and then given her flowers, the penny hadn't dropped. At the moment, she needed him to not feel bad or embarrassed and truly she didn't want to hurt his feelings. "But if it's any consolation that was the best kiss I ever had."

"You're not the first lady to tell me so."

She grinned, amused at the man's remarkable recovery ability, glad her rejection hadn't crushed him...not that she fooled herself into believing his emotions for her ran so deep. But his declaration was too bold to let slide without comment. "Honestly Harry, a few ladies may have said that but don't you think it's conceited for you to repeat it?"

"Only if it's an untrue glorification. Do you think it is—" He ran his finger along the top of the velvet collar of her dress that teased the soft skin of her throat. "—because your admiration of my ability tells a different tale? I find false modesty and the pursuit of compliments to puff one's self up far more tiresome."

From what she observed walking around the keep and bailey, he had a fair number of female fans among the ladies of the castle. "I was being truthful about your kiss."

His gaze dropped from her eyes to her lips and lifted again. "Want another just to be certain?"

"Tempting as your offer is, I need to talk to you about a totally unrelated topic. But I am sorry for the confusion."

"I'm fine." He poured himself a wine and sat. "Talk to me."

"This evening I saw Cedric and Ben brought two men they'd captured to Richard. Were you present when Richard talked to them?"

Harry shook his head. "Richard was busy and will interrogate them later. Why?"

"I know the men are strangers to you but not to

me."

"Let me guess. The men are from the same place you say you are from, the place that we cannot find."

"Yes. I don't know what reason they will give you for their presence here. I can only imagine it will sound as mad as mine. I told you I believed the outcropping contained a powerful energy that brought me here. There's good reason to think they fell victim to that energy as well. If so, they're explanation will likely sound mad too. They must be as confused as I was, as I am, about how I came to be found by you in a year that for me is over six hundred years from my time."

He took a large swallow of wine. "I hate hearing you talk of this bizarre time difference." He stretched his legs out and took another deep swallow of the wine. "Are either your lover?"

"No. I'm not in an intimate relationship with either or even close friends with them. Why are you looking at me like that? Like you don't believe me?"

"Then why are you concerned for them?"

"We are acquaintances nothing more. But I know them well enough to not want to see them harmed."

"Tell me about them."

"They're scientists working on a project involving space. The taller one is Leland Gordon. The other fellow is Anthony—Tony Halliday."

Harry pulled his legs back and half-turned so he could reach the ewer and refreshed his wine. Then he went back to stretching out. "You say Gordon is the family name of the one. Interesting. We had a man here two years ago who went by the name Oliver Gordon. He called himself a scientist. He earned his freedom by creating this thing called a periscope. He gave one to Richard for use by Elysian Fields and one for Prince Edward."

Felicia couldn't believe what she just heard. Oliver Gordon was here! Hope she'd given up on spiked through her. If he was here two years ago, he'd found a way home. Shakira did too. A means definitely existed. She had to figure it somehow.

"Did you follow him after he gained his freedom?" She hoped Harry said yes and could say where Oliver went next and what he did.

"No. He left for France with his associate, Roger Marchand and Electra."

That's four who found their way back, Felicia thought. The way out was somewhere nearby. It had to be and she had to think the outcropping was a link. Oliver and Leland and Tony worked around the outcropping. They wound up here. Why the sisters or Shakira did, she had no idea. Baby steps. One theory at a time, she reminded herself.

"I need to talk to those men first thing in the morning," she told Harry.

"Why the rush?"

"I want them to see they aren't alone. I wound up here like they did. I'd like to know what they were doing prior to finding themselves here."

"I will see if Richard agrees, but it won't be until we are through interrogating them."

When lied to, men like Harry and Richard were unforgiving. Leland and Tony might be flogged or suffer another equally horrid punishment. She had to warn them.

"They maybe too afraid to speak honestly. Let me convince them to tell the truth. I must speak to them first."

"No. Since you've told me at least part of the truth,

we will want to see what story they tell us when questioned."

"Can I at least be present? Please?"

"Maybe, if Richard agrees."

"I'd be very grateful."

His brows danced above wickedly bright green eyes. "How grateful?"

"What a devilish flirt you are."

"One of my many skills."

Chapter Seven

Elysian Fields dungeon, 1359

"We never discussed a cover story in case we were captured," Tony said.

"All that we prepared for in the rush to leave, how idiotic to forget a logical excuse for being on the Baron's land." Tony massaged the bridge of his nose. "Are you having trouble breathing? You sound like you're all plugged up," Leland asked.

"The damp is aggravating my sinuses. I can't breathe through my nose at all. I hope whatever they do to us, they move us out of here before this sinus issue turns into an infection."

"Don't wish too hard. We could find ourselves at the end of a rope. As to a story, got any ideas?"

Tony pressed a finger against one nostril and held the hem of his tunic up to the other. He tried to blow but it didn't work. "Damn." He dropped his tunic hem and hand. "I haven't a clue, but I'd leave out we're time travelers from any explanation."

"Why'd I bring you? I can come up with lame suggestions on my own." Leland hadn't slept and spent the night racking his brain for a reasonable story. Over the last three nights, preparing for the journey and now here, he had maybe slept four hours. Worry and nerves kept exhaustion at bay.

"I can't tell them my real name," Leland said.

"Why?"

"They know my dad, remember? They believe he's in France with Roger. If they know we're related, they'll send a messenger there telling him they're holding me prisoner and expect him to come. What happens when the messenger doesn't find him or Roger? How do I explain his absence in addition to our presence?"

"People often take us for brothers. Let's tell them that. You can be Leland Halliday."

"From?"

"Electra said she and Emily claimed to be from Greenland. They doubted anyone here knew much if anything about the place and would believe whatever they said about the land."

"Sounds good. Do you know anything about Greenland? Because I don't, other than it is a big island between here and Canada."

Tony shook his head. "No, just that it's cold. Does it have Eskimos?"

"How do I know? Don't volunteer information they don't ask for."

"What if Felicia didn't mention Greenland? She doesn't know what Electra told them. If we say we came from there and she's told them different, we're going to be in a world of hurt," Tony said.

Leland stood and bent side to side and then forward to touch his toes. Straightening, he said, "She won't be there for our questioning. Please, these medieval men aren't going to allow a woman to listen in on an interrogation. By the time she's told we're here, if she's told, they'll say we said we came from Greenland. She's smart. She'll play along."

"When they don't hear from us, how long do you think your dad and the others will wait before they send a rescue party?"

A rescue party. The prospect was both a relief and an embarrassment. Here he and Tony were, healthy, intelligent men, the designated rescue party in desperate need of rescue themselves. The men who came would no doubt be the handicapped Simon and Roger, the English enemy, whose life was on the line if he returned. That only added to Leland's shame.

"If my dad has his way, I'd say three days. If Simon and Roger and Stephen can control him, they'll lean toward giving us a little more time, four or five days. I think Roger has the best understanding of our limitations. We're not resourceful knights."

A guard entered the passageway. He brought a fresh bucket of water, a loaf of bread, and four apples covered in bruises. He opened the cell door just far enough to place the food and water inside. He yanked a linen cloth off his shoulder and tossed it to Leland. "Wash the dungeon filth from your faces and hands. The castle steward and Captain of the Guard will interrogate you later. They prefer you to be presentable."

"A horse wouldn't eat these at home," Leland said after the guard left. "But I'm ravenous. I'm eating them."

"My nose is stuffed to the point I've lost my sense of taste, so I don't care. I'm eating them too," Tony said, grabbing an apple.

****

With Harry and Richard next to her at the breakfast table, it took all the restraint she possessed not to ask if they'd decided on letting her be present when they interviewed Leland and Tony. If she was there and if Leland and Tony started to go too far afield with their answers, she might be able to subtly signal them. Harry had to have shared the truth with Richard. The worst thing Leland and Tony could do was to fabricate some nonsense story.

"You're looking very pretty today," Harry said. "You've done your hair differently."

"Thank you, Tildy did it for me." Felicia had no skill when it came to hair. She'd been pulling it back into a ponytail using the same band she had since she came. If she wanted different style at home, she had the advantage of hot rollers. Tildy, Emily's maid, had come to her rescue and braided it for her the night before. Tildy kindly came this morning and fluffed it out, so Felicia's hair made a soft blonde frame for her face.

She took Harry's compliment as a possible open door to ask about the interview. Before she could two knights dragged another knight from the table and began pounding him on the back. The third knight was bent over, a hand to his throat, the other arm flailing, beating air in panic.

"He's choking." Felicia jumped to her feet and ran over, followed quickly by Harry. "Move!" The knights around the choking man wouldn't let her through. "Harry, I can help but they're blocking me."

Harry pushed the two aside. "Let her through."

The choking knight had sunk to his knees. "I need him standing," Felicia ordered.

"Cedric, give me a hand." Harry and Cedric lifted the knight to a standing position.

"Bend him forward slightly." She demonstrated how far and when they did she applied the Heimlich maneuver.

Three times it didn't work, and the other knights shouted for her to stop and let them pound on his back again.

"She's a healer. Let her try," Harry barked and they quieted.

Felicia began to panic, afraid she was failing and the knight would die in her arms. What kind of healer-what kind of doctor loses a patient to choking?

On the fifth thrust, a chunk of bread flew from the man's mouth. He cupped his chest, taking deep breaths of relief. His normal color began returning to his blue face. "Thank you, milady, I shall owe you my life until the day I die."

"Let's hope it doesn't come to that."

"I've never seen a choking man's life saved in such a way. Can you teach me?" Harry asked.

"Yes, it's an excellent thing to know."

"If you've finished with breakfast, we can go outside and you can show me. We'll practice behind the castle. There's lovely spot between the gardens and the cliff with a fine view, and no one will bother us," Harry said, smiling.

"I'm done with breakfast. Let's go."

Harry led her to a spot that overlooked the Severn whose surface sparkled with flashes of light in the bright morning sun. In the distance apple orchards and farmland made up a patchwork of green. "Is this not a lovely place?"

Felicia had been here before. She'd walked along the cliff's path a day earlier but she didn't tell him. She didn't want to spoil his moment. "It's stunning and peaceful. Thank you for bringing me here."

"I'll start. First you'll want to position the person

like I asked this morning, slightly forward, like so." Felicia put her hand between Harry's wing bones a pushed. You're much broader chested than the knight this morning but luckily my height gives me long arms."

She wrapped her arms around his waist, made a fist under his ribcage and repeated her actions from that morning only with the force needed for demo purposes. "You want to make the thrusts quick and forceful to dislodge the food. It should actually feel like you're trying to lift the person off the ground, even though you're not."

She repeated the action twice more, then said, "Try it on me now."

"I've been waiting for you to ask."

He slipped his arms around her and held her tight to his chest without bothering to bend her forward. His arms enveloped her in a cocoon of strength and an unanticipated rush of sensual thrill filled her.

"You didn't bend me," she reminded him.

"You're not really choking." He did a couple practice thrusts. The last was a hair too hard.

"Ooh!"

"Did I hurt you? I'm sorry," he said softly, his warm breath tickling the sensitive shell of her ear.

"No, it didn't really hurt. Only a little," Felicia told him, wondering if he could feel her heart beating against her ribs because it felt like a high-speed sledge hammer to her.

"Shall I kiss the spot and make it better?"

"Are you suggesting your lips contain healing power?"

He came around and facing her, wrapped his arms around her and pulled her close enough to kiss. "Shall we put them to the test?"

She should politely press her hands to his chest and push him away. She should. She didn't come close. She stared like a mesmerized cobra at his lips and told him, "You're an unrelenting smoothie, Sir Harold."

"Smoothie? I don't know the word. But as to the other, I'm more determined than unrelenting. Explain smoothie."

"You know all the right words and moves to charm a lady."

He nodded with a little dip of his head in agreement. Then, he kissed her, walking her backwards into an oak tree as he did. His hand ran down her spine and she knew he had to feel her bloody racing heart for sure. The devil man knew what he was about with women and knew her insides were doing cartwheels with that kiss. No man should know that much about women.

When he finally broke the kiss, he grinned and said, "Like that?"

"Perhaps." She gave him a light push against the chest. "Don't you have some Captain of the Guard duties to attend to?"

"I do."

"Be off with you. I've things to do too. We'll speak later."

"Later." He wiggled his brows and turned to leave.

"I've got to find a way home. I can't afford distractions no matter how handsome or charming," she said quietly to his departing back.

****

Guards tied Leland and Tony's hands and led them at sword point up from the bowels of the castle. The second guard knocked on a door near the staircase. They were told to enter. Inside sat a dignified looking, middle-aged man behind a large desk.

On a chair in front of the desk, rigid and arrow-straight sat the knight Felicia called Harry. None of the affability and warmth he'd shown her in manner and expression was evident now. Just the opposite. Their appearance was being met with steely-eyed scrutiny by a man Leland guessed only needed to look you over once to establish a cold evaluation.

"Untie them and then you may leave," the man behind the desk told the guards.

They did as ordered. He waited until they closed the door before he introduced himself and the knight, "I am Richard Armstrong, the Elysian Fields Castle Steward." He gestured toward Harry. "This is Sir Harold. You've been caught trespassing on Baron Guiscard's land. We want to know your purpose for being here. Need I warn you not to lie?"

"No. We understand there are consequences for misleading you," Leland said.

Harry stood and came over to them. "Hold out your hands, palms up." When they did, he examined them. "Roll your sleeves up now." He turned their arms over and examined them. "No callouses or scars. You're no warriors. That's for certain."

Harry returned to his chair.

"What are your names?" Richard asked.

"I'm Leland Halliday and this is my brother, Anthony Halliday."

"Where are you from?" Harry asked.

"Greenland."

"It's a vast island west of England," Tony added

with a weak smile.

Leland swallowed his groan. He'd specifically warned Tony against volunteering information.

"We've been told about Greenland. Do you think us backward?" Richard asked, his voice moving from even to tight with the question.

"Sorry. I meant no insult."

"You carry only a sword and knife, yet Sir Harold confirms neither of you are warriors. You have no wares. Pray tell, what trade do you pursue with no products?"

Leland figured he might as well tell the truth as far as that question went. They knew from their association with his father what a scientist was or at least had an idea.

"We're scientists."

"Where are your tools? Two years ago we had a man here who claimed such a trade. He made an apparatus for the army to use. He needed tools," Harry said.

Leland didn't have a ready, logical answer. He hadn't anticipated the question, although he should've. Fear muddles the mind. "We aren't here to participate in our trade. We are merely travelers, wishing to see England."

"Harry..." Richard gave a small bob of his head. "Now."

Leland and Tony both watched as Harry went to the door. Leland wouldn't have been surprised if the Grim Reaper in his full regalia of hooded black cloak and scythe stood on the other side. *Just our luck the way everything has gone so far.*

Harry returned with Felicia. He walked her in front of him, an arm around her waist to steady her and one hand over her eyes. He kicked the door closed and then walked her to the side of the desk but kept her standing in front of him. He continued to cover her eyes.

"Making sure no hints are given," he told her.

"I'm going to remind you about lying," Richard reiterated to Leland and Tony and leaned back in his chair. "Do you know this woman?"

Smart move on Harry's part, Leland thought. With her eyes covered from the moment they came in, she couldn't show any recognition. He and Tony had no idea if she'd admit to knowing them.

Their mission was to get her home safely. The less Harry and Richard knew about the time tear, the better. Either Leland or Tony needed to tell her about messaging the others at home using the memory box. Oliver would set up a time to use the machine and hopefully get her back. Harry and Richard would be more inclined to let her move freely if she wasn't associated with him or Tony.

"Do you know this woman?" Richard asked again, more firmly.

"No."

Harry's face darkened. He released Felicia so fast, she staggered a step. Before Leland realized what happened, Harry had a tight grip on the front of Leland's tunic. Utilizing a move he learned in his self-defense class and never thought he'd use, Leland managed to knock Harry's hands away. He wasn't prepared for the swift right cross Harry landed on his jaw. He fell back against a table, arms flailing, knocking things over as he fought to keep his balance.

In front of him, Felicia had taken hold of Harry's arm. "Please Harry, no more. They're afraid. I was too. I am still in many ways," she added in a gentler tone. "They didn't tell the truth because they didn't know what to say to be safe."

Harry dropped his arm. "For you I'll stop."

Leland massaged his jaw then wiggled it side to side testing to see if it was broken and grateful it wasn't. It felt like he'd been slammed with a brick.

"You were told not to lie," Harry said. "You're Tony Halliday." He pointed to Tony. "You're Leland Gordon and your father is Oliver Gordon. You're both from the same strange place Felicia calls home. The only truth in your statement is you are scientists, according to Felicia, and I believe her."

"Why did you deny knowing her? Why would you believe the truth dangerous?" Richard asked.

"We have no indication how you'd view our presence. Since we spent the night in a dungeon, I guess not favorably. If you think the worst of us and were made aware of an association we had with Felicia, those negative beliefs might reflect back on her. The last thing we'd want is to cause her harm, so I lied. I knew Tony would go along with whatever I decided to do."

"You lied for a noble cause. That's your defense?" Harry asked.

"Yes."

Harry snorted. "Horse fouling's."

Medieval times, medieval attachment to the church, Leland gave the religious fealty route a shot, hoping to convince them. "Shall I put my hand on the bible and swear it's the truth?"

Harry mocked the offer with a dismissive wave. "You'll fool none with a meaningless gesture of that sort. Many a time in my early years as a knight, when I suffered from being deep in my cups, I promised the Lord and all the saints I'd never swill ale again. Oaths that never lasted. Put your hand to ten bibles, it holds no credence with me."

Tony took a single step forward. Harry quickly moved in front of him, blocking him from getting closer to Felicia.

Tony raised his hands in mock surrender. "I'm not going to try anything. I truly don't understand what the original offense was that landed us here. We were only walking in the woods. We weren't stealing or threatening anyone, but we're treated like criminals."

"The mute has a voice," Harry said. He pointed to the spot Tony left. "Step back."

"Are either of you going to explain what we did? I've only heard trespassing. It was the bloody woods for pity's sake. Not the palace." Tony moved to where he originally stood.

"You were told. You trespassed. That's enough for the patrol to bring you here to answer for your actions." Richard went to the door and called the guards. "Harry and I will discuss what to do with you. Until then, you'll go back to the dungeon."

"May we speak to Felicia?" Leland asked.

"I will discuss the possibility with her," Harry told him.

"Take them away," Richard ordered. "You needn't bother with ties. I doubt they'll run. A small kindness as you're friends of Felicia's."

"Obviously, you don't believe his story about why they lied," Richard said to Harry.

"Not in the least." He brought a chair over and placed it next to his. "Sit, Felicia."

"I give him credit for coming up with a good

excuse for the lie so fast," Richard said.

"Do you have any idea what you will do with them?" Felicia asked. "I'd really like to find out how they got here."

Richard shook his head. "I'll have Cedric and Ben ride out with them. Since they claim to come from the same place as you, they can point out where their homes are. Let's see if those have disappeared like yours. If so, I'm not sure how to proceed with them."

Felicia knew they'd disappeared. She and Harry rode through the woods through the area Oliver Gordon and his team worked on their project. Their trailers and other equipment were gone. She had no reason to mention the missing structures and equipment to Harry. At the time, she was too caught up in dealing with the fact her home and business no longer existed.

"I have an idea," Harry said. "They're scientists like Oliver. Felicia confirms that. We had Oliver create something we've never seen to earn his freedom. Let's do the same with them."

"Think they can do it?" Richard asked Felicia.

"How to explain? The scientists where I am from have different equipment to work with, far more advanced. No offense. I don't know how much the lack of access to sophisticated equipment and advanced material affects their abilities."

"You're making excuses for them if they fail," Richard said.

"No. I'm saying I don't know what they need to succeed. Science, the science that is their expertise, is not mine."

"I don't see how you can claim your material is so

far more advanced than what we have. Nothing you have kept your home in place."

Richard gave Harry one of those *well said-good point* nods. "He's right."

"Too true, sadly," she admitted.

"Shall we go down and tell them what we want?" Harry asked. "They should be moved to a different chamber as well. One with better light."

"I don't want them on this level. Move them to one of the servant's chambers on the first floor, but I want a guard on their door at all times. Unless Cedric and Ben return tomorrow and say the homes of the scientists are there. Then, you're to take a company of men to where they live and find out how they came to be on this land without us knowing," Richard told Harry.

"Have you decided if I can speak with them?" Felicia asked.

"I have. No, unless you disagree, Richard."

"Whatever you decide on the matter is fine with me, Harry."

"Why not?" Felicia pressed. "I'm not asking to be alone with them. You'll be there or the guard. I told you I'm curious about their presence here."

"Why or how they came to be here, is no matter to you. They just are. That's all you need to know. It is a matter of importance and security to Richard and me."

"But—"

"Leave off, Felicia. The topic is closed." Harry stood and went to the door. "Busy yourself elsewhere. Richard and I have business to conduct."

****

The next day, as soon as they returned to Elysian

Fields, Cedric and Ben escorted Leland and Tony into Richard's chamber. They arrived back during the midday meal. The smell of fresh baked bread filled the great hall. Seats at the tables were filled with the knights, squires, and guards. Servants brought platters of various cheeses and fruits to the tables while others followed pouring ale.

Leland's empty stomach twisted and growled in protest. The bread's scent had a maddening effect since his breakfast consisted of two rotten apples and stale bread.

"It's taking every bit of will power I possess not to pounce on one of those loaves and tear into it like a wild animal," Tony said.

"Me too." Leland eyed a golden crusted loaf and imagined the crunch it would make.

Cedric elbowed Leland. "Quiet."

Only Felicia and two other women sat at the head table. Felicia perked up seeing Leland and Tony as they came down the main aisle. She pushed her chair back but the older woman at the table placed a hand on Felicia's forearm. Felicia scooted her chair under the table again. She gave them a small wave as the four men passed but said nothing.

Richard and Harry sat at the table in Richard's chamber eating their meal. "You two can go," Richard said. "I'll have the guards come up and escort them out when we're finished," he told Cedric and Ben.

Harry turned in his chair, slathering butter over a hunk of bread. "Let me guess. Your homes were gone too?"

"You knew they would be," Leland said.

"I did. Makes sense if Felicia's is, yours would be too." He stuck the buttered chunk of bread in his mouth, slowly ate it, and tore off two more chunks. "You two look ready to swoop down on our meal. Here." He tossed the torn chunks to Leland and Tony.

"Thank you. Really, thank you," Tony said before tearing into his bread.

Leland didn't wait but displayed his gratitude with a vigorous nod.

"We're moving you to a servant's room on the lower level. Once you're shown where you will be housed, you can share a meal in the kitchen with the cook's staff. She knows to let you eat in there," Richard said.

An obvious but in Leland's mind, painful question, hung in the air unanswered. It seemed to him if they were housed as guests, they'd be in a chamber on the same floor as Richard. What were they, exactly?

"Are we here as your guests or prisoners?" Leland asked.

"Neither. Think of yourselves as serfs serving Baron Guiscard." Richard turned to Harry. "Sound right to you?"

Harry peered at them over the rim of his tankard, took a deep pull from it and then set the tankard down. "Yes. They can't be guests. They weren't invited. They can still wind up prisoners, but generous men that we are we're offering them positions with limited freedom."

He'd said it straight-faced. Harry's smug tone hinted at his true feelings of superiority. Leland had a feeling a chuckle would follow the comment, just to twist the knife. Harry didn't disappoint.

"As serfs, that's pretty close to slave labor," Tony said.

"Prisoners or serfs, your choice," Richard said.

"We will act as serfs," Leland said, hating the smirk on Harry's face. "You understand neither of us knows anything about farming. We're not much help in that arena other than lifting and carrying."

Richard tossed them a pear apiece. "You're not going to labor on a farm. We want to see what you can create for us as scientists."

"If the two of you think to wound my pride by lobbing food at me like an animal in the Royal Menagerie, you've failed. I'm too hungry to care." Leland bit into the juicy fruit with enthusiasm.

"On the contrary, it's not my intention to embarrass you. It's been hours since breakfast. I figured you'd be hungry. Speaking for myself, I didn't feel like getting up and handing you the pear." He looked to the side. "Harry?"

"I didn't think about it one way or the other."

"Fine. What do you want from us?" Leland asked around a soft bite. He wiped leaking juice from the corner of his mouth and licked the finger he wiped with.

"Your father made a periscope. Make us something as useful."

Richard said it like they'd snap their fingers and *voila, your wish is our command, oh great Castle Steward.* Leland's imagination went dry as the Sahara at the suggestion.

"Make you something useful?" Tony repeated.

"Yes."

Obviously stumped by the request, Tony pressed for more information, which Leland suspected, correctly, he'd fail to gain. "Like what?"

"You're the scientists. It's up to you to create an item we will find useful. In other words, we've no interest in frivolous nonsense," Harry said.

Tony threw his hands in the air before spreading his

arms wide. "How, pray tell to use your words? We have no tools, no means to draft plans for a *useful thing,* not the simplest hardware of any kind. And no direction from you as to what you're most interested in acquiring."

Harry and Richard bent their heads close and whispered. Richard did the most talking with Harry doing a lot of head shaking, to Leland's chagrin. Whatever Richard was suggesting was probably the most workable for him and Tony and Harry was quashing his ideas.

"We will provide you with material to draft ideas, write them down or draw as you see fit. When you settle on one, we will do our best to provide the tools and hardware you need to assemble it," Richard told them.

"That's it? All that scheming and no suggestions?" Tony snapped.

Harry's eyes narrowed. "Scheming?"

Leland jumped in to save Tony from himself. "Bad word choice, he meant to say, all that discussion."

"Tread lightly, Halliday," Harry warned Tony.

"Listen to him," Richard said. "Proceeding to the main matter, when you go downstairs, send the kitchen spit boy up, if he can be spared, and I'll give him what you need. You have the freedom to walk around the bailey, the lists, and the lower level of the castle, but that's all. You're not to go to the gardens, the chapel, the stable, or the barracks without permission."

"Nor are you to enter this level. Do not, under any circumstance get near Felicia's chamber or attempt to communicate with her here, or elsewhere, unless I am with her," Harry warned.

Richard went to the door and waved the corridor guard over. "I see no reason for you to enter the forbidden areas, but if you must, I will assign additional guards."

"Will we *ever* be allowed to speak with Felicia?" Leland asked.

Harry gave a heavy sigh. "She wants to speak to you but I haven't decided whether to allow the conversation."

****

Leland and Tony sat at a table in the corner of the kitchen. One of the servants came over with a platter of food and a pitcher of ale. "Richard sent word down that we're to feed you in here. I'm Drusilla. If you need more, ask for me. Don't bother Beulah, the cook. She's not tolerant of interruptions."

"Thank you, Drusilla," Leland and Tony said in unison.

When she stepped away, they exchanged a look of mutual panic, that said: *What the devil are we going to do?*

"Do you have any ideas about what we might create?" Leland asked.

"None, nada, zip," Tony said, pouring himself a cup of beer. "They act happy with the periscope your dad made, which makes me think perhaps they'd like a companion instrument."

"What's a companion instrument to a periscope? I've no clue."

"Me either," Tony said with a shrug. "That's as far as I got, which is why I said I've got zip."

England being at war with France for decades now, the only connection Leland saw that made the most sense was militarily oriented. "We're talking a possible military type device."

Four partially-armored knights walked past the

kitchen door. One popped in and gave a petite servant girl with red ringlets kneading bread a pinch on the bottom. The girl squealed, spun around, and blushed at something the knight whispered in her ear. The knight laughed and dashed out.

Leland and Tony watched the exchange with amusement. "She's a cutie," Leland said and shot a glance over at the redhead, who'd woven a bright blue ribbon into her braid. "Not as pretty as Drusilla though."

"I agree. Back to our problem, based on the fortifications and the amount of knights serving here, that's likely the best option," Tony said.

"What goes with a periscope? Have you seen any war movies with Special Forces fellows? They have all sorts of bits and bobs." Leland didn't expect Tony to know many. He was a sci-fi or *Avengers* sort.

Leland was stuck coming up with a war movie himself. His mind was a blank. He didn't see many either, preferring spy thrillers like the Bourne films. "I keep thinking about Jason Bourne."

"He's no help. I can't picture him with any super weapon, not one that we can use. Making a sniper rifle or assault weapon, even if we could is not in order. Whatever we pick, it can't have a huge effect on the order of things. We don't want to change history."

They ate in silence. By the time they finished practice in the lists had begun. "Let's watch for a while. Maybe we'll get an idea," Leland suggested.

The list was set off to the side of the bailey on the far side of the stable. The fenced field had been divided into three different areas of fighting men. The first area men worked with straight maces or morning stars using stuffed dummies as targets. In the second, the men lined up in relay formation taking turns running and throwing lances and spears at various sized painted wooden targets. In those two sections, the men worked in hose and boots, either shirtless or in loose linen shirts and hose and boots. In the last section, the men worked one-on-one with swords, but they wore gauntlets and shirts under breastplates.

Harry walked the length of the field, watching and occasionally calling out corrections. He had changed out of the tunic he wore when Leland and Tony appeared before him in Richard's chamber. Now he wore a loose linen shirt like the others, a breastplate and gauntlets, and a sword.

Leland tapped Harry on the arm. "That boyish looking fellow participating in the sword play circuit isn't doing well. His opponent is pushing him all over the field," he said, wondering about the lad's age and how safe this exercise was for him. His mature opponent had a decade on the lad, which Leland guessed meant that much more experience. "He can't be more than sixteen."

"He's fifteen," Harry told him. "This is an important move for him. He's just gone from squire to knight-in-training. I would remind you that Prince Edward and our own Baron Guy Guiscard were only sixteen when they fought at Crecy."

Harry waved to the young man. "Calvin, come here."

"What do you bet Harry's going tear the poor kid's head off," Tony whispered to Leland.

The lad jogged over.

"Your weight isn't evenly distributed. That's why you're getting pushed around. We all have a strong side and weak side. It's natural for us to favor our strong side but in a one-on-one fight your balance is easily thrown off especially when wielding a weapon. Practice will help you become more aware of your stance." Harry walked behind him. "Hold your sword out like you're presenting it to someone."

Calvin did, and Harry cupped Calvin's elbows and lifted. "You're placing more weight on your left arm. I can feel it. Widen your stance, straighten your shoulders and you should feel the difference here." Harry reached around and patted Calvin's torso.

Harry removed his sword. "Turn around. There's no victory if you're always on the defensive. Come at me and I'll show you some defensive blocks with offensive follow through strikes." They practiced a few then Harry released Calvin to return to his field opponent.

"I thought you'd be a lot harsher with him," Tony said.

"He's learning. Tearing into him today wouldn't help him. Next week may be another story."

"This is what Simon used to do, isn't it, act as trainer-instructor?" Leland asked Harry.

The second the question was out of his mouth Leland wanted to kick himself. He wasn't supposed to know anything about Simon. From the suspicious expression on Harry's face, that same thought occurred to him too.

"What do you know about Simon? Don't attempt a lie," Harry warned.

"Nothing, honestly. I overheard the guard last night mention Simon was missing. They spoke of him like he had a position of some importance."

Harry's expression softened. "Yes, he was Captain of the Guard, a position I am temporarily assigned."

Relieved, Leland smiled and he and Tony watched

the practice quietly. Harry left their side to direct the spear throwers to shift routines. They'd now move to hand-to-hand fighting.

"I haven't seen any weapon we can spin off of, have you?" Tony asked Leland.

"No. Maybe we're underusing a great source in Harry. Let's ask him what they liked best about the periscope." Leland also hoped asking Harry for his input in this way might help get them in his good graces. Couldn't hurt.

****

They waited until practice in the lists ended for the day before talking to Harry. They explained the direction they wanted to take. "What impressed you most about the periscope?" Leland asked Harry.

"I'll show you." Harry led them on foot outside the castle walls into the woods beyond. At approximately one-hundred-fifty meters, he pointed to a painted rock. "Range for our archers depends on the strength of the bowman. Most are accurate to this point. Let's go a bit further." They continued on approximately another fifty yards. "The stronger archers can strike this distance." He pointed to another painted stone.

"How does this play into the periscope?" Tony asked.

"I get it," Leland said. "If the castle were to come under attack, your men on the rampart can use the periscope to spot invaders as soon as they come into range—"

"Without exposing themselves by having to stand and observe," Tony interjected. "Well done, Professor."

Harry nodded. "Exactly. We're hoping for a similar device for defensive or offensive purposes."

"Are you expecting the castle to come under attack?" Leland knew it wouldn't be attacked until the English Civil War. Who was the current perceived threat?

"No, but we like to be prepared for any trouble."

"Tony and I need to discuss it."

"We'll give you a day or so to come to us with suggestions. Let's go back." Harry started walking.

"Have you given any thought to our speaking with Felicia?" Leland asked as they trudged along.

Harry turned and blocked his path. "Why are you so anxious to speak with her? Were you lovers?"

"No. We were friends nothing more."

"And you?" Harry asked Tony who shook his head.

"She treated me medically a few times. Sinus trouble." Tony tapped his nose. "Lovers? No, she's not even my type."

"What do you mean, not your type? Are you saying she's not comely enough for you? She's very lovely."

"She's pretty as can be but there's no magic between us."

"Magic? Do you dabble in sorcery?"

The alarm in Harry's question set off warning bells. Once more Leland jumped in to save Tony's skin and by extension his own. "No! No! It's an expression. That's all."

Harry moved within arm's reach of Tony. "I don't like you."

Tony could react one of three ways. He could retreat a step, which would appear cowardly to a man like Harry. Nor was it in Tony's nature. Or, he could stand his ground, or take a swing at Harry.

If there was any truth to mental telepathy, Leland needed Tony to read his mind now. *For God's sake don't take the bait and swing at him and please don't smart off to the man.*

Tony stood his ground but tempered his answer. "I gathered that."

Leland thought it as good a time as any to break up this pissing contest. "Harry, can't you just see it within yourself to let us talk briefly to her?"

Harry shot Tony a threatening parting glance and then started on the path back to the castle. "I haven't decided. Do not make a nuisance of yourself with repeated requests."

Chris Karlsen

Chapter Eight

The usual meal time noise and chatter that traveled from the hall and greeted Felicia as she came down the staircase was absent tonight.

As she entered the room, she also noticed the lack of playful interaction between the men and servant girls. Each was serious faced and the mood at the tables somber, the men speaking softly among themselves.

"Why is everyone so quiet?" she asked Harry, taking the seat next to him.

"We called off the search for Simon and Emily today. We believe the family drowned."

"Drowned? I'm so sorry. You're sure? Did their bodies wash ashore?"

He held the platter of vegetables for her while she served herself. "No. But, if they were attacked, and even if they dragged Emily off with them, we'd have found the bodies of Simon and Kendrick by now. The only other possibility is they went sailing on the river and the boat capsized or hit rocks and shattered. For some reason it went down."

Felicia knew Emily could swim. All the sisters could. The friends often swam together growing up. Emily's heavy clothing would pull her down. She'd also have a struggle if her son was going under.

"Did Simon know how to swim?" she asked.

"Yes, but not well anymore, not since he lost his

leg. Little Kendrick hadn't been taught yet. If Emily was having trouble, Simon would fight to save her, and they'd both fight for the boy. It wouldn't be unusual for all three to be lost in those circumstances."

Felicia's mind went back to the day she fell and found herself in this strange place. Why had Electra and Esme been gathered with their husbands around that outcropping? What were Oliver and Leland Gordon doing there? If there was any truth to the existence of a sixth sense, Felicia had a ghost of that tickling the back of her mind. That tickle told her Emily and Simon weren't dead. They just weren't here—in *this* now.

"Such a terrible loss for Elysian Fields," she said, going along with their belief.

"He's with his best friend, Stephen, again."

Stephen. They all say Electra went to France with Oliver and a Frenchman named Roger. Logic dictated that the Roger they spoke of was the same as Electra's husband. Could Simon's friend, Stephen, be the same Stephen who was Esme's husband? Felicia wasn't sure how that came about but it wasn't weirder than what's happened to her or the arrival of Leland and Tony.

"What did his friend Stephen look like?" she asked, trying to sound casual.

"Twenty-six at the time of his death, a little shorter than me, brown hair, I can't say what color eyes. I knew him for years but never looked deep in his eyes. It's not the sort of thing I do with men. Oh, he had a nasty scar on his chin. He received a serious slash at Crecy. Why?"

Esme's Stephen had a distinct scar on his chin. "Just wondered. How did he die?"

"He was killed at Poitiers, although we never found

his body, which was odd. We walked the battlefield twice, searching for it."

Maybe because there was no body to find.

"Will there be services here at the family chapel?"

"Yes. You'll notice the squires aren't here tonight. They ate earlier. They're all in the barracks now polishing the armor of the knights they serve. The men will look their finest in Simon's honor."

Felicia looked past Harry to see Richard's wife, Julia, consoling him. His plate had little on it and what was there he'd barely touched. She stroked his arm and spoke softly to him, words that had him granting her a faint smile and kiss to her temple.

The warm sight tugged at Felicia's heart. Grief counseling wasn't her forte. It was an awful failing on her part as a doctor, but no matter what she said, it came out sounding hollow, at least to her ear.

Grief had affected Harry's usual hearty appetite as well. He nibbled at the stew seeming to be satisfied with whatever gravy he soaked up with bread. Felicia waffled on inviting him to her chamber for a goblet of wine and to talk about Simon if he felt like reminiscing about his friend. There were two problems with that, the first being her less-than-sterling counseling ability. She could overcome that just by letting him do the most talking, which was the point to begin with. The second was the potential for him to misunderstand, like the last time she invited him to her chamber.

A wild-ass vision of a romp with Harry flashed into her mind. "Oh God."

"Pardon? Did you say something?" Harry asked.

"No, I...I thought I dropped some gravy on my

dress. I see I didn't." She breathed a sigh of relief.

Where had the vision come from? She'd read a surprising number of people respond to death by having sex with a loved one. Allegedly, it was a form of reaffirmation of life. She wasn't big on psychological mumbo-jumbo. But she'd fly with the babble this time as the explanation fit why she saw herself so clearly on the bed with Harry, her skirt up to her waist, legs tight around his hips, and him not acting chivalrously at all.

Her heart hurt for him. He looked so downcast. How could she not invite him? Obviously, they could talk somewhere else- stroll through the garden or by the river. But Harry would likely be more inclined to open up if they had the privacy of her chamber. That was what she told herself anyway.

"Harry, I understand how hard this must be for you. You fought side by side with the man through some of the worst battles England has known and come out victorious. If you feel like talking, I'm a good listener. We can speak in the privacy of my chamber, if you wish, or anywhere else to your liking."

"Thank you. I appreciate the offer of boring your gentle ear with my memories."

Dinner passed without much more talk from either Harry or Richard and Julia. Felicia stood ready to leave, uncertain whether Harry planned on coming up to her chamber or not. A single overture was sufficient. She wouldn't mention the invite again, lest he really take it wrong.

"Come with me before you go upstairs," Harry said, standing.

He took her by the hand and led her to the kitchen.

At a table by the open back door, Leland and Tony were eating their dinner. Drusilla and a red-haired young woman were hovering, chatting with the men, smiling and flirting happening on both sides.

"Felicia, this is a pleasant surprise," Leland said and stood. He introduced her to Drusilla. "She's from the same village as us," he told her.

Tony also stood and introduced Felicia to the redhead, who Felicia had seen in the hall only at mealtimes. "This is Heather. She and Drusilla have been sharing delightful castle stories with us, haven't you, darling?"

Heather flushed bright pink, noticeable even in the fading light of the summer evening. She giggled and gave Tony a girly punch in the arm. "I told you it isn't right to call me that when we hardly know each other."

Tony winked at Felicia and Harry. "Do you want me to stop?"

Another giggle from Heather. "No."

"It's very nice meeting you ladies." Felicia turned to Harry. "Does this mean you're letting me talk to Leland and Tony?"

"Briefly. Drusilla, Heather, busy yourselves elsewhere. Give them some privacy." After the two maids scurried out, Harry moved a couple strides away and positioned himself in the doorway of the kitchen.

Felicia motioned for them to sit. "Please sit. Not sure where to start. First, did anyone find Chloe? I'm worried sick about her."

"She's safe and staying with Esme and Stephen."

"Thank heavens. We have to talk fast. Is there something you'd like to tell me? Why we're here, for example?"

Leland nodded. He looked at Harry who stared back steely-eyed. Felicia thought for a terrible moment she saw rebellion in Leland's eyes. She feared he might be tempted to engage Harry in a stare-down. Any challenge to Harry's authority could have him terminating the chance for her to talk to Leland and Tony. Common sense prevailed and Leland turned back to her.

She knew he'd have to choose his words carefully. Hopefully, he knew she was aware of his predicament.

"Disregard logic. Think sci-fi. Think H.G. Wells and Hawking."

"I'm way ahead of you. I've figured that part out. Can you tell what means you took for your journey?" she asked.

"Same way as you...the outcropping."

"There's a special path?"

"What's going on here? What kind of conversation is this?" Harry snapped. His tone sent the kitchen maids scurrying. "This is silly jabber. Yes, there are two paths by that outcropping. We took one the other day. Who cares? The three of you carried on asking to speak together and this is all you have to say? Let's go."

"You need to *dig* for the answers," Leland said as Harry put his arm around Felicia and urged her away.

Alone in the corridor, Harry pulled her into an alcove and grasped her firmly by the upper arms. "What did he mean, dig for the answers? What was that code for?"

"I don't know. Honestly. I don't know what he meant. It has something to do with how we all wound up here. That much I swear to you is true. What exactly it refers to, I've no idea."

"Would you tell me if you did?"

How could she answer that without lying? Until this very minute, until Leland suggested there was an answer to her problem, until Harry asked her outright would she tell him the truth, she believed she could lie without remorse. She no longer believed that. Through no effort on her part, when she wasn't looking, as they say, she discovered a damned inconvenient and deep, too deep, fondness for the man. Bloody damn, damn, damn.

How? That was a mystery. The man was arrogant, conceited, and a dreadful misogynist. She couldn't blame him for the last. He was a man of his times but it didn't change the fact that he was a misogynist. And damn, why did all that annoying stuff have to be packed into armored hotness?

"Felicia! I asked you a question. Would you tell me if you did know what he meant?"

How can I possibly tell you I'm a time traveler? "Yes," she said in pathetic acquiescence still not sure.

"You don't sound convincing, but I'll accept your yes as you've not lied to me in the past." He put his arm around her waist again. "Does your invitation still stand for me to come up to your chamber and talk?"

"Yes."

"I'd like that. First, I'd like for us to stroll through the gardens. They're beautiful this time of year."

The sweet scent of roses filled the air as they entered the garden. The setting sun cast the rows of flowers in a warm orange and dusty-pink glow. "The roses are extraordinary. I've walked through here a couple times. Who tends to them?"

"The kitchen staff. They see to the flowers while seeing to the vegetable garden." He drew his knife. "Point out any blooms you favor and I'll cut them for you."

"Thank you." An internal giggle traveled through her. It had been a long time since she'd received flowers from a handsome man.

****

They'd spent part of their time in the garden sitting on a carved stone bench. The arms were made to look like animal paws and the seat was supported on the backs of stone lions. When the sunset light turned from warm pastels to dusky grey, Felicia and Harry left.

"I must check on the men in the barracks before I come to you," he'd said.

She stopped in the kitchen on the way to her chamber and asked Drusilla for something to put her bouquet into. She could've asked Tildy to get her a vase but Felicia had hoped to run into Leland and Tony visiting with the maids. Neither was present when she went through. She'd have asked where they'd gone off to as she heard their movements were restricted but she feared her asking would get back to Harry. She'd no desire to open an interrogation over a nothing incident.

Drusilla gave her a pewter vase whose bowl was banded with pearls and lapis lazuli. "It belonged to Lady Shakira. Sir Guy gave it to her after a trip they made to London." Drusilla looked around and seeing only the spit boy and Heather in the room with them she leaned closer to Felicia. "It was a gift because there'd been an incident and Lady Shakira had been badly injured. It was whispered that a favorite of the queen attacked her and when Sir Guy found out, pummeled him within an inch of his life." She leaned back and with enormous pride said, "That was our Sir Guy. No one hurt what was his. We miss him."

"I've heard nothing but good things about him. Thank you for the vase."

Felicia moved to leave when Drusilla tugged on her sleeve. She handed a short-bladed knife to Felicia. "Take this to trim your stems. It's just sharpened."

For a fleeting second Felicia wondered if sweet Drusilla might help her talk again with Leland and Tony. Dare she ask? The idea died as fast as it occurred to her. If Harry found out, he'd be livid and she didn't want to get Drusilla punished.

"Thank you, I'll bring it back in the morning," Felicia said, turning the knife blade down toward the flowers and away from her body.

In her chamber, two dresses were laid out on the bed. Tildy arrived before Felicia rang for her.

"They're more of Lady Emily's. When we received the official word that the family was lost, I saw no reason not to alter them for you." Tildy held first one then the other up to Felicia, gauging the accuracy of the alterations. "They're nice dresses and shouldn't go to waste. She wouldn't want that. The dark red one was a favorite of Lady Emily's if you're wondering what to wear to the service tomorrow. I think it would please her to see her dress worn to honor her memory."

"I appreciate you thinking of me at this difficult time, Tildy. I'd be happy to wear one of her favorites tomorrow."

"If you don't need me for anything, I'll leave you for the night," Tildy said.

"One minute." Felicia checked to see the wine had been refreshed and it had. "I'm good. I'll see you in the morning."

An hour passed. Checking the candle clock they were well into the second hour since she left Harry. She'd expected him to arrive twenty maybe thirty minutes after they parted. How long did it take to check on the men?

When the wax melted past the two hour mark, Felicia went in search of Harry. Was it bold on her part? Yes, perhaps too bold considering she had mentally set physical boundaries for them to adhere to during his visit. But she told herself it was in his best interest that she offer a sympathetic ear. His dear friend had died--or so he thought. Harry might be sitting depressed, letting dark thoughts ruin his pleasant memories of Simon and their times together.

She left her chamber and since no one was in the corridor, stopped for a moment to listen at Richard's door. Harry might've gone there first to discuss the sad news with Richard and Julia. The only voices Felicia heard were muffled and belonged to Richard and Julia. Felicia continued on through the great hall and into the bailey.

She didn't dare go into the barracks. She rousted the stable boy and asked him to check for her to see if Harry was still in the barracks with the knights.

"I know he's not there, milady," the stable boy told her. "He took Simon's horse, Odin, out well over an hour ago."

"Do you know where he took him?" She couldn't imagine he'd have gone riding in the woods in the dark. That seemed unnecessarily dangerous.

"He's in the field where they hold the jousts."

"Where is that?"

"Beyond the lists. Let me get a torch and lead you there so you don't fall and hurt yourself in the dark." The boy lit a torch off a lamp hanging on the outside stable wall. "This way."

She couldn't imagine riding in the woods but she couldn't imagine riding in the jousting field either, which was almost as dark as the woods. The only light came from the moon or what faint light might be cast from a rampart torch. Then again, Harry had ridden this arena for twenty plus years, he must know the parameters by heart.

She saw the four lights once she reached the edge of the list field. "Are there men out holding torches at the corners for him?"

"No. Simon ordered wooden poles erected several years ago with torch holders."

"Why?"

The boy shrugged. "Not for me to know. Do you wish me to stay?"

"I don't think so but let me talk to Sir Harold before you go." She crossed into the field and waited by one of the torches while he cantered round the opposite end. As he came to the center of the top end of the field, he saw her, waved, and cantered over.

He wore a loose white linen shirt, dark leather breeches, and the tall boots he wore when working in the lists with the knights. His hair was windblown from riding. With none of the accoutrement of a knight--gauntlets, sword, tunic with the Guiscard device, or armor, he looked more like a highwayman than the Captain of the Guard.

"Sorry, I lost track of the time and kept you waiting." He laid his hand on his heart and tipped his head. "Forgive me."

"No worries. You're forgiven. The stable boy wants to know if he can go. Or should I have him walk me back and I will return to my chamber and wait for you there?"

"Ride back with me. Light our way to the stable, Edgar. Then, you and your father return and douse the field torches," Harry told him. "Take my hand." He reached down to Felicia.

She grabbed his hand and he pulled her onto the saddle in front of him. In a move faultless in its execution, she found herself wrapped in the powerful arms of a man who smelled like the outdoors, like the shire itself, a bit wild with its woods and streams and fields of green.

"Why are you out here with Simon's horse?" she asked, seeking a distraction from the rush of excitement she felt when he drew her to his chest.

"A favor to my friend who loved his mount. Odin hasn't had a chance to spend some of his horse energy the last week."

"Interesting name. I wonder why Simon chose it. We haven't been under Viking threat for a long time."

"Guy's horse was named Thor, you know, God of Thunder and strength. When Simon heard Thor answered to Odin and Odin was the sky God and God of War, he wanted that for his horse."

"Ah, kind of cool."

"Pardon?"

"Ignore that." Harry clucked, and Odin tossed his head once and began walking toward the stable. Felicia pressed her back to Harry's chest. Why not take advantage of the opportunity, while she had the chance? "What about your horse? How did you come up with Saragon? It's very unusual."

"It is. I heard the name from an old knight who served the Earl of Manneville. He fought in one of the later

144

Crusades and heard a story of a Sumerian called Sargon the Great who was a warrior and supposedly a great king and all that blather. I couldn't care less about Sargon. I've no idea what a Sumerian is other than a person from a place that existed long ago not far from the Holy Land. I like the name Sargon but I liked it as Saragon better." He rested his chin on the top of her head. "No great mystery. I should learn to tell a better story, shouldn't I?"

"No, that one is fine."

Felicia's hands could easily have rested on the pommel of the saddle. Resting them on his thighs was just as convenient. She chose them.

Warm under her palm and tight against his thigh, the buttery soft leather breeches were smooth as a second skin. A fine horseman, Harry held the reins in the light clasp of one hand. Odin responded to Harry's subtle leg cues, his firm thigh muscles flexing with the strength the cue demanded beneath Felicia's fingers and hands.

"Are you afraid?" he asked, pulling her attention from the feel of the rise and fall of his thighs.

"No, why do you ask?"

"Your breathing has grown noticeably faster."

His other hand he'd kept pressed to her middle. She'd been too preoccupied with those thighs to shield the desire he brought out in her. He stirred a mix of excitement at the potential of what a sexual rocket man she imagined he'd be. Dread tempered the joy of her imagined encounter. At some point she'd lie to him or at least mislead him, and she dreaded that day. That day wasn't today or tonight. Tonight started off being about him not her fantasies. Nothing was going as planned.

His thumb is stroking the bottom of my breast.

"You've strong hands for a lady."

"What do you mean?"

"Your grip on my thighs is remarkably fierce."

"Oh, sorry." Embarrassed, she loosened her hold.

"Don't be."

At the stable, Harry jumped to the ground and lifted her down. "I'll be up to see you shortly. I swear I won't be waylaid this time." He gave her waist a squeeze and ran his thumbs along the bottom of her ribs, tickling and arousing at the same time.

"Perfect," she said in a girlish voice she didn't recognize as hers for many years.

She started for the keep but turned after a couple steps. "Harry—" she called out before he entered the stable.

He stopped.

"You do know I planned on talking about Simon with you, don't you?"

He smiled. "See you soon."

Felicia hurried to her chamber. She grabbed her still damp panties that she'd washed earlier from the windowsill and hid them. Next she attempted to recreate Tildy's fluff job on her hair. Hard to say if she succeeded as she tromboned the mirror, pulling it closer then extending it out. The medieval mirror reflected a rippled version of her like a pond someone had thrown a stone into. Medieval women in movies never had these issues.

She glanced out the window. No sign of Harry in the bailey. She might have time to ask Julia if she had a vial of perfume. It occurred to her she didn't know if such a thing was available in 1359. Julia had perfumed soap. Harry said so. But a vial? On the rethink, best not inquire. Julia would ask why. Even if she didn't, she wasn't stupid. She'd figure out Felicia was getting prettied up for someone and more than likely Harry. She spent the most time with him. Another thing Felicia didn't know was whether Julia gossiped or not. Nor did she know if Harry liked to brag about his conquests by naming names, neither of which she needed.

Felicia checked herself in the mirror again. "Just what do you know, Felicia?" she asked the terrible reflection. There was a knock at the door. "Guess you'll find out about Sir Harold. No, you won't. This isn't a date. You set rules for tonight. Duh."

She opened the door and was pleasantly surprised. The heat of a blush warmed her from throat to hairline. If she was as red as she felt, so what? He looked oh-so-fine. Harry had dampened and combed his hair back. He'd changed out of his everyday black boots into better ones that had been polished to high sheen. They reminded Felicia of the ones worn by the Queen's Horse Guards.

Harry stepped inside and looked around. "Who's here?"

"No one."

"Who were you talking to?

"Myself. I can't believe you heard me." A bolt of panic shot through her. How much had he heard? The date part? The rules part?

"Was it a good talk?" He said it straight-faced but the snicker was unmistakable in the tone.

"It served the purpose. Don't you ever talk to yourself?"

"No. Please, I live in a barracks with fifty men and their squires. Even at night when everyone's asleep it's never truly quiet. There's always snoring or grunting and other manly noises. I relish the rare moments of quiet I get."

Made sense. Now that he brought the topic of noise up, she'd put quiet and serene at the bottom of the castle's adjective list. Castle activity generated a lot of noise with the variety of needs. It started with the stirring of the household servants at sunrise and grew with the traffic of tradesmen coming and going. The sounds as they conducted their business were joined by the barking, bleating, and whinnying of animals on the property.

"It's not too terribly loud in the bailey at this hour, but if you prefer, I'll shutter the window," Felicia offered.

"Leave it open. I'm not upset by the noise. I simply enjoy the quiet when it comes. May I?" He gestured at the ewer of wine.

"Absolutely. You're my guest. I'll pour." She poured two goblets and handed him one. She pointed to a chair. "Please sit."

Harry led her by the hand to the bed. "Let's sit on the bed instead."

"The bed? Ah, that wouldn't be very proper."

"Hosting me in your chamber alone without benefit of a chaperone is not proper either. Those hard-backed chairs aren't comfortable."

He led her to the bed. "Sit," he said and taking her wine, put both their goblets on the bedside table. "Sit."

She didn't move, a flurry of reasons for not obeying ran through her mind, none sticking.

"I understand. You don't trust me. I'm not asking you to get naked, Felicia. I'm asking you to sit on the bed where it's more comfortable. Or maybe you don't trust yourself, Hmmm?"

"Shut up." She smiled and sat on the edge of the mattress.

Harry knelt and started unlacing one of her shoes.

"What are you doing?"

"You're on the bed. Take your shoes off." He pulled the first shoe off and then the second. "Odd looking things," he said, examining her Reeboks.

"They're made for comfort."

"They make your feet look big."

"Thank you for noticing."

"Mockery? I'm offering the compliment of saying it's nice to know you're not vain."

"Stop. You're headed down a rabbit hole."

"I've no idea what that means." He sat next to her and removed his boots. "Scoot over so we can sit together."

She did, and he adjusted the large pillows behind her back and then beat the remaining ones into the shape he wanted for himself. Resting against the headboard with the pillows propped up was nicer than sitting in the chairs.

"Here." He handed a wine to her. "You wanted to talk with me about Simon." Harry sipped his wine. "What to say about the man? He was one of the few men I've known in my life who earned the respect of all he served with. He was brave, honorable, and fair. If you had asked me who, of all the knights do you want fighting next to you? I'd always have said, Simon Boatwright. He was already a squire when I came. His father died when Simon was a boy. Since his mother was a maid at the castle, the old baron brought him here to live. Simon only knew the life of a knight. When he lost his leg, he never thought a decent woman, a woman other than a tavern wench, would ever find him worthy."

"But Emily came along. I've known her all my life. He couldn't be with a better lady."

"True. She was the best lady in the world for him.

149

She brought light and laughter back into his life. I am glad he found such happiness before the end came."

"Did the knights like her?"

He shrugged. "Well enough, I suppose. We, me included, didn't interact with her much other than when we had our lessons. She showed great patience with us. Mature knights can be as childish as the kennel lads at times."

Felicia didn't doubt that for a minute. "What lessons did you have with her?"

"Most of us didn't know our letters. She taught us how to read and write."

"Are you glad you learned?"

He thought for a long moment before answering. "I guess. Truth be told, I haven't had a need to use it yet."

In his world, he'd probably never need it. Castle business was conducted by Richard. Harry didn't handle or see the ledgers. Any important document he wanted read he'd bring to Richard or take to the local monastery for a monk to read to him. Math was far more useful for him to know. Monies won at jousts or gambling he did have the math skills for as did the other knights from what she overheard. In the good weather months, many toured on the jousting circuit. Harry had told her Elysian Fields held a couple big events every summer. They were profitable for hosts.

"It was kind of you and the others to sit through your lessons without complaining. I assume you kept complaints to a minimum and didn't hurt her feelings."

Harry chuckled. "We complained bitterly to Simon. Every one of us. We hated the lessons. So boring. We just complained out of earshot of Emily."

"If you don't mind my saying, I thought you'd be

more upset with Simon's death. You seem—" She searched for the right word. "Rather unfazed, considering how well you speak of him."

"I knew he was dead after he'd been missing the second day. I saw no other reasonable explanation for the disappearance of the entire family."

"Richard and the other men held onto hope for several more days."

"I can't explain it other than I instinctively knew. I wasn't at ease sharing how the loss of my friend affected me. I mourned in my own way. Early in the search, most of the knights still held onto the false hope the family would be found. It served no purpose to discourage them."

Felicia empathized. "I've family who believe me coldhearted over my lack of what they feel is sufficient emotional display at funerals and the like. Tears come. They sneak up on me at unexpected times usually when I'm alone and a memory of the person occurs."

"Tears are no measure of the heart. I know women who can cry at the snap of my fingers."

She took his hand in hers. They sat quietly like that for a while until they finished their wine. The back of her fingers rested on his thighs. He still wore the buttery leather breeches. In the warmth of the chamber, his body heat radiated through them twice as hot as when they rode from the field. "I'll pour us another," she told him.

"Stay here. I'll bring the pitcher." Harry got up and brought the ewer over and replenished their wines. "What had you planned to say to me to cheer me?"

"I hadn't prepared a speech or script. I thought I'd play it by ear, see how downcast you were first. I wanted you to remember the good times. I honestly am not the best at raising people's spirits when they've suffered the death of a friend or loved one. You'd think as a doctor, or healer if you prefer, I'd have gotten better over the years. I haven't. But I thought I'd try."

"I appreciate you considered my feelings. Is that the only reason you invited me to your chamber tonight?"

"Yes." He didn't say anything, just held her in his gaze that recognized a lie for what it was. "No."

He brushed his lips over her temple, skimming her cheek on a path to her mouth that had her heart pounding.

"Such kindness from such soft lovely lips," he spoke the compliment a feather's distance above hers, his breath tickling and enticing her. He kissed her, deep and hard. Laying her hand back onto his thigh, he raised her skirt to the top of her thigh.

She moaned as he slid his palm up her leg and cupped the soft fleshy inside of her thigh. She drew in a sharp breath. Harry's leg tensed as her grip on his thigh had reflexively tightened. Now the back of his knuckles brushed the fine hairs between her legs. Every nerve ending in her body fired. His fingertips danced and circled around and along her opening. She groaned and lifted her hips, wanting those fingers to delve inside her.

She closed her legs around his hand and leaned into him, moving her hand from his thigh to cup him. The trace of air from his soft moan teased her temple. The wine became an annoying impediment to pleasure. She handed him her goblet. "Put this on the table," she whispered. "Yours, too."

As soon as the chalices touched the wood, Felicia climbed on top of him. She tucked her skirt and chemise up to settle herself on his leathered legs unencumbered by the yards of clothing. His chest rose and fell, the breath flowing in waves over the sensitive skin of her throat as she tunneled her fingers through his hair and grazed his jaw with her lips.

With a deft touch he undid the buttons he couldn't see on the back of her dress. She lifted just enough to allow him to push the bodice and sleeves down exposing the curve of her breasts under the thin cover of fine linen and ribbon. Barely touching her skin, his fingers drew a path over the curve up along her collarbone, stopping at the well at the base of her throat. He pulled her closer and grazed his lips from the well to her ear, nuzzling the now hyper-sensitive skin.

His mouth traveled a maddeningly slow journey from her cheek to corner of her lips. She thought she'd lose her mind if he didn't kiss her like he'd kissed her that morning.

"All I know is want for you."

His confession shattered her control as he took possession of her with another touch of his lips to hers and the deep possession of her mouth with a breath-stealing kiss.

He ran his hands down her ribcage and then snaked them up slowly, letting his thumbs tease her nipples. Lust fired through her veins. He kept her mouth busy with another mind-numbing-kiss and she ached to do something to relieve her fiery need.

She untied the laces on his breeches. He raised his hips and she tugged them down and pushed aside the cloth undergarment he wore, releasing him. He broke the kiss as she slid down to take the silken tip of his arousal in her mouth.

His hands on the delicate straps of her chemise, a long, low groan escaped him as she teased the tip with tiny licks. He pulled the straps down with a ripping sound, freeing her breasts.

"Sit up." He did and she removed his shirt.

Before she tried to do it herself, he had his breeches off. Naked, he sat on the edge of the bed and ordered her to stand in front of him.

She stood with her back to him and he finished undoing her buttons. Then, he had her face him and he removed her chemise the rest of the way. When he pressed his mouth to her inner thigh, she clasped his head in her trembling hands. She closed her eyes and just let the feel of his warm lips on her thighs take over her senses. His hair tickled the curly nest between her legs. He moved to her belly and then kissed each hipbone. He blew soft air on the circle of wet left behind. He pulled her down onto his lap. "Who are you really, Felicia?" he asked, thumbing her breasts.

"Nobody," she whispered. When she could stand it no more, she pushed him back. "I need you inside me. Now."

They made love once more during the night before Harry fell asleep with her in his arms. Felicia lay awake, her mind heavy with a thousand emotions. She'd been made love to before but never by a man like him, a man who generated such bliss and such guilt in her.

A tear rolled down her cheek onto his arm. He moaned but didn't wake. He's a tough knight she told herself. Maybe saying goodbye won't bother him the way it will her.

I never thought I'd like him this much.
Another tear.
She turned so it landed on the pillow.

Chapter Nine

"I'm going to leave before the servants wake and see me leaving your chamber."

Felicia woke with a start hearing Harry's voice. She'd left the window open all night so they'd enjoy the cool evening breeze. She rolled over and saw the dim grey light of dawn had only just begun to break through. The chamber remained dark as night.

"Can you see to dress?" she asked, sitting up. Harry was already at the foot of the bed.

"Yes, enough. Only your chamber is dark. The corridors have torches that burn all night as does the great hall. The servants that tend to them during the evening will be eating in the kitchen at this hour, which is why I should leave now."

She could tell from the sound of his movements when he had his breeches on and slipped his shirt over his head. The mattress dipped as he sat to pull on his boots.

She should say something but what? She'd like to ask if he planned on visiting her a second time. But then she boomeranged back to the issue of stringing him along when she intended on returning home. But who knew when or if that would come about? Was it so terrible to enjoy Harry's company while they had this time together? She slid her arms around his waist and rested her chin on his back as she wrestled with her conscience.

Harry shifted a half turn and tugged her to him for a deep and sensual kiss. "I'd like to spend the evening with you again tonight unless you prefer me not to."

The challenge to her good conscience vaporized with his asking. "I'd like that."

He kissed her a second time and stood. "I'll see you at breakfast."

"I'd like that too. I'm counting the minutes." Felicia tried to go back to sleep after Harry left but couldn't. She sat in bed contemplating what she'd do to pretty herself up with no real cosmetics available.

Julia was still the alewife to the people in the surrounding area. She told Felicia it was what she'd done to earn money before marrying Richard. Richard didn't mind her continuing with the work. Julia went into the village every morning to conduct business. Hitching a ride with her shouldn't be a problem. When Harry showed her the village, she'd noticed a woman who sold perfumed soaps from a cart. She'd buy a scented soap for bathing and for her hair and maybe a ribbon or two if the woman had any.

"What am I thinking, I've no money. Damn, damn, damn." She slammed her hand on the mattress. She hadn't been without money since childhood. Even then she had change. The Tooth Fairy was a generous soul as were her grandparents.

A dark solution danced into her head. Emily probably had those things and everyone thought Emily dead, which meant some of her beauty items weren't needed. Would it be in bad taste to ask Tildy if she could borrow some of those soaps? Her better self-asked, "It's extremely bad taste, Felicia, a horrid thing to suggest...but nonetheless, practical," her less-than-better-self replied.

She waited for sunrise before getting out of bed. Tildy had to help her get dressed every morning. The gowns all had a bazillion buttons down the back, which no woman on her own could manage, even if she were a contortionist. Tildy would arrive shortly before breakfast to help her get ready.

Felicia had finished her morning ablutions and personal needs when Tildy knocked and entered. She brought a dress of fine green wool with a full white linen apron embroidered with colorful flowers that took the dress from plain to charming.

She turned the bottom of the apron up to inspect the stitch work. Felicia knew what careful and tidy stitches on a human looked like. To her way of thinking they shouldn't be messy on cloth either. The workmanship on the back of the apron showed equal skill as the front.

"Did Emily embroider this?" Felicia asked, curious if she learned the art while living here.

"No. Lady Emily did embroidery but she was never good at it. Bless her, but she tried." Tildy smiled at the memory.

Felicia couldn't put off asking for the soap any longer. Whether this was the best time or not, who knows? The pleasant memory of Emily might work for her, might not. "Tildy, I see how much you cared for Emily. In spite of losing her, you've been kind to me and brought me her dresses. You brought me the soap the servants use for my baths. It's hard on my skin. It's drying. Would you consider letting me use Emily's soap? I assume she used a nice one like what Julia uses."

"She did. She and Julia both liked the lavender-scented soaps. I think she'd be happy if I gave them to you. She was generous that way. Anything else you like or need?"

"Some ribbon for my hair."

"I'll bring her box of ribbons, too."

****

After breakfast Harry said goodbye and headed for the lists to work the men. Felicia wouldn't see him until the midday meal. She headed for the kitchen in hopes of finding Leland and Tony. With Harry busy, she'd take advantage of the freedom to go and do whatever she liked, and that was a visit to the outcropping. First she wanted to see if Leland and Tony had more information to give her. They had to if they knew how to move people back and forth in time.

They weren't in the kitchen. She asked Drusilla if she knew where they'd gone. The poor young woman broke from churning butter and wiped the sweat from her face onto her apron. "I believe they went to see Richard about some tools they needed but after that I don't know."

"How long ago did they leave?"

Heather stopped plucking a chicken and said, "I saw them with Richard as he left the hall. That was a bit ago now."

"Thank you. I'll get out of your hair now." Felicia clarified before the baffled servants asked. "It's a saying from my home."

She went in search of Leland and Tony, but she was thinking about Drusilla and Heather and what nasty jobs they had. The callouses poor Drusilla must have from working that dasher, beating cream into butter, not to mention sore shoulders. Heather didn't have it much better, pulling pinfeathers from a chicken carcass. Felicia grimaced at the idea of the tedious job.

"Romantics can talk Age of Chivalry all they want. Once the hand kissing and bowing is done this business of women's work in the medieval world doesn't just suck, it sucks and blows, as the Americans say."

"Pardon milady, did you say something?" the cooper asked as he unloaded a barrel from his cart.

"No. I didn't mean to speak out loud."

She spotted Leland and Tony talking to the blacksmith. Tony had a stick and drew an image in the dirt for the blacksmith, while Leland appeared to explain the diagram.

Felicia called out and went over to join them.

"Excuse us, Ormond," Leland said and they moved out of earshot of the blacksmith.

"I've deduced the way back for me, for us, is that outcropping. How does it work?" Felicia asked low to make doubly sure Ormond couldn't hear since he wasn't hammering at the moment.

Leland glanced over his shoulder and then he and Tony leaned in as he started to tell her about the memory box. "Arrangements for travel time are made through a memory box."

"Where is that?"

"Let me finish."

"Finish what?" Norton, their guard, asked. "I leave to take a piss and right away you're conspiring with your heads together conjuring up mischief." He gestured to their threesome's circle.

"He was about to describe for her what we planned on making for Richard and Harry," Tony quickly explained.

"She'll learn soon enough. You should be on your way, Lady Felicia. They need to get back to their assignment," Norton said.

"Of course, I'm going for a walk in the woods now."

"On lovely sunny days like this, my mum loved to dig in the garden. She was always walking around with a shovel." Leland's pointed look spoke more than the words.

"A shovel." Leland had lost his mind. How the deuce was she going to walk through the gates with a shovel, allegedly for a stroll in the woods, and not arouse the guard's suspicions? "It is lovely. I'll look in the garden shed for a shovel-like tool. Maybe dig up some wildflowers on my walk."

"Back at it, you two." Norton gave Leland and Tony a shove toward Ormond's booth. He didn't follow. Instead, he placed a firm but light hand on her arm. "Did Harry say it was all right for you to walk in the woods?"

Blast Norton for asking. What to say? Dare she lie? Harry's time in the lists during morning sessions took him up to midday. She should be able to get to the outcropping and return with no problem. Harry needn't be the wiser.

"He's fine with it."

"Really?"

She didn't like the sound of that but she was committed to the lie now. "Really."

"Be careful. Do you wish me to find someone to accompany you? A male servant perhaps?"

She shook her head. "I'm not planning on being gone long. I look forward to the time alone."

"Still, be careful."

"Always."

She hurried to the garden and in a shed found an array of shovels, none suitable. All were too big but on the wall hung a bunch of trowels. She took the sturdiest, stuck it in her apron pocket, and went into the woods.

****

Armed with the information about the memory box, Felicia circled the outcropping. She kept her eyes on the ground looking for a disturbance in the dirt. It made sense that recent messaging had to have occurred to notify Simon and Emily when they were to be there. The problem with the soil around the rock was nowhere did it show signs of digging. Lots of trample marks, some hers, some Harry's from the other day. Some were no doubt left by Leland and Tony. She had to assume Simon and Emily too. A few of the smaller prints looked like they belonged to a woman's boot, the kind women around the castle wore. The prints definitely weren't Felicia's size nines. Leland and Tony didn't say if you arrived and left in the same spot where the box was buried. Maybe you didn't.

After a dozen times around the rock, she gave up searching for the easy clue of finding a turned soil spot. "Why can't these people do something normal like marking the rock itself? Paint a white X to mark the place where they should look down and dig. Pirates, Indiana Jones, lost treasure of the Knights Templar—who doesn't mark their secret spots? Didn't they ever watch old movies with treasure maps? What the hell?

Felicia figured to start at the place she was transported from and dropped to her knees. She began to tap the ground hard in hopes of hitting an object. Leland hadn't had a chance to tell her if the memory box was metal or wood. She assumed if it was buried to keep it from discovery by the wrong people, they used metal.

Her strategy was to work a meter at a time. First

pounding and then digging down at least a half-foot. She'd never finish by midday but she had nothing else to keep her busy. After the meal, she'd come back and work another meter-long section. It would take several days to complete the circumference of the outcropping. No other options for getting home existed, so however long it took, she'd make the effort.

They hadn't any rain in the last week and her arms paid a price, trying to make progress. The dry soil took two hands on the trowel to dig a hole the width of a long envelope. She guessed that sounded like a reasonable size for the box.

Finally she worked her way to the end of the meter. Without looking, she slid her knees back but the rest of her was stuck. The skirt of her gown was caught on something. She turned to see what and saw it wasn't caught on anything but held down under a large, black leather boot. The boot belonged to a pair that sat at the end of her bed last night.

"What are you doing?" Harry moved his foot off her skirt and lifted her up by the arm. He took her trowel and shoved it in his sword belt.

Think fast. Think fast. Think fast. Wasted instruction. Her mind was a big, fat, blank.

"Your silence tells me you're seeking a credible lie to tell me. Do not lie to me, Felicia."

She couldn't say; *I'm not in a position to tell the truth. You wouldn't believe me.* The best she could offer was a half-truth. "Leland suggested I'm right about this outcropping. It possesses some power we were swept up in and ended here, at home but not home. He's a scientist, as you know. He and Tony believe the power may radiate from the earth up into the rock."

He showed no reaction. She hoped it meant he hadn't rejected the theory out of hand, but was assimilating what Leland and Tony suggested and was processing the possibility.

"By radiate do you mean transmits?" he asked at last.

"Yes. The sun, for example, radiates heat rays."

"You're digging to find what?"

"I don't know. Something, anything that is out of the ordinary." She wished to be honest to the point of saying a metal or possibly wooden box.

"You seek a unicorn. No such power lies in the earth."

"I've nothing else to do with my time. Can't hurt to look."

If she blinked, she'd have missed the flash of pain in his eyes. "Even now? You're that unhappy here?"

Was she? No. But that no carried a condition. Harry. He made this time and place bearable. To her dismay, she had no measurable way of knowing how deeply he felt for her. Other than that tiny flash of pain in his eyes and his confession that he'd miss her if she burned at the stake, he kept his feelings to himself.

She had to answer him. "It's not that I'm terribly unhappy." With careful consideration to her choice of words, she explained, "I don't fit in here. I've no lady friends. I can't blame them. They don't know what to make of me." She stepped into him and laid her palms on his chest, hoping her despair could be transmitted through touch. "In my home, a healer like me helps a lot of people. I'm not allowed that opportunity here. Surely you can understand how isolated that makes me feel."

"What about Tildy? She likes you."

She wanted to grab a handful of shirt and shake him. *Tildy? Tildy? What about Harry? Does he like me? How much? For how long?* Lord have mercy but men were thick witted at times. How the devil did they get a leg up on us women politically?

"I like her too—she's sweet but she has her work to do."

"I don't mean to suggest you perform a maid's duties."

"I understand you meant afterward when she's socializing with her friends from the staff. Even if I were welcomed by them, I can't sit around embroidering linens and gossiping. I am sorry Harry. That's not me. I need to find something more useful to do. I'd be lying if I said I don't want to search for a way home."

"What if you had a more powerful reason to stay?"

Fear of what he'd say next grabbed hold of her. Her breath temporarily caught in her throat. Part of her wanted him to say the words telling her he wanted her to stay and part of her panicked at the thought. Both parts battled in equal measure. Why couldn't she have Harry in the twenty-first century?

He asked a question. She'd roll the dice and see what he said. "I guess it depends on what the powerful reason is?"

She stared into his eyes and he into hers for an eternity in silence. An elephant sitting on her chest would weigh less than the crushing weight of emotions this wait gave her.

Apparently, Harry wasn't going to say the words— *I want you to stay.* Relieved and disappointed, she let go of his shirt front and moved back a couple of steps. "How did you know to find me here?"

"Norton came to me at the lists and told me you went for a walk in the woods. He said you told him I allowed you to do so without an escort. He's not a fool. He doubted I'd agree to that.

"You've searched for your clue long enough this morning. Come back to the castle with me." He wrapped his arm around her waist. "Spend time in the garden. Enjoy the sun. After the midday meal, I'll have Cedric take over the men's afternoon list practice. We'll go sailing on the river. It will be nice, relaxing."

It sounded as pleasant an afternoon as she'd conjure up if he'd asked her what she wanted to do. Tomorrow, she'd return to the rock and search more. She had to, no matter what Harry hinted at. Hints carried little weight.

"Did Leland and Tony tell you what they planned to make?" she asked, changing the subject, genuinely curious.

"They're making an eyepiece similar to the periscope that Oliver made. It brings far away items into closer sight. You hold it in both hands."

"Binoculars?"

"He called them something else."

"Field glasses?"

"Yes. We've sent to the University of Oxford for special magnifying glass lenses they need. A lecturer at the university named Bacon invented a special glass with that feature. The Prince told us about it."

"If they work, will you free Leland and Tony?"

Harry shrugged. "Look a fawn." He pointed to the youngster as it darted away. "I wonder where the doe is?"

He had no intention of telling her what he and Richard planned. She told him they were the ones who said a clue to getting home might lie buried around the outcropping. He knew she'd enlist their help the minute they were released, if she knew when they were freed.

****

Harry met Felicia at the entrance of the hall as she arrived for the midday meal. He took her by the hand and led her toward the kitchen. "We're not eating in the hall."

"All right. Where are we eating or is it a surprise?"

"It's a surprise. You'll like it."

As they passed through the kitchen, Heather handed him a wicker basket. "Here, sir." Then she gave him a wine skin. "And your wine."

They left through the garden and walked toward the path to the river. "Are we having a picnic?"

"Yes, but downriver, away from prying castle eyes."

A red rowboat with the Guiscard swan painted on the bow sat on the riverbank. She'd wondered if the boathouse farther down the river belonged to the baron. She hadn't explored the interior but it looked like it held three rowboats this size.

"Is the boathouse down there castle property?" she asked as Harry set the picnic hamper and wine bag inside the boat.

"Yes."

"How many rowboats do you own?"

"Two. The baron has a larger fishing boat as well which is housed there during severe storms. Get in." He assisted her into the boat and once she was settled, pushed the boat into the river. He waded out up to his knees before hopping in and taking the oars.

They continued on the river until they came to a cove with straight sides and a semi-circle at the top. The funny shape reminded Felicia of a jigsaw piece.

Harry rowed to the left circle and when the nose of the boat hit the bank, he jumped out and pulled the boat up farther onto the shore.

Felicia gathered her skirts and the picnic hamper and sat on the edge of the boat ready to ease onto the bank. Harry lifted her down the rest of the way instead. "This way," he said, taking her hand.

They walked along a Monet-worthy path bordered by twisted ancient oaks and thick with shrubs of various sizes and variegated greens and bordered by twisted ancient oaks. The path ended in a glade surrounded by bushes covered in wild roses.

"This is beautiful." Setting the basket down, Felicia went from rose bush to rose bush sniffing and admiring the different shades of pink flowers. "How did you find this spot?"

Harry spread a blanket he'd brought from the boat and looked up. "Do you really want to know?"

"I get it. This is your cool spot to take chicks."

He mimicked her gestures. "What is this that you did with your fingers?"

"Air quotes."

"Air quotes? Your answer begs an explanation."

"It's a retro phrase that people used to say."

"Air quotes, retro phrase..." He gave a little shake of his head. "I'm still mystified. Don't bother to explain," he told her, raising his hand. "How is it we are both speaking English yet we are not?"

She grinned, appreciating the irony. "I'm ready for wine."

"I'm ready for wine and food. I'm ravenous."

Felicia stuffed a chunk of bread with cheese and nibbled at it between sips of wine, eyeing Harry with curiosity.

"You're staring."

"I'm wondering why you haven't married. You are a man of good station, Captain of the Guard—"

"That's only recent."

"Still, Richard wouldn't have appointed you if you weren't a well-respected knight. You're handsome. You have a lot of charming ways with the ladies, as you've said more than once. As a potential husband, you've a lot to offer a woman. Why hasn't a lady snapped you up?"

"I'm not familiar with the term *snapped me up* but I take your meaning. I don't wish to leave a widow or children without a father."

"There are married knights at Elysian Fields."

"True. It's a risk they're happy to take. I am not. I've fought in brutal battles and been fortunate enough to come home unscathed. Who's to say how long my good fortune will hold?"

"I've seen a few widows doing different jobs at the castle. You said Guy made provisions for wounded knights to remain at the castle for the duration of their lives. I can't imagine the widows of knights killed in action would be turned away."

"They aren't. Many of the widows you've seen are wives of dead knights. The children who are the kennel boys and work as the kitchen staff errand boys are their sons and daughters."

"There you have it. You wouldn't be leaving a widow or child in a hopeless situation."

"Sir Guy provided for the families. He's dead. Who's to say what the young Baron will do when he takes control? I won't chance sending a widow out to beg or worse."

Men throughout history from the Egyptian dynasties up to the early twentieth century sought male heirs. "Don't you want to have a son to carry on your name?"

He shook his head. "I've two brothers to carry on my family name. I imagine at least one of them has had a son."

"You don't know?"

"No. We haven't spoken since I left home."

The information did not fit her vision of life in this time. It wasn't as though people here had the terribly busy lives that modern people have with their work and commuting and all the other niggling things that fill our day. She imagined life here was so much simpler. She imagined there'd be occasional days his family would visit the castle just to see Elysian Fields and to see him. After all, he was the only knight in the family. That had to be a source of pride. If nothing else, she thought they'd meet with him at the village inn and catch up with each other.

"Have they never visited you?"

"No. They have farms to work."

"Can they never leave the fields for a few hours?"

"I suppose. If they don't, so be it."

"You never go to them?" He shook his head again. "Don't you wonder what is happening in their lives?"

"A little, but I was neither a favored child nor an especially wanted child. Just one of several. I think you need to be special to be missed. Conversely, I feel no pressing need to see them." He said it in a matter-of-fact tone and Felicia believed he'd long ago shed any hurt caused by the distance from his family.

He set their goblets of wine down. Gently cupping her chin he tipped her head, bent and kissed her. "That's to ease your worried heart. I saw pain for me and the estrangement from my family in your eyes. Worry not. Blood doesn't always make for family. The men I fight with, eat and drink with, laugh with, suffer the rigors of war with, they are my brothers. The servants in the castle, men and women, we share the good and not so good in our lives are my family. The sadness of losing Simon and Emily, the happiness of a new birth, holiday cheer, the joy of the summer's festivals fill my world. My life is not empty. I'm not lonely."

"Good. Now kiss me again."

They stayed kissing for a while, touching without speaking, sharing an intimacy that usually belongs to longtime lovers. "There's a pretty pool nearby that feeds into a stream. Would you like to see it?"

"Yes."

Beyond the wild roses bushes lay a wide path where an old stone wall stood, its stones fallen in places and overgrown with ivy. "Somebody must've lived here once. Who built the wall, I wonder?"

"Probably a small farmer taken by disease during the time of the Black Death. Our area wasn't as devastated as others, but we still lost a fair number of people to the plague."

Black plague struck England several times. Felicia rifled through her memory of school history lessons from two decades earlier. The worst plague years were 1348-1349, this had to be the timeframe Harry referred to when he said they lost many in the area. Her stomach flip-flopped remembering when it returned to England: 1361. That put Harry at risk again. Would he believe her if she warned him? What could he do about it even with advanced knowledge? Her medical training didn't prepare her for preventing the plague, not without modern means. She had no words of wisdom to offer or any idea how to stop a rat infestation of the magnitude that triggered plague.

They reached a pool, a black mirror that reflected the willows and colorful shrubs surrounding it. The perfect reflective surface rippled with activity at the top and bottom. Flat, rocky shelves dotted the place where an upper stream fed the pool then narrowed and fed into another stream. Felicia loved the graceful white swans that floated along from the mouth of the stream through the pond, down to the lower stream. They traveled in pairs with their lifelong mates.

"I love swans. They're so elegant and graceful."

From under one of the rock shelves came a single black swan, flapping his wings and sailing at a rapid pace past the others. Harry pulled Felicia in front of him and wrapped his arms around her. "That's me, the black swan."

"Why do you say that? You're not black-haired or dark-eyed."

"It's nothing to do with my looks. You're one of the white swans, the fairest of diversions in my life. I am the black swan in your life, a peculiar personage you don't know how to decipher."

"I disagree. That description diminishes you and what you are to me."

He leaned down and kissed the sensitive skin beneath her ear and then took her hand in his. "I am more then?"

"Yes. In the beginning, you were a mystery, part of a place I didn't know how to decipher because I didn't know how I got here. You were never a peculiar personage, not in the least. To me, you've become the unanticipated firestorm."

"I like the sound of that." He drew sensuous circles on her inner wrist with his thumb. "Where do you burn the most?"

"The heat is mobile. It travels."

He raised her hand, brushed a soft kiss across the palm then asked, "Do you swim?"

"I do."

"Let's go in the pool. It'll be nice on a warm day like this. Oh, there goes the second black swan, must be the penne, flapping its wings that way." He began unbuttoning her dress.

"Is a penne male or female?"

"Female, now that the flapping has stopped, see how she tucks her wings back in a penned manner?"

For a large man with large hands, he worked her buttons with remarkable speed. When he finished, she turned to help him. He opened his mouth to say he didn't need help, she could tell, but he caught himself before the foolish words came out. Instead, he allowed her to undress him.

Only his shirt and tunic were available to her. She could get the breeches off but his boots were an issue. "You have to sit down for me to remove your boots," she told him.

"I'll get them."

She punched him in the arm as he bent to pull a

boot off.

"What was that for?"

"Declaring the last swan was a female due to the flapping. She hadn't tucked her wings yet. What a bounder."

He chuckled and continued attending to his boots. "You're holding my tunic against you like a shield, why?" he asked after he stripped down. "I've seen you naked."

"I'm not concerned about you seeing me. I've never been naked in public."

"You're not in public. You're in a glade surrounded by woods. I don't think rabbits and squirrels care much about your state of undress."

"Have you ever been naked in public? Not in an isolated clearing like this but where other people can see you?"

He took his tunic from her, folded it and set it on the ground. Holding her hand, he led her to the pool. "Yes. When we're on campaign we all take advantage of rivers and streams we come across. After we fill our water bags and the horses drink, the men strip down to wash off the stink of battle."

The water didn't get past her calves when she pivoted and started for the embankment. Harry grasped her by the wrist and held her back. "Where are you going?"

"It's icy cold. Where did this water come from, the Scottish Highlands? How can you bear it?" she asked, seeing him wet up to the chest and not a goose bump on him.

"You'll get used to it."

"I don't want to."

He pulled her toward him, embraced her and floated backward farther into the water. "Better? Warmer?"

"Yes." It was, a little but she didn't want to admit

that and give up floating in his arms. She'd endure the water. She locked her legs around his waist and her arms around his shoulders and pressed her cheek to his. Her shivering lessened.

More swans joined them from a stream that fed the pool. Once she got used to the water the cool was a welcome relief on the warm day. In her own time, she'd put on shorts and a light top. Here she had to wear the forty pounds, or so it seemed, of the hot and heavy wool clothing women were forced to don to be considered decent.

Harry released her. She tested the depth and found the water wasn't over her head. She easily bounced on her toes off the bottom. She didn't dip her head under the water. Pond water struck her as too icky to stick her face into. Harry hadn't dipped under either. She stretched out and enjoyed the freedom of a swim. She circled the pool and did a few laps from the top to where the pool narrowed. Harry swam next to her, stroking out twice as many laps as she did with his greater reach and strength.

She was floating on her back, catching her breath after the laps when Harry said, "Want to get out?"

"Yes, I'm getting cold again."

They climbed out and lay down facing each other on the blanket Harry had spread. "Drusilla packed pears. Do you want one?" Felicia asked. She folded her arm under her head and dragged her nails across his chest.

"No."

She moved teasing fingers toward his belly. His quick inhale gave her a peek at the fine line of brown hair that revealed that not all men are adversely affected by cold water. Harry had recovered masterfully and when he threw his leg over her, she had firm proof of his recovery.

Lucky me.

He moaned as Felicia slid over on top of him. She refused to let him move, holding his arms down while she ravaged him with kisses. From his lips and jaw, she moved down, kissing and nipping his shoulders, then his chest, her thumbs stroking nipples and ribs. When she reached his belly button, she kissed the area and left warm wet marks that she blew on and made swirls around with her tongue. Harry groaned again and tried to pull her up, his every sound music to her ears. Right here, right now, she had power, however short lived, and it felt oh so fine. This was the most power she'd had since landing in this strange place.

She knocked his hands away. "You realize I have complete power over you, O Mighty Knight?"

"You do. I am enjoying yielding to you, milady."

She continued down his tensing body. He threaded his hands through her hair as she took him in her mouth.

"Enough. My turn." He rolled her over to start a path with his mouth, and tongue, and hands that started at the dip between her breasts. His hands fanned over her ribs as he paid homage to each breast before continuing his journey down. The barest touch of his thumbs aroused the sensitive skin of her hipbones to be followed by the caressing warmth of his lips. Those warm lips on the inside of her thighs worked wonders urging her legs apart.

"Harry—please..." she begged in a breathy whisper.

Cupping her bottom, he lifted and buried himself in her. A chivalrous knight even in that heated moment, he let her set the rhythm and waited for her to finish before finding his own satisfaction.

After, he lay down next to her and she rested her head on his chest, listening to his pounding heart beat as fast as hers. Behind them, a loud, high-pitched squeak sounded. She thought of one of Chloe's stuffy toys when under doxie attack. That squeak was followed by a series of them.

"That's one way to kill a moment. What is that noise?" she asked and rolled off Harry.

"That is one of your beloved graceful swans, a black swan to be exact. They make a hideous noise. The very opposite of what you expect from them."

"I'd like to put my chemise on at least. I've always been rather shy about being naked. "

Harry smiled and said, "We'll have plenty of time to be naked."

They both dressed. Conversation over the meal had a new ease that came from their new intimacy. The tear in time or whatever Leland and Oliver wanted to call the thing she got caught in, turned her world upside down. Harry turned it upside down and on its side another way.

Felicia never gave much thought to falling in love. She considered herself a fatalist regarding love. If she fell, great, if not, then the world wouldn't end. The sun would still rise, the earth still turn. She had friends, a loving family, and a satisfying career.

But Harry made her question what falling in love felt like because she just might be falling. This chauvinistic, arrogant, medieval man, of all the men she might fall for, how had Harry possibly stolen her heart?

Should she tell him the true ability of the memory box? She trusted him with the secret. "Harry..."

"Hmm?"

"I..." Renewed uncertainty came from whether he'd believe the truth of what happened. If he did and she had the opportunity to get home, would he come with her? Why not?

She'd convince him how wonderful he'd find the future. He'd only seen Gloucestershire and the counties on the way to London or the port when they sailed to France. At home she'd drive him the length and breadth of the British Isles. He could see all of the country he fought so hard for. He'd enjoy the convenience of electricity and indoor plumbing and running hot and cold water. She'd buy a handful of DVDs and he could watch the exciting war films like *Dunkirk, Henry V., Saving Private Ryan, King Arthur*. He was bound to find the future thrilling.

"I've something to tell you, something you'll find hard to believe but don't judge right away."

"Have you committed treason, murdered someone, or delved into witchcraft?"

"Certainly not."

He smiled. "I believe you're on safe ground. Go on."

"I..." She took a bracing breath. "I'm trying to think how best to start."

"Just say what you want to say, Felicia. But first, lay down next to me."

She stretched out by him again. Lacking the courage to look him in the eyes when she blurted out the truth, she focused on the clouds passing overhead. "I told you that buried at the base of the outcropping might be a clue to the power contained within it. There's more. Buried is a box that will allow Leland, Tony, and I, learn the exact means home. You see our home is truly here but we're from a different time. That's why things weren't the same for us. We're from the future. Please, please don't think me a mad woman for telling you."

Felicia waited for a comment, a laugh, or an

expression of shock, anything but silence.

"Harry?" She mustered the courage to sit part way up and look him in the eyes. Her response came in the form of a throaty rumble as he slept. Had he heard any of what she said? She shook him awake. "Harry. Did you hear what I told you?"

"I'm sorry. I dozed off when you started in about the base of the outcropping. What was the rest?"

No way could she summon up the courage to repeat the opening of her time travel confession. "Never mind, we'll talk later."

Chapter Ten

Harry spent the night with her again. He didn't bring up the conversation he slept through at the swan pool and neither did Felicia. She told him she'd tell him at a later time and she would, when there was no way around it.

Maybe he'd find out the time travel issue from Leland or Tony. Then Harry would naturally confront her with the truth. He'd be angry she kept that secret, but she'd overcome his anger with two-pronged logic. One, she'd argue she hesitated to tell him because it does sound mad. After all, he warned her not to speak to anyone else about her idea the outcropping might have special power. Second, when she did try to tell him, he fell asleep. Those arguments should ease some of his anger.

"Do you wish me to come to you again this evening?" Harry asked.

"Of course."

The dawn breeze ruffled Harry's hair as he stood in the doorway ready to return to the barracks. In that moment, Felicia couldn't decide which Harry she preferred—casual, hair free, shirt loosely tucked into his breeches, his black, heavily creased boots, and his sword and sword belt draped casually over his arm. Or, the Captain of the Guard Harry—Sir Harold, hair pulled into a queue, shirt tucked under a tunic with the Guiscard device or under his breast plate, black boots polished to a high gloss, his sword sheathed and worn. Both made her heart beat faster whenever she saw him, even at a distance.

She closed the door behind him and went to the window, watching for him. When he entered the bailey, she followed the shadowy form she knew was him with her gaze.

"What am I going to do about you, Harold Quarles?"

****

After breakfast Felicia hurried to the kitchen hoping to catch Leland and Tony.

The scientists were finishing breakfast when she arrived.. Leland had scooped the last of his eggs onto a spoon while Tony crafted a sandwich out of fried egg.

"Good morning, Felicia. You look well," Tony said and took a bite of sandwich.

"Thank you, you two look none the worse for wear."

The yolk on Tony's sandwich was just runny enough to soak the soft part of the bread. Her mouth watered with envy. The sight made her lust for a fried egg and tomato sandwich. She hadn't seen any tomatoes at the castle and doubted they'd reached Europe from the New World yet. When, or if, she ever got home, she'd have a giant sandwich loaded with tomatoes and cheese, with an egg on top.

"Drusilla and Heather take excellent care of us." Tony winked at Heather who giggled. "Did you go to the outcropping yesterday?" he asked Felicia.

"I did and I brought a trowel. Obviously, I couldn't bring a shovel," Felicia said in a quiet voice so not to be overheard by Heather. "It's going to take me forever to dig all around the rock. I wish you'd marked the spot the box is buried."

Tony looked over at Leland. "I don't know. I went where Leland and Oliver told me. Is it marked?"

Leland, who'd been drinking milk, swallowed. "Yes. There's a bright silver streak of mica the length of your forearm running through the granite. The box is buried in the ground right below."

Felicia could've hit him over the head and would have if anything handy had been within reach. "Why didn't you tell me? I spent the entire morning digging with that ridiculous trowel in the dry dirt. What a pain."

He shrugged. "Sorry. I forgot."

"Our possible route home and you just forgot to give me some clue? How does something that important slip your mind?"

"I don't know. I've had building the binoculars with Tony on my mind."

"You're an idiot. If I get back ahead of you, I'm telling your father he raised a twit."

He offered a nonchalant shrug to the insult. "He's heard it before. Are you going out again today?"

"Yes. Why wouldn't I? How deep is it buried?"

"Half-meter."

"A half-meter! Seriously? It's going to take all morning to retrieve the box. That's if Harry doesn't come along again. Your guard snitched me off yesterday. Harry turned up and brought me back to the castle."

"Speaking of Harry," Leland gestured for her to bend down. "Come close."

She did. Tony had finished his sandwich and came over to hear what Leland wanted to say.

"Is it true that you and Harry have a thing?" He

wiggled his brows.

"Who told you that?"

"Drusilla."

Reflexively, Felicia shot a glance across the room at Drusilla. "Where'd she hear that?"

"From Tildy. I take it the rumor is true then. You wouldn't be asking who else knows if it wasn't."

"My questions are not an indication of guilt. I am curious about the source of all the gossip. How can Tildy know such a thing?"

"Oh please, Felicia. We live off the kitchen so we spend a lot of time here. This is the one room all the servants stop in and talk. There are no secrets in a castle. There are eyes and ears everywhere."

"We do hear it all," Tony confirmed.

Did Harry know people were talking? Should she ask? Whether he knew or not, the point was moot now. All of Elysian Fields apparently knew. In her other life, she'd never been the subject of gossip. Rather ironic she had to travel seven hundred years to find herself the stuff of wagging tongues.

"You two best not be blabbing about Sir Harold and me and tell the others the same. She pointed to each in turn. "If he hears about the gossip, I don't think it will go well for any of you." She hoped calling him Sir Harold added oomph to her order. From the smirks on Leland and Tony's faces, it didn't.

"She's peevish, which means it's true," Tony told Leland with a smirk.

Felicia stormed out but not before grabbing a turnip from the bowl on the table and lobbing it at Tony. Typical scientist, his skills were all above the neck. He tried to catch the vegetable before it hit him but bobbled the attempt and was struck in the chest.

"Ow. What was that for?"

"Not telling me about the mark yesterday."

"Not fair, we had an audience."

"Excuses, excuses."

Felicia found the trowel where she left it in the garden shed and headed back to the outcropping.

At certain times of the day, when shadows covered the side of the rock with the mark, the symbols were nearly impossible to see. You had to know where to look. In the morning light and on her knees, Felicia found the mica streak without much effort. She began digging and after close to an hour, she hit the box.

"Finally." She pulled the box out of the ground. The lock had a small padlock attached, which was clamped shut. "Come on!" Leland hadn't mentioned a key nor that the box even had a lock. "I'm going to kill him."

She wrapped the box in a linen towel from her chamber. In the process, she discovered a key had been taped to the bottom. She tried it in the padlock and the box opened. Inside, the team on the other side had placed a cell phone, a pen and notepaper.

"There are no cell towers here. I can't text or call." She stared at the device, baffled, feeling more medieval in her ignorance than like a modern woman. "What other purpose does this serve?" She looked up when she asked the question as though the iPhone man would appear to answer. She turned the phone over in case she missed some clue attached to the body but didn't see anything.

Felicia placed it back in the box. She wrapped the metal box in the linen and returned to the castle. She had to track down Leland and find out about the phone's purpose. They were working in a three-sided canvas booth next to the much larger and wooden blacksmith's booth.

Leland and Tony stopped working as she approached. She lifted a corner of the cloth for them to get a peek. "I see you found the box," Leland said.

"I did. Where's Norton?"

"He's off talking to the blacksmith. We have a few minutes to ourselves to talk. You look inside?" Leland asked.

She nodded. "What am I supposed to do with this? I know what to do with a cell back home. What use is it here?"

"It's solar powered. I'm sure my dad put a video on it with some instructions. I'm sure he's concerned for our safety. Let him know we have to fulfill this condition to gain our freedom. He'll understand. Tell him you're able to return ASAP."

"No, I don't want to leave you two here. You wouldn't be in this position if you hadn't come to rescue me. It's not right I go alone," Felicia said.

"We'll be fine. We'll make their instrument, they'll have no more use for us and send us packing. We'll be able to return a few weeks behind you," Tony told her. "You can't pass on an opportunity to go home."

Anxious to see the video and make arrangements for getting home, Felicia asked, "How long does it take to charge?"

"Sunny day like today, leave the phone on your windowsill for three or four hours. That should be enough. I'm not sure how long the charge lasts. I never asked my dad. He handled the messaging. I'd put it on the sill first thing tomorrow morning as long as the maid stays out."

"Norton is returning," Tony said and busied himself with a portion of the metal lens holder.

"Let us know what you find," Leland said.

"Absolutely."

Felicia went straight to her chamber. The maid had already been there and tidied up. Felicia's room faced west, which was a lucky break. She had the benefit of hot afternoon sun. She laid the phone on the inside portion of the sill so if it fell, it would fall on the bedroom floor. But to be on the safe side, she placed a pillow on the floor for it to land on.

Next she sought out Tildy. "Tildy, my chamber is clean and I won't need any additional help today or this evening. Please tell the maid not to bother turning my bed down."

Tildy gave her a sly smile. "You'll have all the privacy you need, milady."

Felicia's first thought was to deny a relationship with Harry. A quick denial would only confirm the rumors. They knew what they knew. "Have a nice night, Tildy."

She prowled the corridors of the keep and the castle grounds the rest of the afternoon, going over again and again how she'd have to face saying goodbye to Harry.

When she couldn't stand the wait any longer, she hurried back to her chamber and turned on the phone. The battery was at half but the video was there like Leland said. Oliver asked for everyone's condition. Once he received an update on the situation, he'd send instructions how they'd arrange to bring them home.

Simon and Emily were also on the video. Simon addressed his message to Harry. "Harry, I'm not sure when or if you'll see this. If you do, be assured we are safe. I didn't want to leave Elysian Fields, but Emily has a life threatening illness. She needs modern medical treatment. I can't explain how Oliver and Leland managed to move us through time but we are still in Gloucester, England, only it is 2018. I hope no harm has come to Leland and Tony. They traveled back to rescue the doctor, Felicia Wycliff, who was mistakenly caught in the transfer I am told. Oliver is working on their return. I know Richard will have made you Captain of the Guard. The men look up to you. There's no better leader for them. That's it. Take care, my friend. See you on the other side." He nodded as he said the last. A soldier's code she guessed, probably a reference to meeting again in death.

Oliver came on again and suggested that the details involved in bringing them home would be confirmed in writing, which is why he included the pen and paper. Good idea, Felicia thought. Before he signed off, he lifted Chloe up and shook her paw as a hello to Felicia. She kissed her finger and touched the screen where the dog was. "My wee punkin."

The new noisy activity in the bailey meant the knights and others were headed into the keep for dinner. She put the phone in the box but took it out right away and put it on the sill. It wouldn't be dark for a couple of hours. The sun wasn't as bright as in the afternoon but a little more sunlight couldn't hurt.

"You've hardly touched your food," Harry said at dinner. "Is something wrong?"

"No. I'm not very hungry tonight." An honest answer and a partial one. She'd been lost in thought, people watching and absorbing the environment. This might be one of her last dinners at the castle. The time here had given her the rare opportunity to experience real medieval life. Only a handful of people she knew of shared that experience with her. Did they miss it, she wondered? To have seen Elysian Fields, a ruin in her lifetime, in all its Norman splendor was something she'd never forget.

She hadn't made any true friends, just Harry. But the people had been kind to her, a weird stranger dropped into their midst. Their time with Emily and Shakira probably had a lot to do with the last. The castle folk liked them and as a result were more charitable with her. That plus the fact Harry protected her. Without him, who knows how far their charity would extend?

Harry finished and pushed his chair back. "I will see you later than usual this evening. I have business in the barracks."

"I shall wait with bells on," Felicia said, pushing the sad thoughts of goodbye from the forefront of her mind.

"Do you have bells?"

She laughed. "No Harry. This is another we're speaking the same language but we're not moment."

He grunted, gave her hand a squeeze and left.

Felicia went to find Leland and Tony. They were sitting outside on the bench by the kitchen door, looking relaxed and talking over ale. Harry kept them under Norton's watchful eye only during the day. The gates were locked at night, which made escape difficult. Guards patrolled the ramparts and stood watch in the towers. In addition, Harry threw in the added warning that if they did try to escape, they'd wind up in the dungeon. Their kitchen quarters weren't much but they were clean-ish and as comfortable as the rest of the servant's quarters.

"Did you charge the phone?" Leland asked.

"Of course." The kitchen door was open while the staff went to and fro. "Let's walk and talk," she said. "You break for the midday meal the same time as we do, right? I see Norton eating in the hall."

"Yes," Leland said.

"I'll eat fast and hurry down with the phone. You can get a message to your dad. I'll bury the box in the afternoon and we await instructions."

"Are you in a rush to hook-up with *Sir Harold?* Tony asked her.

"No. He has business in the barracks. We're meeting afterward. Why?"

"Have a beer with us."

"I'll have a bit of wine with you." She went in the kitchen and found a pitcher of wine from the meal and poured a half goblet. Then, she joined them for a stroll around the bailey.

"In spite of the threat against you to make some useful item to gain your freedom, do you feel a special thrill being here, at Elysian Fields while it is still a grand castle?" she asked. "I mean, we're not making history but we are part of the life and times of those who are or will be. That's special. To me, at least."

"I'd agree. I have no desire to stay but I do feel this is such a unique and special adventure, I'm thrilled to be part of it," Tony said.

"Me too, this time, and let me add the caveat, so far. This journey isn't over," Leland said. "I'm not sure I'd wish to repeat the journey here or anywhere else."

Felicia sipped her wine and had to admit Harry added much to her warm feelings. "True, I suppose I'm romanticizing this. You've worked on time travel for so long and now you've achieved it. You're here. Isn't this how you pictured it?"

She expected they'd want to expand their experience, that, in spite of being held hostage, they'd have been enthusiastic. Their lack of response surprised her. "You're disappointed, then?"

Leland took a deep breath. "Not disappointed but adjusting is harder than I imagined. I could do without the smells, especially in the area of personal hygiene. Not all are bad but take the blacksmith we often work next to, good glory. The man works up a sweat during the day and a body odor to match. It clings to him like armor. It brings a tear to the eye some mornings."

Felicia snickered. "I can't disagree. There are a couple guards that walk the corridors who've made me wince when they passed."

"I miss electricity. Not so much for the convenience of flipping lights on and off. I miss the ability to work into the night on the binoculars, for instance. Even in the daytime we have to do the detail work outside in the bright sun. Those are the big downsides to me. An upside is the nature and heart of the people. In the main, they are delightful. Too superstitious for my taste but we've laughed together, shared family memories, complained about the same folks. I am saddened by fact they must accept a limited future for themselves. They are born in a certain economic strata and that is where they will die. But that said, being sturdy English stock they carry on."

"If I may add to his upside comment," Tony said. "They appreciate small pleasures that folks in our time don't." He smiled and said, "Take Heather: the cooper's wife paid her tuppence the other day for helping with chores. It was a joy to see how excited she was about buying new hair ribbons with the money."

Leland and Tony had grown attached to Drusilla and Heather. Felicia wondered if they'd hurt leaving them behind the way she would leaving Harry.

"As for me," Tony continued, "I appreciate how fresh the air is. With the exception of the night we spent in the damp dungeon, my sinuses haven't bothered me at all. It's the clean air. There are no noxious fumes drifting over from motorized boats on the river or dirty air from Cardiff or the highways. The sky is bright blue, not a speck of haze."

"We have gorgeous blue skies too," Felicia balked.

"Not blue like these. Look up. They are the color of Gainsborough paintings. And when it's quiet, it's a true quiet. I shall miss the peacefulness of this time."

They went back to the bench and talked for a while longer about their work on the binoculars. They talked quietly since half of the kitchen staff was inside cleaning up. Others passed by on their way to the garden to gather vegetables and fruits for the next day.

"What adjustment was hardest for you?" Felicia asked Leland.

"I am fonder than I should be of Drusilla. I want to design a tool or instrument to make her daily work easier but I can't. I can't interfere and give her an invention before its time. Bad enough we're handing over field glasses."

"I understand. I know if I stayed, I'd have trouble dealing with diseases I could cure in my time but not here. Ah well, nothing we can do about that." Felicia finished her wine and stood to go. "I'll see you tomorrow."

****

Felicia entered her chamber. The light outside had begun to fade, casting shadows in various corners of the room. She lit a thin, wooden stick off the candle clock's flame to light the larger candles on the table. The corner by the window where Harry sat filled with light.

"What is this?" Harry asked. He held out his hand with the baffling black square object in his palm.

Felicia jumped a foot at the sound of his voice and pressed a hand to her chest. "I thought you had business with the knights," she said in a breathy voice.

"I finished. Answer the question."

His tone was deliberately sharp and challenging tone to cover his chagrin. In a million years he'd never admit to his ignorance of what the strange device was used for or his fear of the harm it might cause through a source he couldn't predict.

"You never want me to lie to you. So I warn you be prepared for a truth you might never have wished to know." She extended her hand. "May I?"

He turned the device all around, checking for a means to indicate it might be a weapon. Nothing looked suspicious. "For now." He handed it to her.

"Want to sit on the bed while I explain?" Felicia asked, taking the device.

"No." He hooked his foot around the leg of the other chair and pulled it over next to his. "Sit. Talk."

She cradled the odd object and stared for at it. Harry leaned back putting added distance between himself and the object. He couldn't tell if she expected it to do something or if she was fashioning an answer. "If your hesitation is to concoct a credible story, do not. Whatever the unwelcome truth, I will have it and not a tale."

"You asked for truth. Well, here goes." She took a deep breath, let it out and spoke the truth. "I'm not from this time. I'm from this place, but in the future, as is Leland and Tony. That's why we know our way around the area, especially the land belonging to Elysian Fields and Stroud. It's why the buildings we are used to seeing aren't here."

"If you weren't a woman, I'd beat you for taking me for a fool. Only a madman or fool would believe that rubbish. How little you care for me that you do this with no remorse."

"Harry, I tried to warn you about what I had to tell you."

He grabbed the device from her. Again, he turned it over several times in his hand. He ran his fingers over the clear window and the strange backing, which was softer to the touch than the front. He tapped the screen. "What is this material? Where does it come from?"

"The future."

He grasped her wrist hard and yanked her closer. "Do not dishonor me or yourself with vile lies."

"I'm not lying. I swear on my soul. I'm not lying. It's called a phone. Give it to me and I'll show you what we call a video of people you know. You'll see what I am telling you is true."

He released his hold on her wrist and handed the phone back to her. She turned it over and pressed a small metal bar on the side. Felice used her finger to rapidly scroll past odd pictures, stopping on one. "Here you go," she said and showed him the screen.

Oliver's face appeared. Shocked silent, his breath caught in his chest as though a horse stood on him, choking off his air. He stepped away from the sight, resisting the temptation to shake Felicia until she made the picture cease to exist.

"No, it's the devil's work." It didn't matter he cared nothing about the devil this thing she held had no place in this world. He batted the phone from her hand. Felicia leaped and stretched, attempting to catch the phone before it fell. She caught the edge just enough to alter its direction. The phone landed on the pillow she placed on the floor.

"Thank God. Don't do that again. You could've broken it," she snapped at Harry.

"Evil should be destroyed."

"It's not evil. Is it catching fire in my hand? No. Is the smoky mist of a sorcerer's trappings spewing from it? No. Stop with the devil talk. I don't believe it's your nature to go along with the ravings of priests and their rantings about the devil. You're not a churchie sort of guy."

"You've the right of it, there. I don't believe in the devil. War taught me no fallen angel could do to man what we don't already do to each other." With a tip of his chin, he asked, "What is this then?"

"It's simply a tool, a means of communication from the future, nothing to do with the devil or God. It is a tool the way the periscope Oliver made for you is and the way the binoculars will be." The video had continued to play. She held tightly onto the object. She pressed a horn-shaped picture on the screen and Oliver began talking. "Just listen as Oliver is explaining how I wound up here."

Harry listened without comment nor did he attempt to attack the phone again. Felicia stopped the video when Oliver finished. "Do you understand Oliver had a means to bring Simon and Emily here and I arrived here during the process?"

"I understand this is a magical instrument made from material I am not familiar with. To convince me, perhaps you can conjure the face and voice of Simon whose exact end is questionable. Why should I trust Oliver? He was an Englishman traveling in the company of the French enemy...bah, a traitor if ever there was one. Richard should never have talked Simon into letting them go."

"Speaking of Simon, let me play more of the video." She let the recording proceed to the part where Simon came on and spoke his message specifically addressed to Harry.

A host of emotions made their way into Harry's thoughts as he listened and watched the image of Simon. A hint of sadness first at the sting of losing a friend, then anger and the sense of betrayal of his memory of Simon. Simon knew there'd be undeserved mourning for him and the family. The voice of logic reminded Harry that Simon left not on a whim but with cause. The logic did little to dispel the anger. In the end after Simon finished and Oliver came on again, disbelief and confusion fueled Harry's reaction.

"If you are from the future as you claim, then my future is your past. You know what it holds." Her conciliatory expression changed to caution. She started to balk, which he anticipated and cut her off. "I don't want to hear an excuse. You ask me to believe this mad declaration. I ask you to provide more proof. I am owed that."

"What do you want to know?"

"When will I die? Is it in battle?"

"I cannot tell you that. I am not a seer. Being from the future doesn't give me a looking glass to all the past. Even if I did know the details of your death, I wouldn't tell you. Somethings are in the hands of destiny or God or Gods, if you prefer."

"I can face my fate. If you're from the time you say, then you must know."

"Again, I'm not a seer. I don't know when your death occurs or Richard's or Julia. I can tell you the destiny of some well-known figures from this time. For us, it is history and we are taught certain facts."

He gestured open-handed. "Indulge me."

"The king will outlive the Black Prince. The Prince will contract a fever on campaign fighting with Spain. He will suffer for several years with the illness. When the king dies, the Prince's son, a boy named Richard, will be crowned. They men in power and the people grow to hate him and will imprison him in the Tower where he'll die."

Edward of Woodstock wasn't someone Harry ever thought of dying without being king. He was one of the heartiest, most able-bodied of men, especially for a royal. "The Prince will never rule. Such a fine man and soldier. What a terrible loss for England. What of our war with France? Will we win?"

"Yes but the victory won't last. Henry the Sixth, another king decades from now will suffer from a madness inherited from his mother. He too will be usurped and die in the Tower."

"What of England? What becomes of us?"

"England will have its struggles, like many countries, but she is strong and survives. There's a time when she will be the mother country to many colonies."

It occurred to him that all the campaigns against France, past, present and future were ultimately a lost cause. The men's lives lost, a waste. But, all she said might be nonsense.

Felicia reached over and tucked her fingers into his hand. "Harry, what are you thinking?"

"I don't know what this thing you hold is, but I know the story you tell cannot be true. No person can move through rock."

"We're not moving through the physical elements that comprise the rock. There's a metaphysical, an unseen feature that allows an opening through time, a doorway for lack of a better word."

"How is this transfer through time achieved?"

"I don't know. Leland does. He worked with his father on the system."

"When Emily and Electra came here, they were dressed in the same fashion as you. Are they from the future too?"

"Yes, they're friends of mine."

"Why did they come?"

She shrugged. "I don't know. I wasn't aware they had until you talked about them. Emily is considered a missing person and her mysterious disappearance generated a great deal of gossip."

Harry stood and slipped his hand under her arm. "I'd like to learn more about this so called doorway. Let's talk to Leland. Bring that talking thing."

When they reached the scientists door Harry didn't bother to knock. He threw open Leland and Tony's door, kept a tight hold on Felicia's arm, and kicked the door shut behind them. Leland and Tony had been playing cards. They both froze, nervously glancing from Harry to Felicia back to Harry.

Leland's apprehensive gaze dropped to the phone in her hand. He laid his cards on the table. "I think I know why you're here."

Tony saw where he was looking, sighed and set his cards down too.

Harry jerked Tony from his chair and pushed Felicia into it. He turned to Leland. "Tell me about how you move people through time."

"My father and I discovered that when hit with enormous electrical power for a short span a force within the outcropping opens a tear in the fabric of time. We don't know what about that particular rock is the origin of the tear or why nothing around it possess the same quality."

"What is this electrical power you speak of?"

"We have a machine that mimics super lightning. You've seen how powerful lightning is and the damage it can wreak." Harry nodded. "After many experiments, we learned how to create a similar force, maybe not quite as strong as nature but enough to open the time tear."

"If you had this ability, why didn't you utilize it immediately to bring me back?" Felicia asked. "I might've been attacked or worse while you left me here. Thank heavens Harry brought me to the castle."

"The machine's power is limited. We've developed it to the point of one super strong blast but then there's a period of twelve hours needed to restore power. We knew you'd have moved on by then," Leland explained.

"You should've tried anyway."

Harry was too proud to show his disappointment, hearing the depth of her zeal to return. He'd have thought her fervor to go back might've lessened in the past weeks as they grew closer.

Right now he wanted to know more about the phone. Harry left but returned a moment later with a chair, wine, and two goblets. He poured wine for Felicia and himself in the goblets. Leland and Tony had tankards of ale.

Harry took a long pull of the wine. Everyone else drank in silence.

A long uncomfortable minute passed before Leland spoke. "Believe us Harry, we've no desire to stir your blood more than we already have. We meant no harm to anyone here. We came to help Felicia," he explained.

Harry took the device back and scrolled with his finger the way he'd seen Felicia do. He scrolled until he found Simon's image. "I don't believe this image of Simon is true." The more they said, the more suspicion grew in him. He turned to Felicia. "I'm trying to decide your purpose in showing me this falsehood. You knew it would wound me. He was my friend. If you can mimic lightning, you can find a way to mimic my friend."

"Harry...I—"

Leland quickly spoke up. "The man in the video is Simon. Not a trick. Our science was able to achieve this."

"If your science is so brilliant, you must have more you can impress me with other than a picture of dubious origin." Harry sat back in the chair. "What else have you? And no blather about dead kings in our future."

"In our time, we'd amaze you. But, we came for Felicia not to bring flashy bits and bobs to amaze you. We hadn't planned on getting captured. And frankly, we wouldn't bring anything too modern with us. That'd be too dangerous," Leland told him.

Tony perked up and interrupted, "I brought something. My eyesight is flawed. I can't read writing that's close up clearly. I need what we call eyeglasses. They are a distant cousin to the binoculars we are making for you. They have two lenses set in a frame that rests on your nose and ears. As a precaution in case we were caught, I didn't wear them. Instead, I wore contact lenses. I'll show you." Tony bent and lifted one from an eye.

Harry grimaced. "What is he doing? Stop!"

"I'm not hurting myself." Tony showed him the contact in his palm. "I've one for each eye. They're made of a special soft and pliable material that is curved to the eye's surface but made to correct vision problems." He extended his hand further and gently squeezed the contacts. "They're pliable to make them easier to work with."

Harry looked unconvinced of their specialness. "Is that all?"

Leland looked at Felicia. "My dad said Prince Edward made Electra show him her gold crowns. I don't have any crowns."

"Me either. My fillings are porcelain."

"I see it's up to me again to save the day. I have two molars crowned in gold. When we get back, you both owe me a bottle of Johnnie Walker Blue," Tony told Leland and Felicia. "Harry, in our time when you have a bad tooth, you don't have to pull it. You can clean the rotten portion out and cover it in gold. You save the tooth that way. Want to see an example?"

"Show me."

Tony opened his mouth wide and tapped the side of his jaw where the crowns were. Harry peered inside Tony's mouth, spotted the crowns, and gestured with his finger. "Open more." When he did, Harry removed his eating dagger and leaned in again.

Tony pulled away and shot a hand up. "Whoa, whoa, whoa."

"If I wanted to stab you, I'd have done it long ago. Open your mouth again."

A sour-faced Tony did as he was ordered.

Harry tapped each crown with his dagger and then sat back, putting his dagger away. "Seems to me you could find a better use for gold."

"Do you believe us now?" Felicia asked.

"I remain uncertain. How can I be alive here and Simon alive there? I am in 1359 and he is in 2018, when I am long dead. Explain this."

Tony had left the room and come back with a bowl of flour.

"I can offer only a theory," Leland said. "We believe we're functioning on parallel worlds. The time tear connects the two. The theory we favor is that the worlds can exist simultaneously because each has its own place, its own timeline for lack of a better word. My dad and I think, but aren't certain, that the only difference is our world is slightly ahead of yours in actual time."

While Leland explained the parallel world theory, Tony smeared a thin layer of flour on the table and drew what looked like a modified version of the universe. Harry recognized the universe from a sketch Emily had made for a lesson she gave the knights.

Leland continued, "By behind you, I mean that when we've brought people back there's a difference between how much time they have experienced passing here and what has actually passed in our real time. A brilliant scientist called Einstein theorized that space-time is curved and that accounted for the difference."

Harry sat quiet again. With one sweep of his arm, he cleared the table. Goblets flew across the floor. Felicia's wine splashed on the wall, the floor, and Leland's shoes. Felicia flinched and sucked in air, Tony and Leland recoiled, Tony nearly knocked over his chair.

Harry stood, his green eyes dark with rage. "What a wicked, selfish lot all of you are. You treat the people here like landscape for your experiments, background to be dealt with as needed. Why do you people keep coming?" He fixed on Felicia. "You disturb our lives. You injure people without remorse."

"That's not true." Felicia reached for him but he remained out of arm's length.

"Some incidents have been accidental. We don't know what happened to bring the sisters other than it was not planned, neither was Felicia's coming here. Don't blame them. They triggered others to come to their rescue. We came to bring Felicia home," Leland said.

"The point is—you tinkered and tampered, testing until you found a way to open a tear in time. Now, you cannot control the results of your toying with the natural order. Once Felicia is returned home, once you've fulfilled your duty and made the binoculars you promised, you two go. Then leave us be." Harry paused at the door and in a low voice repeated, "Just leave us be."

****

Harry didn't come to breakfast. Felicia had mixed feelings about that. She wanted to grab and hold onto every opportunity to be with him, to hear him speak even if it was only to offer her bread. Another part of her ached with the knowledge of how much he hurt and she was a big contributor. She hadn't slept well and sat at her chamber window watching the sunrise. That's when she'd seen him leaving the stable on Saragon.

After breakfast, she brought the box and a trowel and walked to the outcropping. Leland had recorded a message for his father about their binocular project. She had recorded a brief message and confirmed everyone was in good health. She also wrote the same on the paper provided per Oliver's request.

Felicia had dug half the distance down she needed to when a horse whinnied behind her. She turned to see Harry jump to the ground. He tied Saragon to a low branch of an alder. He drew a proper shovel from a leather loop attached to his saddle and came over to her.

"How deep does your box have to be buried?" he asked.

"Half-meter."

"In words I understand."

"This much further." She showed him with her hands. "Why are you helping me? You made it clear last night you don't like any of us."

He kept on digging and said, "I never said I didn't like you. I care about you more than you know but you've made it clear you've no desire to stay. Your happiness lies elsewhere. I'll help you go there."

He had the hole dug to the right depth in three shovelfuls. He stepped aside while she nestled the box inside the spot. Harry filled the hole and tamped down the loose earth.

"Thank you." Felicia sensed she should respond to the comment about her strong desire to go home. She hadn't tried to be diplomatic expressing her wish. She'd been candid because it was true. Why did the truth ring so bitter when she heard the words spoken back?

"I'll give you a ride to the castle." He lifted her

onto the saddle, untied Saragon and mounted.

Harry said nothing on the ride and neither did she. If he was using silence to make her feel guilty about leaving, she refused to allow it. She had every right to want to go home.

Felicia stayed in her chamber until the midday meal. Harry missed that meal too. When she finished eating she visited with Leland and Tony until they had to return to working on their project. Harry was a no show for dinner as well. She itched to ask Julia or Richard about his absence but thought, why? He wasn't going to starve. He was likely eating in the barracks. Obviously, he wanted to avoid her. So be it.

I won't feel guilty.

The next day Felicia dug up the box and checked for news. Oliver and the others were ready for her. She was to be at the outcropping the following morning approximately an hour before midday. That was a busy time at the castle and the least likely time anyone would look for her. Not that many people had a reason to seek her out but it was a precaution Oliver wanted to exercise.

She chose the prettiest necklace Emily owned to wear the day of the journey. She didn't plan on keeping it for herself, but Tildy said Simon gave it to Emily. Felicia thought she would love to have it again. Harry still avoided coming to the hall for meals so Felicia sought him out. She waited outside the barracks for him. She wanted to say goodbye.

She grasped Harry's arm as he stepped out the door. "I'd like to speak to you alone."

He led her to the end of the building where he said the men didn't pass by on their way to the lists. "What is wrong?"

"Nothing. I wanted to say goodbye. I am leaving later this morning. If all goes as planned, that is."

"What time?"

"Around 11. Harry, I...I." She hadn't intended on baring her soul but what the hell, she was going. "Harry, you made a frightening journey special and happy. I will feel the loss of you forever."

She waited in real time maybe only ten seconds. Any other day to count out, one thousand, two thousand, and so forth to ten thousand, the seconds pass in a few blinks of the eye. But when you're waiting for the words that can change the course of your life, those seconds pass like years.

When the words didn't come, Felicia said, "Goodbye, Harry." She turned and started to walk away.

"Felicia."

She spun ready to rush to him but couldn't move. He encircled her with his arms and held her tight to him. One hand pressed hard on her lower spine, the other cradled the back of her of her head, his devastating kiss lifting her onto her toes. The kiss stole all the air from her and she stole what she needed back from him. Elation filled her. No man kissed a woman like that if he intended on letting her go. It had to mean he'd come with her to the future. Didn't it?

Her fingers tunneled under the top of his breastplate and curled over the muscles of his collarbones.

Harry broke the kiss but continued to hold her, touching his cheek to hers. "Goodbye, Felicia," he whispered. Releasing her, he walked away.

He'd reached the barracks door before it dawned on her he truly wasn't going to change his mind. He wasn't going to walk back to her. She turned and hurried toward the gates, her chin up. She repeated the mantra: don't cry, don't cry, in her head as she passed through the portcullis and over the drawbridge. Her pride refused to shed a tear but not for any good reason. No, because she still held onto the ridiculous ray of hope he'd change his mind and she didn't want him to know she cried over him.

She arrived at the outcropping early. She estimated it based on the time on the kitchen candle clock when she said goodbye to Leland and Tony. That time combined with how long she spent with Harry and walking to the rock put her arriving with approximately a half-hour to spare.

She plunked down directly in front of the mica streak on the rock. Instead of dwelling on her hurt, she tried to concentrate on what she'd do with her first day home. Cuddle with Chloe topped the list. Take a hot shower, brush her teeth with a proper brush and paste, change into comfortable jeans and a top, and go to a good local takeaway that served something besides stew or bland porridge. She considered several foreign options. Indian curry sounded best.

"Come on Oliver, zap me already. I want to come home." She stood and stretched. She closed her eyes, willing Oliver to hear her. "Come on, come on, come on, let me get this debacle over."

"Felicia!"

Opening her eyes, she saw Harry throw the reins over Saragon's neck. He jumped down and ran to her, pulling her into his arms. "Stay." He kissed her savagely, a kiss insistent on bending her to his will. "Stay."

Felicia didn't have a chance to answer. One moment she was in his arms, ready to remain in the medieval world, the next they were caught in a whirlwind. Everything around them spun too fast for her to identify. Sights passed in a blur of greens, blues, and browns. She clutched his shirt tight in her fists truly afraid one or the other of them might spin away to a different time and place. She didn't remember any noise the last time. She thought she heard Harry call her name but his voice was drowned out by a high-pitched whirring. Then the two of them were on the ground, tossed there by a powerful force.

Chapter Eleven

She rolled over onto her hands and knees and waited for her stomach to settle. Prone to nausea when turned in circles, she avoided carnival rides. Fortunately, she didn't feel a need to throw up and her stomach calmed quickly.

Harry was on his hands and knees as well. He spit twice. "I've a terrible taste in my mouth like I drank a tankard of salt water. Ugh. He tried to stand but lost his balance, flailed and beat the air and managed to stay upright. "Are you dizzy?"

"Yes, but it's passing. I was the last time too. Oliver activated the machine. This is exactly how it was for me before. My mouth is also crazy watering."

Harry had found his feet. "Is that all there is?"

"What do you mean?"

"If I'm traveling across centuries, I expected to experience more."

"Like what?"

He made a circling motion with his hands. "I thought I'd be hurled through time and land on my feet like so." He stopped the circle motion and put his fists on his hips like an arriving conqueror.

"Like an invading Viking on the prow of his ship,

you mean?"

"Not exactly but rather like that, yes."

"Sorry to disappoint."

The outcropping was nowhere in sight. As far as the eye could see the landscape was green fields with an occasional hill. "Viking hopes aside, where's the outcropping?"

"Where are Oliver and the others? He said they'd all be here to greet us." Felicia spun around and wide-eyed asked, "Where are the woods?"

"Good question. You had the woods in your time, yes?"

"Yes, they've been there forever."

"This looks like it might've been farmland until recently but I can't see any identifiable crops. There's no evidence of woods ever being here."

Felicia shook her head. "We can't have landed in the right place."

Harry looked around. "Nothing is familiar to me. This isn't the Baron's land. Where are we, do you know?"

Felicia took the hand he extended to help her to her feet. "No."

"Does this look like your time in anyway? Is it close to where we should be?"

"I can't say one way or the other. We have green fields in the twenty-first century too and our farmland is similar. I need to find a village and I'll know more."

"As we don't know if this land belongs to friend or foe and until we do, let's try to stay out of the open as much as possible," Harry advised.

"We've no reason to think we aren't in England still."

"Allow a soldier his caution."

"No harm is being cautious."

Harry took her in his arms. "I'm sorry."

"What for?"

"We're in this situation because of me. I should've have spoken my heart and asked you to stay when you came to me outside the barracks. You would never have gone to the transport spot and this mishap wouldn't have occurred."

"Don't blame yourself. I seriously doubt your presence made a difference. From what you said, Electra, Roger, and Oliver left together. They traveled to my time without any glitches."

His rueful expression softened. The contrite frown disappeared. He wrapped her in his arms and held her close. Tipping her chin up, he confessed, "I am embarrassed to admit I never gave you the credit you deserve. You are a remarkable woman. The way you handled yourself, an unwilling traveler to my time, is nothing short of admirable. Most women, most men for that matter would've fallen to pieces. Here in a time and place we're not sure of, I can deeply appreciate how you managed to stay strong."

"I can't lie and say I'm not scared. But I'd rather be scared with you than without you. What matters most to me is you wanted me to stay. You came to me. You've unbroken my heart."

That made him smile. "I've never broken a heart before."

"You still haven't." She kissed him.

He pointed to a white cottage and clasped her hand in his. "Shall we?"

"It's sort of silly to be scared. Landing in the wrong spot doesn't mean we landed in a bad spot. The people who own the farm can tell where we are, I'll borrow a phone and call Oliver to pick us up," Felicia said. "You're going to love the modern world. Wait till you feel how good a hot shower feels. Wait until you see television. You don't have to rely on visiting minstrels. We get entertainment from around the world in our drawing rooms now. Food from around the world is minutes away by car. Cars—wait until you see how fast you can get places. I'm going to have so much fun showing you my world."

She slipped her arms around his neck and gave him a sloppy, wet smooch. "Can't wait. And yes, I made that deliberately messy."

They walked for several minutes through the fields. As they did, Felicia noticed the unusual emptiness around them. "You know what's funny, I mean funny peculiar, not funny laughable," she asked.

"What?"

"Not one of these hills has animals grazing. It looks like excellent farmland, the house ahead looks to be a farmhouse, yet I see no sheep or cows or horses. That's peculiar."

"I agree."

They crossed over a knoll covered with yellow wildflowers. When they were halfway to the farmhouse Harry said, "Have you noticed how badly chewed up this field is? A large body of people had to have crossed it. A lot of horses too, judging from all the manure piles. There are numerous tracks from heavy wagons as well."

Harry picked up a handful of dirt and rubbed it between his hands. "This is excellent soil, good for crops. No farmer would willing allow people and horses to tear up his fields this way. There something very wrong here."

A short time later they reached the farm. The orchard attached to the garden offered the first cover of trees for them. They crept into the barn and found it empty.

"No animal has been here in quite some time," Harry said.

"How can you tell?"

"No feed is stored. The loft is empty. The doors on a couple of the stalls are broken. The farmer couldn't secure his livestock. There's no tack or equipment for handling animals. Very strange."

They left the barn and eased up to the back of the house. No voices or sound came from inside. "Stay here. I'm going to explore," Harry said. He drew his sword and slowly moved along the wall toward the front of the house. A few minutes passed and he returned. "There's no one there. It appears abandoned."

Felicia followed him inside. The cottage consisted of two rooms with no furniture. Broken wooden pieces lay around that might've once been parts of a table and chairs. So little remained she couldn't say for certain.

"This is bad," she said.

"What do you see? What's so bad other than the place is a shambles?"

"It's what I don't see. There's no appliances—no fridge, no stove, no sink with faucet for running water, no microwave, nothing a normal kitchen would have. This is really weird."

"I don't know what those things are but I'll take you word for it. Let's look for food and press on."

To their disappointment not a crumb of food could be found anywhere in the place.

"I saw pears on the trees. We'll have to load up on

them until we find a village," Felicia said.

Outside Harry stepped away while she gathered fruit. She'd moved onto the well and was in the process of drawing a bucket of water when he joined her.

"Do you hear that hum?" he asked and finished pulling the bucket up for her.

She nodded. She'd become aware of it when they neared the cottage. The sound wasn't specific and easy to identify, just a low, deep hum. "I didn't know what to make of it. Do you know what it might be?"

He cupped her cheek and kissed her forehead and then said, "I'm afraid I do. That's the sound of an army readying for battle."

She didn't believe him. He had to be wrong. "No, that can't be. Why do you say that?"

"Felicia I've been in many battles. I know what the lead up to them sounds like. What you're hearing is the hum of frightened men unsure if they'll see another sunrise talking among themselves, the whinny of cavalry horses getting tacked by squires, and knights checking their weapons. I think we're about to come upon the body of people who crossed the farmer's fields. It explains this abandoned land."

"How far away do you think the camp is?"

He shrugged. "The way sound travels over flatland like this, maybe a mile. Not far."

They'd have to view the warring armies to learn where they were and know the timeframe. No planes had passed overhead since they arrived, nor had any bombs fallen, nor had there been the sound of machine guns. The elements of modern warfare she'd seen in movies and read about in school. "If a battle is to come, heaven knows what that might mean for us." She pulled in a long breath and let it out slowly. "No choice but to press on. We'll eat while we walk."

Harry nodded. "We must."

His estimate proved right. About a mile away from the house, they climbed a knoll covered in dried grasses. Felicia and Harry crawled on their bellies to the edge of the top. Below an army in red uniforms with tall black hats was forming columns. Farther off to the left, men in blue uniforms and similar hats were forming skirmish lines. Felicia knew instantly the horror of what she was viewing.

"Dear God, no."

Chris Karlsen

Chapter Twelve

"Do you know who these armies are?" Harry asked.

"Sadly, I do. They're English and French."

"Damnation, we are still fighting the French in your time," his disgust and frustration heavy in his voice. "Will we ever not be at war with them?"

"That's the problem, Harry. We aren't at war with the French in my time. We're allies. This isn't my time. It can't be."

"Can you place what war this is?"

"It's the Peninsula War. We studied it in school. It took place in the early 1800's. A great but bloody and brutal English victory known as Waterloo came during the war. We defeated the previously undefeated Bonaparte of France."

Harry studied both armies. Felicia suspected he was calculating the odds for victory each had. "Which are the English?" he asked.

Both sides flew their flags. Harry wouldn't know either. Neither the Union Jack nor the French Tri-color existed when he fought the French. "The men in the red uniforms."

"More the pity, the French are better organized and have the numbers on their side. But the same was true at Crecy and Poitiers and we defeated them then, perhaps the day will be ours again now. When does this great victory occur? Is this the day?"

"I'm not sure how close we are to the date. The Battle of Waterloo occurred on June 18, 1815. But I can't tell just from seeing this where we are in the course of the war."

"Felicia, do you have any idea why we didn't find ourselves in your time?"

She shook her head. "None." A terrible realization followed on the heels of the nightmare that they'd landed at the wrong time and in the midst of a war. "It's worse than that. We aren't even in England. We're somewhere in Belgium."

"Belgium?"

"You know it as Flanders. I don't know what went wrong with our exchange." She began to tremble uncontrollably. She wrapped her arms tight around his neck and burying her face in his shoulder where the breastplate didn't cover. "How will we get back?" she whispered, unashamed of her panic. "I don't know what went wrong or how to fix this."

Harry held her and slowly stroked the length of her spine. "Shh, we'll figure this out together."

She calmed and stopped shaking. Panic wasn't the answer. She enjoyed a few more minutes in Harry's arms and then pulled away and turned her attention to the action on the field.

To her horror, a man exited from a white tent with two flags flying in front of it, one the Union Jack, the other with a fancy standard she couldn't decipher. Felicia squinted to get a better look at him, fearing she already knew he was the most important man in the English army, the Duke of Wellington. Who else flew a standard of such elegant design on the battlefield? He wore a short red jacket with a black sash. Gold braiding hung from epaulets covered with more gold braiding. His uniform confirmed her fears.

"Shit."

"What now?" Harry asked.

"That man," she pointed, "is the Duke of Wellington."

"How do you know?"

"I've seen a dozen portraits of him." She looked over to the French side and the white tent flying the Tricolor. Tied next to the tent was a great, white stallion. Napoleon was always pictured on a white stallion. "I'm afraid we're about to witness Waterloo."

Chris Karlsen

Chapter Thirteen

"We have to find a better place to hide," Harry said, surveying the scene in front of them. "If we're discovered, our presence on the battlefield is too hard to explain. We're not Flemish and English civilians have no business here. Both sides will take us for spies."

Harry was right. Unfortunately, no immediate solution came to her. "Problem is; I'm not familiar with this country. Even if I were, it would be a different landscape, a different environment from my time. I've no idea where we'd be safe." Felicia glanced back at the farmhouse. "What about the farm?"

"It won't be safe after the fighting starts. There will be desertions—always are. They'll probably take refuge there. We could get overrun. Once they killed me, they'd take their time abusing you. They'd show no mercy to a woman."

Harry studied the two sides as they formed up. "Artillery has come a long way. I see why you say this is a bloody and brutal battle. To a soldier like myself, though, all wars are." He watched the Duke relaying orders to his officers. "Who is the English duke again?"

"Wellington."

"Based on his tactics, artillery on the flanks, foot soldiers between, and cavalry bringing up the rear, I believe we can hide by that waterway without discovery." He pointed to a bank of green lining the area behind the English camp. "The horses won't notice us with the noise of the guns and screams and clash of men. As soon as the duke signals charge, we must make a run for the bank."

Wellington mounted his stallion. Bonaparte had mounted several minutes earlier. He'd donned a black tricorn hat, a fashion of the period. Felicia thought they were stupid looking; flat at the edges with a rise in the middle. The wearer looked like he plunked a mantle clock on his head.

Napoleon spent time riding up and down in front of his lines. Felicia assumed he was calling out how they were fighting for Liberte, Egalite, Fraternite, and all that French revolutionary jazz.

"What remarkable weapons those cannons are," Harry said. "If we'd had just one that size at Crecy, there'd have been no need to fight at Poitiers."

Out of place as the thought was considering the carnage about to occur, Felicia saw an unexpected elegance as both sides formed up. The field was a sea of colors. Waves of color with the English infantry in red uniforms and white trousers, behind them the cavalry was dressed in deep blue. The English's royal blue was a different shade than the darker blue of the French infantry. Behind them, the French cavalry wore in green. "I have to wonder, if both armies have regiments in blue, how does one soldier in blue, in the confusion of battle, recognize the enemy blue from that of their own men?"

"You go after the one trying to kill you." His expression remained placid except for the faint grin of amusement at his answer.

"I was serious," Felicia said.

"I was too."

The French Emperor and the English Duke took up their places at their lines. At their commands, the first shots were fired.

The ground trembled. Harry jumped. "God's teeth. What a noise, much greater than our cannons. Time to run. Ready?"

Felicia gathered her skirts, Harry grasped her hand and they bolted for the embankment. As soon as they reached the top of the slope they dropped down and lay flat on their bellies, while keeping the battle in sight.

"I see the commander you call, Wellington, and the French leader...what do you call him?"

"Napoleon Bonaparte."

"Bonaparte and the Duke remain observers out of the conflict. At Crecy and Poitiers, I rode with Sir Guy in Prince Edward's column. The prince never sat back. He entered the fray along with us when we charged. A leader must earn respect. It isn't done by watching alone."

Felicia couldn't think of a twentieth century general who jumped into the mix voluntarily. "Times change and both Wellington and Napoleon have fought in previous battles."

Harry snorted. "The Prince never stopped engaging,' he added in a superior tone. Harry pointed to an infantryman loading his rifle. "What is that long weapon they fire?"

"A musket. It fires a ball about this big." Felicia made a circle with her thumb and middle fingers. "Nasty thing. It can travel through you, a clean through and through wound. But more often than not, it will strike a vital organ on the way. Or, it can bounce around inside you doing all kinds of damage to bones and organs and muscles."

He squinted and leaned forward. "What's under the shaft that they're using as a stabbing device?"

"A bayonet. It's a sturdy knife that attaches under the barrel. That's what that shaft is called. I don't know how it attaches exactly. I've never handled a musket, just seen pictures."

"Clever." He eyed them with the appreciation of a man groomed all his adult life for war.

"Hmmm...yes, when it comes to killing each other we are a clever species."

The artillery on each side fired again and again, the ground vibrating with each shot. Felicia wondered how many men working the guns suffered hearing loss from the deafening blasts.

The English infantry lines had broken. There were approximately two hundred meters between where she and Harry lay and the rear lines. When they retreated to the embankment, she thought that distance sufficient. As the distance shortened with the French pushing hard against the English lines, two hundred meters now appeared not much of a safe zone. Finally, the English lines held their ground but the safe zone had now begun to fill with the wounded.

Line after line of men fell victim to the other side's muskets. Enough men were wounded and dying now for their cries to be heard over the roar of guns.

Many men would survive the wounds they received, if they received treatment in a timely manner. "They need medics to do triage."

"Medics?"

"In modern battles, certain men are designated as medics. They treat the injured with temporary means until the wounded can be transported to a secure location with better equipment. Many of the injured will bleed to death or have their wounds become septic unless they are treated in a timely manner.

"Look at that poor fellow." She pointed to an English soldier turning from the battle lines. He held onto his throat with one hand and stumbled toward the embankment. Blood oozed between the fingers at his throat.

The soldier raised his arm and looked right at Felicia. She swore he mouthed, "Help me."

An officer next to Wellington raised the regimental colors and then dropped the banner. The cavalry, in columns, charged. They were met with a furious counter charge by the French cavalry.

"My God, what chaos. The horses are stepping on friend and foe alike," Felicia said. The lines of men with muskets had broken apart. Some men had room to continue firing, while others had resorted to hand-to-hand combat or bayonet work.

"Savage chaos is a better description."

A steady stream of wounded men now staggered or crawled from where the fighting was most intense. They filled the empty space between the embankment and fighting. One man made it to the foot of the embankment before he dropped to his knees. Like the fellow with the throat injury, he looked Felicia in the eyes and said loud enough for her to hear, "Please." Then he fell forward.

"I can't watch this and not help." Felicia stood.

Harry quickly scrambled to his feet and held her back. "What do you think to do?"

"I'm going to help them."

"No, you're not. It's not safe. You'll get yourself hurt or killed."

"I can't sit here and watch men die. I'm a doctor. I can treat them. I can save some. Let me go."

Harry drew his sword. "You know this is a mad idea, don't you? Don't bother to answer. If you must go, I'm going with you."

They hurried to the man with the throat wound first. A musket ball had passed through his neck. The wound was almost certainly mortal but she felt for a pulse just in case. "He's dead. Bled out. Let's move on."

At the time he'd collapsed the spot where he landed had been free of wounded. Now many lay scattered there. She went to a soldier who wailed in pain as he rocked back and forth, holding his arm. "Let me see."

He shook his head.

"I can't help you, if you don't let me see the injury." She turned to Harry. "Give me your knife." He did and she pushed the soldier's arm out of the way and cut his jacket sleeve. "Your arm is broken."

"One of our cavalry rode over me as I fought with a Frenchie on the ground. Bloody bastard." He eyed Harry suspiciously. "What are you?"

The soldier looked barely out of boyhood. His beard mere fuzz yet but he should recognize what Harry was. "I'm a knight, stupid lad."

It dawned on Felicia what confused the soldier. She'd gotten used to seeing the knights in armor and hadn't noticed Harry still wore his. "He doesn't understand why you're wearing a breastplate in that style. The ones used in this period are different."

"Oh, I wondered why he didn't know a knight on sight." Harry started removing the armor. "I'll put it under my tunic."

Felicia helped him buckle the breast and back plates together the way his squire would and then returned her attention to the soldier, inspecting how bad the break was.

Harry knelt beside the soldier and examined his musket. "Show me how this works."

"What kind of knight are you?"

"Not important. Just show me how this works or I'll break your other arm."

"Harry really?" Felicia scowled.

"I have to protect you and this seems a nice addition to my sword."

The soldier handed him his powder bag, wadding packets, flint, and rod for loading the musket ball. He explained how to measure the powder and set off the load.

"I'll set this but I'll need to splint it afterward. I need material for the splints. Can you gather some branches from the trees by the waterway for me?" she asked Harry.

"I don't want to leave you."

"I'll be fine. I have to have splinting material. Leave me your knife. Just hurry back."

All around them soldiers writhed in pain. "I guess I don't have to warn any of this lot but keep a sharp eye for any who are walking wounded. Kill anyone who looks at you wrong. You understand me?" Harry asked.

She nodded. Walking wounded could easily become marauding outlaws. She gave a fast look around and seeing no one who appeared threatening began cutting the skirt portion off of her chemise bodice. When she finished, she cut the skirt up into strips.

Harry returned with a bundle of branches. "I tried to choose those that were closest in size to one another." He shrugged. "Not a lot of choices."

"I'll make do."

"Where did you get the bandages?"

"I cut up my chemise. If you would, cut the strap from his musket. I'll use it as a sling." Harry did as she asked. "Hold him down as I set the bone." She warned the soldier. "Sorry, this will hurt, but I'm trying to save your arm."

Harry put the strap in the man's mouth. "Bite on this."

She'd have to apply traction to straighten the bone before splinting. "Got him?" she asked Harry in a loud voice to be heard over the volley of guns. He nodded. He'd seen broken bones being set and understood the pain involved.

She gripped the soldier's arm tight and pulled, hard and fast. The strap muffled his scream and he attempted to jerk up, but Harry pressed him tight to the ground.

"The worst is over, soldier," Harry reassured the young man as he removed the strap from his mouth.

Felicia worked fast and they moved onto the next injured man. He lay motionless, staring up, pale even for an Englishman. Perspiration beaded his forehead. He might've been taken for dead but he blinked.

"He's on the verge of going into shock," she told Harry. "Where are you hurt?" She asked, kneeling next to the wounded man. The ground trembled with constant cannon fire. Officers shouted orders, trying to be heard over the battle. "I can hardly think with the noise—the cannons, the muskets...and..." She covered her ears as wounded men and horses screamed.

"The din of it all?" Harry squatted alongside her.

She nodded and dropped her hands.

"Battles are all a nightmare of noises kings and generals care little about. They don't want men to think. If given too much time to think, the armies would drop their weapons and go home to their farms," Harry told her.

Felicia put her mouth near the ear of the wounded man and repeated the question. He didn't answer. She opened his jacket and lifted his blood soaked undershirt. "You've a bad slash under your ribcage."

The man moaned and cried out as she prodded, trying to determine how deep the wound was. "Am I going to die?"

"Not if I can help it. I'm going to do what I can to clean and bandage your cut. I wish I had a needle and thread."

Harry cut away the cleanest portion of the soldier's shirt. "Use this to wipe the worst of the blood and any dirt away. I'll hold the flesh together when you're ready to wrap."

Felicia perked up as an idea popped into her head. She patted the man's cheek so he'd pay attention and she asked, "I assume this being the Duke's regiment, it passed through Bruges. I've been given to understand all you fellows loaded up on the gin brandy the town's known for. Do you have some left?"

The soldier looked to Harry as though seeking permission to tell her the truth. Harry said, "Tell her."

The soldier nodded.

"Where is it?"

He handed Felicia his water canteen. "There's not much."

"I don't need a lot. Harry, dig out his musket wadding, would you?"

She poured the brandy over the wadding. "I'm not sure this will work but I have to stop the bleeding. With no ability to sew the bleeder closed, the best way is to stuff packing in the wound. This brandy is the only way I can think of to sterilize the packing. If I must use this type of alcohol, fine Cognac would be better but I'm sure that's out of his paygrade."

"You lost me," Harry said.

"Not important."

Finished with the soldier's packing, she reassured him he'd be taken to the field surgeon soon. A reassurance she couldn't know was true.

She and Harry stayed bent low and scrambled over to another wounded man. Seeing the raised portion of his uniform trousers covering his thigh, Felicia had a sick feeling about his injury.

"Can you help me?" the man asked.

"Maybe." She tried to sound encouraging knowing the odds were against her. She cut his trousers open and confirmed her worst fear. He had a compound fracture and the bone had severed the femoral artery.

Harry laid his hand on her shoulder and gave her shoulder a sympathetic and consoling squeeze. With his battle experience he knew there was no hope not unless the man was taken to the surgery in the next few minutes, which was unlikely.

"How bad is it?" the soldier asked.

"You need the surgeon to mend the break. Lie quiet. The more you move, the worse you make the wound bleed." She looked over at the distant surgeon's white tent and told the soldier a comforting lie. Unlike the young man with the slashed side, this man had no chance of getting to the tent in time to stop the heavy flow from the severed artery. "The surgeon's assistants will tend to you soon."

Before they reached the next wounded man, behind them a voice said, "You two, come with me."

They turned and found a middle-aged soldier with corporal stripes pointing a musket at Harry. "Drop the gun," he ordered Harry.

"Are you blind? Did you not see she's treating the wounded? I need the rifle to protect her."

"Drop the gun." The corporal jabbed the bayonet toward Harry's chest.

"You're costing English lives," Harry snarled and threw the musket to the ground.

"Come with me," the man ordered still making prodding motions with his bayonet.

"Where are you taking us?" Felicia asked.

"To the surgeon. Start walking. That's his tent." He indicated the white tent.

When they entered the corporal had them stand off to the side as the surgeon operated bare-handed removing a musket ball from a soldier's arm. Felicia cringed. So unsanitary. If she were a gambler, she'd bet as many men died of fever, gangrene, and tetanus as died from their wounds.

He finished and ordered the injured man taken to the hospital barracks. He came over to where Felicia and Harry stood. Wiping his hands on a clean linen cloth, he addressed Harry, "I'm Captain Crosswell, the regimental surgeon and a personal friend of the Duke's. Are you her husband?"

Harry placed his arm across Felicia's torso. She didn't need him to tell her to let him speak for the two of them, at least in the beginning. He had to say they were married. An unmarried woman traveling with a man they would assume was a whore. She saw no good end to that assumption.

"Yes, she is. We didn't do anything wrong," Harry added.

"I'm told your wife was treating men on the battlefield. What is she playing at? Treating the injured is serious business." Based on his expression, he rated her on par with horse manure.

"We know. No one questions your role as surgeon. In our village, she is a skilled healer. We were on our way home to England and accidentally found ourselves in the midst of battle. As a healer, she only thought to render aid to our wounded English."

"May I speak, Captain?" Felicia asked.

"You may."

"Obviously my abilities can't compare to yours. But many of the wounds weren't life-threatening, just cuts, slashes, and broken bones. All injuries that as a woman, I am able to treat in the field. I can sew the slashes and set many of the bones. It saves you time and to use your talents on the more serious wounds."

Crosswell was silent for a long moment and she feared he'd still turn down her offer. "There is truth in what you say." He sniffed and continued, "No woman will ever understand the workings of the human body the way a man does. There'll never be women surgeons. However, I do see the advantage to freeing up my time by letting you attend to some of the less serious injuries."

She held her tongue and dug her nails into her palms as Crosswell waffled on about the inferiority of women.

Glancing around the surgery, Crosswell asked, "What do you need from me to help out there?"

"A needle and thread, two buckets for water, bandage material, and splints."

Harry spoke up. "I could use an extra set of hands for security. It's hard to keep watch over my wife and lend her the occasional hand as well."

"I'll give you Corporal Skaife." Crosswell gestured to the corporal who escorted them to the tent. "Out of curiosity, why two buckets of water? You only need one to dip a cloth to clean the wounds."

"One is for me to rinse my hands between men. The other is for boiled water to wash the wounds and to sterilize the needle and thread," Felicia explained.

"Rinse your hands every time before moving to the next man?"

She nodded. "I believe it prevents cross-contamination." She hoped maybe that explanation might plant the idea it was worth him trying the same.

Crosswell snorted his disapproval. "That's a foolish waste of time. Silly feminine thinking. Exactly why I said women can never be surgeons."

"Can I just have a bucket to rinse my hands?"

"Fine. Gather what she desires, Skaife."

"How did you know we were out there?" Harry asked.

"Skaife saw you when he brought that man with the musket shot in his arm to the surgery. I'm satisfied you mean no harm and I must return to my injured. Are you sure you don't need anything else?"

Felicia thought the boiled water wouldn't last long

as a sterilizing system. "Do you have any lye or lye soap?"

"Not handy."

Felicia thought why not take a shot in the dark and ask for cognac. Crosswell could only say no. "Cognac, if you have it. It's not the best for sterilizing but worth a try."

"How you go on about sterilizing. I don't have any but the Duke has a goodly store. Skaife will run and secure a bottle. I'll make it right with Wellington."

"Thank you."

She, Harry, and Skaife were an hour into triage and treatment. Wellington's artillery, which had been decimating the area where Napoleon had the highest concentration of forces, suddenly stopped. The English guns pivoted and began an assault on a French flank. Felicia glanced over to Wellington who sat mounted in the same place he started, off the right flank. In the crush of helmeted combatants a grey-haired man on the French battlefield moved among the throng of men but carried no weapon. Felicia quickly realized he was treating the wounded. He stopped to nod his gratitude to the Duke and Wellington returned the acknowledgement.

"My goodness, it's Dr. Larrey," Felicia told Harry. "We read about this incident in medical school."

"What incident?" Harry asked.

"Yes, what's going on?" Skaife also asked.

"Napoleon brought the best French doctors on campaign with him. Larrey is the best of the best. His fame was...is," she corrected herself to present tense. "Well known among officers of all sides. Out of respect, Wellington turned the guns to allow the doctor to work."

"How do you know about him, if you're not French? This sounds like information a spy knows." Skaife said. He retrieved his musket, which he'd laid down while helping treat the wounded. "What exactly were the two of you doing here anyway?"

As Skaife raised the rifle, Harry pushed the barrel of the musket down. "My wife's younger brother ran away to join the army. He's underage. The family fears he will be killed. We came to search for him. He'd spoken of wanting to join Wellington's regiment. We haven't found him."

Skaife didn't looked convinced. "How does she know about this French doctor?"

"Just gossip we heard traveling the countryside on our search. My wife being a healer heard about him from other women like her."

The battle had finally ended, at least for today. She wasn't sure how many hours passed when they finally finished. Skaife had replaced the buckets of water a dozen times. All the splints were used along with the bandages. She'd gone through the Duke's cognac and wished now she'd kept a few swallows for herself and Harry. After washing her hands in the waterway and splashing water her face, Felicia plopped down and rested against a tree. Never had she been this exhausted, not even during her residency.

Harry dipped his whole head in the water, shook like a dog, and then smoothed his hair back. He joined her still dripping.

"Hey," he leaned forward and cupping her chin in his fingers, tilted her face toward his. "You're crying. Why?"

"Those men I had to ignore when they begged me for help. I didn't have the materials to save them. I've never had to look in a person's eyes, a person desperate for my help, and ignore their pleas."

"You said it yourself. You didn't have the materials to save them. Be honest, if you were allowed in Crosswell's surgery, could you have saved all of them?"

She shook her head. "But in my time, I could've saved most. I just feel such a failure. I'm trained to do everything in my power to maintain life. *First do no harm.* Walking away is doing harm."

"Wasting time on a man you know you can't save in the long run costs the lives of those you can. You had to make horrible choices but you have to view it as sacrificing the few to save the many." He wiped her cheeks and chin with his thumbs then kissed her. "No more tears."

She took several deep breaths letting the tears subside. She rested her head on his shoulder. "On a different topic, cheers to you for thinking fast on your feet with the story about looking for my younger brother."

"I'd like to take credit but can't. The story is true. A woman came to our company in London prior to us departing for our last campaign in France. She was searching for her son."

"Did she find him?"

"Don't know."

"There you are." It was Skaife standing at the top of the embankment. "Come along again. We're off to the Duke's tent."

"Why does Wellington want to see us? Are we in trouble? You told him Crosswell gave me permission to work, didn't you?" Felicia blurted in a panicked rush.

"It's not my place to question why the Duke does what he does. Just stop fussing and come along."

Harry climbed to his feet and helped her up. "He's right. We've no say in the matter. Might as well get whatever he wants to do to us over with."

"Good grief," Felicia said, looking at her blood stained dress. "I'm about to meet one of the most famous men of the period and I look a filthy mess."

"Soiled clothing may be the least of our worries," Harry said flatly.

****

The rich scent of beef wafted from the area of Wellington's tent a dozen strides before Felicia and Harry reached the entry. A sergeant was preparing the Duke's meal on an outside campfire. Harry's stomach rumbled first followed by Felicia's. They exchanged a mutually ravenous look. Considering how their luck had gone since departing medieval England that morning, she figured neither wanted to think about where or when their next meal would come. The thought about that morning made her pause. They'd only been gone from Elysian Fields the better part of a day. It seemed like a lifetime.

"What's wrong? Why'd you stop?" Harry asked.

"Nothing. My mind wandered for a minute."

"Move along," Skaife said. "Wait here," he told them and went inside. A moment later he moved the tent flap aside. "The Duke will see you now."

"Come. Sit. Private Howe, pour wine for my guests," Wellington instructed a young man who stood in the corner.

The Duke sat on a padded stool at a table covered in white linen with a silver ewer in front of him. He drank red wine from a cut-crystal glass. On the other side of the table were two more padded stools. A bunk was set up on one side of the tent with a portable military field desk on top. A trunk similar to old fashioned footlockers sat on the opposite side of the tent.

The Duke looked much like he did in official portraits, which surprised Felicia. She'd always heard portraits of well-to-do men and women were painted to please the commissioner and not painted for accuracy. In the privacy of his tent, Wellington wasn't wearing the gold-braided, red uniform jacket with black sash seen in many paintings. He wore a white silk shirt like the one shown but had undone the cravat portion. His white uniform trousers and black boots had been brushed of battle dust. His dark brown hair bore wisps of grey at the temples and had started to recede. He had a better jawline, stronger than most nobles of the period and a bumpy, long nose.

Felicia and Harry sat but neither ventured to speak, waiting for Wellington to go first. "You may leave, Skaife."

"Sir." Skaife scurried out.

"Please don't hesitate. You must be thirsty. Drink." Wellington gestured for them to drink the wine. "Are you hungry?"

"Starved," Harry said.

"What about you, Angel of the Battlefield?"

"Pardon?" Felicia thought he'd mistaken her for someone else. A pity. If so, he might rescind the offer of food.

"That's what some of the men are calling you or so I'm told by Private Howe. They saw you and your husband tending to the wounded, saving lads who mightn't have lived long enough to get to surgery. Thank you." He took a sip of his wine. "Other than Angel of the Battlefield, what are your names?"

"Harold and Felicia Quarles," Harry told him.

"Please thank your men for the kind words and in

answer to your question, yes, I'm ravenous too," Felicia told Wellington.

The sergeant they'd seen cooking brought in three bowls of beef stew and a basket of bread. Felicia was in heaven. Beef. She'd never been fond of lamb and the kitchen at Elysian Fields served lamb a lot. She relished the nights they had chicken or fish.

"I'd like to show my appreciation for what you've done," Wellington said. "Skaife said you searched for a relative but didn't find him. I'm afraid I can't help with that. As you know, unless he's a noble or is a commissioned officer, our rosters aren't well kept."

"We understand." Felicia smiled.

"What else can I do to help you?"

What could they have him do, she wondered? Money to find transport home would be lovely.

Harry answered as if he'd read her mind. "We need a way back to England."

"Yes," she piped in, interrupting the sopping up of stew gravy with her still warm bread.

"I'll arrange accommodations for you on the ship taking my most seriously wounded men home. While on the topic of accommodations, if you wish, I think we can find a tent for you to retire to this evening."

"We'd appreciate the use of a tent," Harry said.

Felicia thought—oh, please find a tent. She didn't relish the idea of sleeping on the cold ground.

Wellington turned to the soldier called Howe. "I assume Lieutenant Arnold remains in the surgery tent?"

"Yes, sir."

"Will he survive?"

"Probably not."

"Such a shame, Arnold is a good man," he said with resignation. Prepare his tent for the Quarles, see to their needs."

Howe nodded. "Sir," he said and left.

"Is there anything else you have immediate need for?" Wellington asked.

"Your Lordship, you may think this a frivolous womanly issue but I'd really like to have my dress washed of the blood and residue of battle." She hung her head so he wouldn't see and closed her eyes briefly to force the worst images of the wounded from her mind.

"It's not frivolous, Felicia. If it is acceptable to Harold, come tomorrow morning and I will have my laundress wash your gown. You may remain in your tent wrapped in a blanket until she is finished." Wellington looked Harry up and down then. "Your tunic, I'm sure you are aware is unusual. I can have it cleaned at the same time or if you prefer, I will have a replacement given to you. One more in keeping with what the other men wear. I know of a major who is tall and broad like you. He should have a shirt to spare."

Harry, being no fool, understood his tunic raised questions better left unasked. He accepted the offer. "I'd like that, sir."

They took their time over the meal. Wellington asked about their lives in Gloucester. Felicia let Harry do most of the talking. He had a knack for creating a truthful sounding storyline. For his part, the Duke talked about his family and his hopes for the war ending soon.

When they finished, Private Howe led them to Arnold's quarters. Lieutenant Arnold's tent was sparsely furnished compared to the Duke's. A second cot had been set up in addition to the one Arnold had. A small chest stood in the corner next to a stand with a pitcher and basin. A small rickety-looking table and stool were by the chest. On top of the table lay a gold framed miniature of a blonde woman in a light blue gown with blue ribbons woven in her hair.

As soon as Howe left, an exhausted Felicia sank onto one of the cots. It had clearly been slept in the night before. The blanket was thrown back and the pillow still held the shape of Arnold's head. The other cot had been made up with fresh linen. Felicia was beyond caring about fresh bedding.

"I feel like a cannon rolled over me. I can't remember ever being this tired. Are you tired or exhilarated after a battle?"

Harry joined her on the cot and put his arms around her. "Weary beyond belief. Any soldier will tell you, emotions are so intense prior to the fight it is like walking on a knife's edge. Then, in the midst of battle your need to survive overwhelms all else. When all of those emotions are expended and the battle is over, the body and mind are drained, empty. You only long for the relief of sleep."

He helped her undress and gave her a glass of wine. "Drink and after, sleep. Let your mind be at ease. You saved many men. Fewer women will be widows and children will have their fathers."

She laid down and Harry covered her with the rough blanket. He poured himself a second glass of wine, sat on the other cot and propped his feet on the chest.

"Aren't you going to rest?" she asked.

"In a bit. I'm trying to work out our future."

"Our future..." That was as far as she got before falling asleep.

The next morning Harry hid his armor and he and Felicia went to Wellington's tent. They were given breakfast while their clothing situation was sorted out. The irony of the meal brought a smile to Felicia. As a child, her mother gave her soft boiled eggs with the top off and a thin strip of toast dipped into it. Like mothers everywhere over England, she called them eggs and soldiers. Here Felicia was with the real life versions. Worry whether she'd ever see her mother again darkened the sweet memory. Felicia refused to let it take over her mood.

After their clothes were cleaned, Skaife came to them with instructions from the Duke. He'd written they were to remain in Arnold's tent until the wagons left the next day for the port and the ship home.

"If we make our way to Elysian Fields again, then what?" Harry asked as they returned to the tent.

"Remember when you first met me I said Elysian Fields doesn't exist anymore. It was destroyed a century and a half before this war. The important matter is communicating with Oliver. Hopefully the message box is still there."

It dawned on her that with no money they might be hoofing it on empty stomachs making do with nettle soup until they reached Gloucester. "Do you have any idea where we will dock once we get to England? How will we get to the shire?"

"Southampton most likely. As for getting to the shire...how are your feet?"

Chapter Fourteen

Elysian Fields-1359

"Come on, Norton. Call Richard over and we'll see if he agrees," Leland suggested.

"If it means you'll stop yammering at me, I will. Richard," Norton called out to the steward who was having a discussion with a delivery man. Richard looked up and Norton continued, "These two want to talk to you."

Richard dismissed the deliveryman and came to where Leland, Tony, and Norton gathered. "Go ahead, speak your piece," Norton told Leland.

"Richard, must we still have Norton guarding us? We've no place to go or funds to travel on if we did. I know he'd rather be searching for Sir Harold and Felicia. Tony and I would like permission to leave the castle to test what we've done on the field glasses. I swear we are not planning an escape."

"What do you think?" Richard asked Norton.

"I prefer to look for Harry. These two have given me no trouble. I say let them be free to do whatever it is they need to."

"How far do you wish to go for these tests?" Richard asked Leland.

"No further than the granite outcropping." Leland

and Tony discussed whether they'd let them go that far, out of the sight of the men in the towers. They had to take a chance and push the boundaries of Richard's trust. They wanted to verify Felicia and Harry returned to her modern time.

"All right, if Norton isn't concerned then I'll take his word," Richard said. "I'll expect to see you back here by the midday meal though."

"We'll be here," Leland and Tony replied in unison.

****

Along the way to the outcropping, the scientists stopped to test glasses. "We need to grind the lenses down more. There's a fuzzy edge I'd like to see if we can eliminate," Tony said and handed the glasses to Leland. "See what you think. They're all right the way they are, but I think we can do better."

They'd been forced to create something useful for Elysian Fields. In spite of being put in that position, both wanted to do a good job.

Leland raised the glasses and agreed. "I wish we had a way to adjust the lenses. But a regrind it is."

At the outcropping, Leland began digging with a trowel they'd taken from the garden shed. A short time later, after fast digging, the scrape of metal brought nervous excitement. Reassurance Felicia and Harry were safe dominated their talk on the way to the outcropping. That, and the sad topic of leaving Drusilla and Heather when the time came for them to go home. Leland especially had grown attached to Drusilla.

Tony stood to one side as Leland opened the box and read the message. Leland looked stricken. "No! No, no this can't be."

"What?"

Leland handed the message to Tony.

Felicia never made it here. Is she still there with you?"

"Where the deuce can she and Harry be?" Tony asked.

Leland shook his head. "Lost in time somewhere."

Chris Karlsen

Chapter Fifteen

"Signage...it looks like town signage." Felicia broke into a run, Harry right behind. "It is. *Chipping Camden, Painswick, Stroud*, we're in Gloucestershire, finally." The three shire towns displayed directional arrows next to their names. She threw her arms around Harry and squeezed him in a tight hug. "I could kiss the ground. We're a half day's trek to the outcropping and another chance at going home."

"We're not out of danger, yet. If Elysian Fields is a ruin, as you say, we can hide there until Oliver arranges transport. But, that's if no nefarious types have taken up residence."

She groaned and released him from her hug. He was correct but it didn't mean she needed or wanted to hear logic right now. "Harry, let me have my moment. Don't rain on my parade"

"Rain on your parade? Should I ask?"

She shook her head and waved off the question. "Everything you say about danger is true. I just don't want to hear the bad possibilities yet. Let me enjoy being back home or at least a lot closer to home."

He stared at her for several long seconds, looking like he wanted to say something. He wasn't the stoic warrior knight he acted in front of the men he trained all the time. He let his guard down in private. She knew him well now.

They'd shared the intimacies only lovers do. They'd also endured a raft of problems. She'd seen the subtle changes in his expression when troubled: the slight furrowing to his brow, the hard line to his mouth, the firm set to his jaw. She also knew when he held his true thoughts back and when he switched to stoic knight to shield her feelings or hide his. She waited to see if he'd say what bothered him. Instead he extended his hand. "Let's get started, shall we?"

She took his hand and slid her arm around his waist. "What's wrong?"

"Nothing."

"Liar. Talk to me."

He stopped and brought her around to stand in front of him. "To me, as long as were together, I know I can make a home for us, a good home, where I believe you'd be happy. But I'm reminded in these last minutes home for you means more than just being with me." He tipped her chin up and brushed her lips with a light kiss. "Tell me, when I came to you that day at the outcropping when you planned on returning to your time and I asked you to stay--would you have?"

Good question.

"Yes." That part was true. She wanted to be with him but not part of the world he lived in. She'd have stayed and no doubt spent day after day trying to convince him to come into her world. "Because I love the life I had doesn't mean I don't love you. I can love both."

"Can you? I'm not so sure."

His hair hung loose and messy the past week. It was never messy as Captain of the Guard. Sometime onboard ship he'd lost the leather band he used to tie his hair back and neither of them had access to a comb.

Threading her fingers through his loose hair, she pushed it back from his face and kissed him long and hard. She stopped when she ran out of air. "I am."

When she pulled away, he gave her a crooked smile and clasped her hand. "Let's see how Elysian Fields looks and then dig up your memory box."

****

They reached the ruin by early afternoon. The depression that was once the moat had overgrown with grasses and weeds. Nothing remained of the wooden drawbridge, which was no surprise. Various size blocks of the Cotswold stone used for the castle curtain wall lay scattered. The ruin hadn't changed much between this time and Felicia's time. Not that she could see.

At the edge of the forest, Harry told her, "Stay here until I say it is safe to come further. Stay out of sight. Get behind a tree."

She did as ordered.

He drew his sword from its scabbard and walked around the exterior of the ruin first, using trees and wild shrubs for cover. Then he cautiously moved into the area of the broken battlements, through what had been the portcullis and into the bailey. Several minutes had passed when he reappeared and waved her over.

"I take it we will be the ruin's only occupants," she said, joining him.

"No one has been here for a long time. No one has even come to steal the fruit and vegetables from the old garden. There's not many but a few still on the ground and on the vine." He held the rusted head of a broken spade in his hand. "I found this where the stable used to be. Thought it would be handy for digging up your box. We'll visit the

247

outcropping and then I'll go to the river and see if I can catch a fish for us."

"Sounds like a plan."

Keep a nice, steady pace. Do not get over anxious. That was her mantra all the way to the outcropping. Felicia was desperate to run to the outcropping but after Harry's comment questioning her affection, she had to hold back.

When they got to the spot it looked like recent digging had gone on. She hoped Oliver was responsible and that he kept attempting to message her and hopefully hear back. Harry began digging fast into the dry soil. What was left of the spade head snapped in two but he was able to finish with the partial piece. He pulled the box from the ground. Felicia knelt next to him and together they opened it.

She skimmed over the initial exchange between Oliver and Leland establishing she hadn't arrived home and confirmation she wasn't still at Elysian Fields. Leland advised his father that Harry had also gone missing. He and Tony speculated he was with her but they couldn't be sure. Both father and son expressed grave concern for her safety, if Harry wasn't with her. Not knowing where she was in time and place fueled the greatest concern. No one, not Oliver, Leland or Tony had any idea where or how to begin looking for her. No one had an explanation for why they failed to bring her through to the right time.

"Not good, not good at all." Felicia rocked back onto her heels.

"Stay calm. You've told me all along how clever Oliver and Leland are. There's no reason to believe they won't figure out what went wrong." Harry removed a pad of paper and a pencil from the box. He studied the pencil for a few seconds, then sniffed the end, and ran his thumb over the eraser end.

"It's a writing instrument," Felicia explained before he asked and tapped the lead end.

Harry wrote an H on the corner of the paper. "Handy thing. And this?" he asked, pointing to the eraser.

"That deletes the writing."

"That's troublesome."

"How?"

"The temptation to write what you shouldn't is stronger if you know you can say it then erase the words. It is too easy to spill your true thoughts when they are best kept close in silence."

He gave her the pencil back. "Tell whoever opens the box next, be it Leland or Oliver, that we are together and safe, for now. Advise them of the timeframe, that it is June, 1815. Finally, they know from our communication we're here but we should advise them we haven't explored the immediate area. Because we're safe at the moment, a threat we don't know about may exist. In other words, hurry and get us away. We'll keep checking the box."

She did as Harry suggested and afterward he reburied the box.

"Now about this fishing idea—do you think we can cook over a small fire or will that attract too much attention?"

"I know a shielded spot that should be fine for a fire. The thought of raw fish too grim?"

"Eww, yes. Eww. I can't even stand sushi."

"What's sushi?"

"Raw fish they wrap in pretty decorations and try to fob off as a delicacy."

"This is popular?"

"Oddly, yes."

"Have you tried it?"

"Two pieces, just to shut a friend up."

"And it was horrible?"

"No. The pieces I had were good."

Harry's brows furrowed, which she expected. "I'm confused. You can't stand it even though the little bit you had was good?"

"Because I didn't have the icky fish ones but veggie ones. Completely different."

With a slight shake of his head, he pulled another piece of paper from the box. He opened the note and compared the date with the others. "This one is more recent. Bad news." He handed her the note.

Her hunger forgotten, with trepidation she took the note. It was from Leland to his father.

They've stopped searching for Harry and Felicia. There are rumors-bad ones starting. Some of the men and household servants are growing dangerously suspicious of Tony and me. They say Felicia came here looking like Emily and Electra, dressing and talking and acting much the same and much different than the local people. Then, we arrived and Felicia knew us, too. If that wasn't bad enough, Simon and Emily disappeared and now Harry and Felicia. The word sorcery is being bandied about. Not out loud yet, the castle steward is keeping the worst of the rabble-rousers at bay and the pitchforks and torches at a distance. But I'm not sure how long that will last. These are superstitious folk. Our commitment to making the field glasses is finished. Tony and I will stay a short while longer in case Felicia and Harry return. We cannot remain long. It is too dangerous for us.

"It was bound to happen. Too many unexplained incidents," Harry said.

"I know."

"Richard is well respected and holds a great deal of power over the people. If Leland and Tony manage to leave soon, they should be fine. I trust they will. They are aware of how dicey the situation is." Harry gave her the box. "There's a pad of paper and what appears to be another writing instrument inside."

"Wouldn't it be funny if Leland and Tony wound up here with us?"

"No," Harry snapped when the words were barely out of her mouth. "I've my hands full enough watching over you."

"They might not be warrior knights but they have skills. They're smart. They are scientists after all."

His physical response was immediate.

"Save the eye rolls," she said, getting testy.

"Scientists serve no purpose to our needs. All they can do is conjure up nonsense that I can't use. No, they need to go to their own time straight away. Worry not about them. Tell Oliver to get us back."

"You're not being fair to Leland and Tony. You can't say they wouldn't come up with something helpful for us."

"I know what is tried and true. I know strategy that has worked for our fighting men. What I know about your oh-so-smart scientists is they created a condition that has us in a century that neither of us is familiar with and not what they intended. So, pardon me if I don't share your confidence in them."

He stalked off, which he was wont to do when after

a tense exchange. Felicia followed quietly searching for a counter to his argument and failing. That more than anything pissed her off. Damn him and his logic.

****

Three days passed with no word from Oliver or Leland. "This is discouraging," Felicia said.

"You don't want to think this but we need to consider our future if we find ourselves here permanently."

Harry was right. That possibility had invaded her thoughts the past days with no word of rescue. She pushed the idea from her mind. At some point, she'd have to deal with it. This time period was a real pickle. At least in Harry's own time, he was a knight. He had a profession. What could he do here? She didn't dare insult him by asking. It wasn't just Harry. What the devil could she do to contribute other than see if a local healer or surgeon would take her on as an assistant? If Crosswell was typical of the men in the profession, she wouldn't exactly be welcomed with open arms. *What a pickle.*

They'd ventured into the local village. It didn't have a name and didn't exist in modern times. Felicia believed it might've disappeared during one of the World Wars. A number of small villages had. The men had gone off to fight and when too many were killed, the women left and moved back to their families or to the cities to find work.

Harry and Felicia offered their services around the town. He earned a small wage doing heavy labor for some of the older tradesmen at an age where they struggled. Felicia helped with cleaning and serving in the tavern in exchange for meals for her and Harry. It was the same type of work they'd done to make their way to Gloucestershire from Southampton. The owner's wife of the local tavern also let them use an empty vat to bathe and wash their clothes.

"Not much of a life I'm providing for you, is it?" Harry asked as they dressed.

"Not your fault. It's not anyone's. We'll just have to keep checking the box. Let's stop at the outcropping on the way to the ruin." She peered into the ragged linen the tavern wife had given her. Felicia had fashioned it into a hobo-like carrier for their food. "At least we have real food."

She eyed his visibly thinner torso. She'd no creativity when it came to food. At home most of her meals were microwaved and eaten on a tray in front of the telly. Harry cleaned and gutted the fish he caught. Her contribution was limited to running a stick through the carcass and holding it over the fire. The edible veggies and fruits she offered up as is. She really had no idea what to do with those. "My food preparation has taken its toll on you. Sorry, but cooking isn't my forte."

Harry cupped her chin. "Oh darling, I love you too much to tell you the truth and respect you too much to lie. Let me put it this way: it's true your cooking isn't your strong suit, but I've been thinner."

"Really? When?"

"The Poitiers campaign."

The minute he said it, she remembered her history of the hunger that ravaged the English army.

Harry continued, "By the time we reached Poitiers, we'd run out of supplies. All of us, knights, foot soldiers, archers, all were living off dandelion soup, which is exactly what is sounds like, dandelions boiled in hot water. The morning of the battle the Prince ordered us to break camp and make ready to return to Bordeaux, our province in France. We'd resupply there."

"We were told in class that King John mistook your activity as forming for battle."

"He did. In response, the French formed up. Hungry, weak and outnumbered as we were, the Prince was never one to run from battle. He ordered us to assault positions. As you know, we did go to battle and won, *decisively*. You know why?" He answered before she got a chance. "Because we're better fighters than the French and always have been."

He leaned in, the excitement of the victory in his eyes and his gestures animated as he described the aftermath. "We put King John and any nobles we could ransom under guard by our baggage. We took the food supplies, armor, weapons, and horses from the remaining knights. The food was distributed to all. The armor and weapons we distributed to our soldiers and archers. The horses we brought back to the nobles we served."

"What about the weapons their foot soldiers carried. You couldn't let them go with those?"

"No, of course not. We made a pile of them along with the wicked crossbows the Genoese mercenaries carried and made a bonfire of the lot. The Genoese were downcast because they wouldn't be paid. Some of the French foot soldiers took the defeat to heart. We reminded them they'd be feeling much sadder soon. In a few weeks, the Dauphin would be taxing them into rags to pay his father's ransom," Harry said with a light chuckle.

He's shown more pride and vitality in the retelling of that day than in anything that had happened to them since being transported to Waterloo. Concern over how he'd react to the modern world had troubled her, picked at her psyche when she watched him work or even when he held her. But listening to how he spoke of being part of that great victory, succeeding at what he'd trained all his life to do, concern was morphing into dread. She was beginning to fear how he'd adjust to her world. He'd have Simon and Stephen to talk to and that would help. It should help. Would and should. Creeping dread colored the words.

"Shall we stop at the outcropping? Maybe we'll find a message," Harry said.

"I'd like that." Felicia bundled the cheese round, loaf of bread, and two chicken legs the tavern owner's wife gave her back into the linen cloth. The food was manna from Heaven to Harry and Felicia.

****

They set their hunger aside to first check the box. Harry used the broken spade head and dug fast. He retrieved the box from the hole and handed it to Felicia. "Here. I've never been superstitious but in this I am relying on all your modern wishes for luck to work."

Felicia opened the box. "There are two new notes." She stared at the folded paper but made no effort to unfold it.

Harry bumped her shoulder with his. "What are you waiting for? Read it."

"I'm nervous. I'm afraid it's bad news."

"Want me to do it?"

She shook her head and opened the paper.

"This is a good idea of Oliver's," Harry said, reading along with her.

Oliver had made a list of all the environmental factors when he came through both times. He did the same with Simon and Emily. He'd even included factors from Alex and Shakira's experience. He explained he searched for what was different. What had caused Harry and Felicia to not come through to the right period? It wasn't age differences, at least he didn't believe so, since everyone who had successfully gone through the time tear varied in age. That left the environment. He wanted her to make a list of everything she and Harry could think of going on around them the day she was scheduled to travel.

"No worries. Between the two of us, I think we'll get most if not all pertinent details." She tucked the note into the sleeve of her dress and pulled the second note out.

"I agree," Harry said after they'd both read it.

"Leland said he and Tony were going to make every effort to leave the castle and be free to attempt their return to the modern world. The only thing stopping them might be if Richard imprisoned them for some ginned-up reason. Do you think Richard would do that?"

Harry shrugged. "For the most part, it depends on them. The people have no logical explanation for Simon and me disappearing. They'll look to cast blame. If Leland and Tony do anything to draw additional suspicion their way, combined with the rumors they mentioned already hanging over them, Richard will do what he must for their safety and to keep the peace among the castle folk, including imprisoning. Wouldn't you?"

She'd like to think she'd have the courage to not respond by locking the men away. That said, in a world filled with superstitious people and strange beliefs of all kinds, for everyone's safety, she might imprison them.

"They're smart enough to be extra careful with what they say and do." Felicia didn't know either well enough to swear to the last. "I hope they are," she added low. "Let's eat and brainstorm as much as we can recall from that day."

"Brainstorm? In other words, compare what Oliver has listed to our day?"

"Yes."

"You should've just said that," Harry muttered.

They sat at the base of the outcropping and laid out their small hoard of food. Felicia nibbled on bread and cheese as she ticked off the things that were the same. "You want my chicken leg?" she stopped to ask Harry.

"No, you eat it. I know you're hungry."

"I need to write Oliver back and I don't want to mark up the paper with greasy fingers. It might make our answer too hard to read."

Harry pulled his dagger from his boot and scraped the chicken meat from the bone. Then, he jabbed the knife into a piece and handed her the knife. "Eat."

Felicia wolfed the chicken leg and wrote the list Oliver wanted as she and Harry recalled what they could. "The list isn't very long."

Within minutes they spotted the one major difference. "Weather," they said simultaneously.

"We need a good summer storm. If not over us directly, close by. In my summers, we have several over July and occasionally into August." Felicia was desperate for him to say the same months and the weeks the worst storms occurred corresponded with her time.

"It was the same for me. We may be out of here shortly, if we're lucky and the storms come early. Generally we can see when a storm is brewing and we can advise Oliver." Harry peered over to see what she was writing. "Are you letting Leland know?"

She nodded. "I'm telling him that we're still rolling the dice on the time. Hopefully we have a storm that lasts for more than a day as a fallback day if we need a second attempt. Leland and Tony need to do whatever voodoo necessary to get free of the castle."

"I don't know what voodoo is but I take your meaning. Richard will free them. With the rumors they refer to traveling through the servants, he'll want them away from Elysian Fields. They're becoming millstones."

When she finished the notes, Harry buried the box and then turned his attention to the west toward Wales.

"What are you looking at?"

"Most of our summer storms come out of Wales and into the Bristol Channel. I am wishful thinking that soon I will look to see the horizon change to wicked grey. Until then," Harry said, "We'll return to the village tomorrow and continue to work where we're needed."

Not what Felicia wanted to hear. More mopping up disgusting tavern floors and taking cold baths. Ugh.

"What will be the first thing you do when we arrive in your time?" Harry asked.

The question surprised her. He hadn't shown much interest in what would happen if she got home.

"I will hug and kiss my dog until she demands treats for more love. Then, I'm going to take a hot shower, put on comfortable clothes, and order a pizza. Except for the hugging Chloe part, the rest is second to my showing you my home and all the conveniences of the modern world."

"Where is this hot shower?"

"I have a large bathroom...it's like the most glorious garderobe imaginable only with more useful items."

She kissed him, a lingering deep kiss. She sensed he still doubted how strong her love for him went. She loved him with all her heart. That wasn't the problem. Truth be told, if forced to choose between staying in the modern world or returning to the medieval, she couldn't swear to being one-hundred-percent certain she'd choose the medieval. The strength of his character made him an excellent knight. And his being a knight was the issue for her. The thought he'd likely go off to fight in battle again and might die, leaving her alone in the medieval world turned her stomach inside out. That worry came to her more and more as returning to her world seemed within reach. Guilt over the possibility he was right to doubt always swamped her. Why else would she waffle on staying or going? The issue wasn't a reality yet and might never be. She pushed the fear from her mind and continued, "I have a huge shower, big enough for two people. I can't wait to show you."

****

Felicia nattered away as Harry dug out the box like they'd done the day before and the day before that. "With all our grey winter weather, I never thought I'd hate sunny days. I now hate sunny days. Every night I wish for a thunderstorm."

"Here." Harry brushed the dirt from the box and handed it to her.

"Oh my God." Felicia threw her arms around Harry and hugged him tight.

"What?"

"Oliver has given us information on an upcoming two-day storm and when to expect it. We're to show here early 7:00 a.m. on those mornings. He will make the transfer attempt then. If we miss the first day, we have the second chance. This is fantastic news."

"It is but how can he know what days we have a

storm coming?"

"Remember I gave him the day we arrived back at Elysian Fields. A week has passed so he worked off that."

Harry looked skeptical and took the note from her to read it for himself. "I still don't understand how he can do this."

"He either medieval fan site, members are super into the time period and know how to work out the regional weather. But more likely he Googled weather history." She explained, knowing he would question what Google was, "Google is an information source we have. It can tell you about most everything in the world. You have to be specific at times, though. I once searched Moroccan leather bindings. I was curious about a book I wanted to buy. I won't tell you the initial responses I got from that broad inquiry. Nasty stuff!"

She folded the note and put it in her skirt pocket and then wrote the same instructions for Leland to find. According to Oliver, the storm would arrive at the end of the week and hover for a couple of days.

Chapter Sixteen

Finally, the storm rolled into the shire with thunder and the lightning they hoped for. Felicia and Harry hunkered down by the base of the outcropping.

"Are you afraid?" Harry asked as they waited for the transport time. Both had been too excited to sleep and went to the outcropping at dawn.

"Not afraid, but nervous. I just want everything to go as planned."

They were still talking when the familiar feeling of his world turning inside out took over. He couldn't maintain his balance and fell to the ground. As he fell, Harry had a vague image of Felicia falling as well. Only seconds later, the confusion and disturbance in his physical world passed. He swallowed numerous times, his mouthwatering like crazy again.

Felicia rose up on her hands and knees but remained in that position for a long moment, unsteady and looking like she'd topple over again.

"Are you all right?" Harry, on his knees as well, put his arm around her waist.

"Yes. How are you?"

"Good."

"Felicia..." Oliver hurried toward them.

Felicia threw her arms around Harry's neck and gave him a big kiss. "We're home," she said, turning at the sound of Oliver's voice. "We're safe and home." She cupped Harry's face in her hands. "I could kiss the ground. But you're far more fun."

Both of them were grabbed and helped to stand. Oliver planted a kiss on her forehead. "Thank heavens this worked. I couldn't be sure. It's all still experimental."

"Thank heavens is right. You have no idea how happy I am to be home," she gushed.

"How do you feel? Any unpleasant after effects? I didn't have any but what about you?" Oliver asked.

"Like I got shot out of a human cocktail shaker but otherwise good." She hugged Oliver again. "I'm so glad to be home."

Next to her, Harry quietly watched them. A sudden new kind of doubt stirred as to whether the place he now found himself was where he should really be.

Oliver released her and she slid her arm around Harry's waist and held him tight. "Oliver, I'm sure you remember Harry, my knight in shining armor, from your time at Elysian Fields."

"We saw each other in passing but never really spoke," Harry said.

"It's good seeing you again." He shook Harry's hand.

Coming up were Stephen and Simon. Simon's gait was wobbly as he hurried on a metal blade attached somehow to his leg.

Harry trotted to him, embracing the man. "Simon, I thought I'd never see you again." Harry stepped back, taking in the sight of his friend. "Everyone at home believes the family drowned when no trace of you could be found. Felicia showed me the picture of you and your message to me. I wanted to believe the message true but doubt remained." He embraced his friend again. He released Simon and fixed on Simon's metal leg. "What is that device on your leg?"

"It's what they call a blade leg. It allows me to maneuver without need of a crutch. I didn't want to try one at first but I'm happy I let Emily talk me into a test time." Simon rolled his pant leg up to reveal more of the blade. "I'm still working on getting used to it. I'm not completely steady on it but I can walk, run, and jump wearing this."

"Amazing." Harry turned and wrapped his friend Stephen in a firm bear hug. His friend wore an odd covering on his eyes that looked like dark glass fixed in a wire frame. He didn't know what to make of the covering but he'd ask about it later. At the moment just seeing Stephen was a miracle. "You're here too-another miracle." He patted Stephen on the back and then released him. "We all thought you dead at Poitiers. Seeing you both...I don't know what to say."

"I almost died but that's a long story. Now you're here, we'll have plenty of time to talk."

Harry eyed Stephen's white cane. "Have you become crippled since coming here?"

Stephen removed the dark glass eye cover. "No. My injury at Poitiers left me blind. The cane is an aid to help me function in unfamiliar surroundings. It is also a symbol to other people that I am blind."

"No." Harry had seen a number of blind persons over the years. He recognized Stephen's limited movement as the same. He hugged Stephen again. In their time, blindness was devastating. If a person had no one to help them, the blind usually wound up beggars. "Blind...I'm sorry, my friend."

"It's not as terrible as you imagine. I'm a celebrity now and earn a fine living," Stephen said, smiling as Harry let go of him.

"Celebrity?" Harry looked to Felicia.

"He's well-known, famous."

"Well-known for what?"

"I'm a popular singer," Stephen explained with a broad smile. "I used to sing for pleasure at Elysian Fields and to impress the ladies. Now I am paid to sing."

"Why didn't you tell me he was here too when you talked about Simon?" Harry asked Felicia.

"I didn't want to get your hopes up. I had a strong suspicion the Stephen you talked about was the one married to Esme, but I couldn't swear to it. Simon was a different situation. He and Emily disappeared the day I found myself back in time. I'd seen Oliver and Leland doing something with a black machine when my incident occurred. I put two-and-two together."

She gave Stephen a hug. "Speaking of Esme, where is she?"

"Home. Oliver brought us here."

The four of them joined the rest.

"Where's Chloe?" Felicia asked.

Oliver smiled. "I knew that would be your first question. She's at my place ready to go home with her mom."

Felicia sighed with visible relief. "Good, good, good. What of Leland and Tony?"

"They finished the field glasses. He says Richard is happy to have them out of his hair. The quicker, the better. With the rumors of magic and witchery swirling around them, it's getting dodgy for them to stay. I'm working on bringing them soon," Oliver reassured her.

"Alex gave me some clothes for Harry that I have packed. He said they were close in size. My Range Rover is parked just up the path on the road. I figured you'd want to go home right away and settle in and relax."

"You guessed right. Can we go now, please?" Stopping suddenly, Felicia looked from Oliver to Harry and back. "How would Alex know about Harry and his size?"

"It's another story for another day," Oliver said.

Harry wanted to hear the story now. From the look on Felicia's face she was as curious. But she kept her curiosity to herself more anxious to get home than hear the tale. As for him, he was also happy to go to Felicia's, to cleanup and eat. He craved any offering she had on hand that could be warmed and eaten with little fanfare.

The group climbed the path to the road. Harry came to an abrupt halt at the sight of the large black carriage on wheels. "This is the vehicle Oliver refers to? This strange looking metal carriage?"

Felicia looped her arm through his. "This is a relatively modern invention. For lack of a better description, metal carriage will do. The car has a gas engine that propels it at the chosen speed of the driver."

Her explanation didn't enlighten to his satisfaction. "I won't ask what a gas engine is. Is it far to Oliver's? Can we walk to where we're going? I don't care for the look of this means of travel. I've had enough of strange travel for today."

"We can walk to Oliver's trailer and to my house from there but it will be faster if we drive—a lot faster. Plus, you have a chance to talk more with Simon and Stephen."

Felicia rose on her toes and kissed his cheek.

"You'll be fine riding in a car. Trust me, this is safe. You're going to be gobsmacked by the speed."

"Your description does little to convince me." Not much in his life left him gobsmacked. He doubted this carriage would stir gobsmacking excitement.

About to climb in the front seat, Simon noticed Harry's hesitation and came over. Felicia mouthed *help* and Simon tipped his head in understanding. "What's wrong, Harry?"

He shook his head and didn't budge. "I don't care to ride in this metal monster. Courage I possess. A sense of adventure, I do not, not unless driven to adventure like recent events forced upon me."

Simon took a turn at convincing Harry. "It is quite safe, Harry. It takes getting used to but once you do, you'll be pleasantly surprised at how fast the folks here go from one place to the other."

Maybe...maybe not. Simon had a rascally nature that few but the knights he was friends with ever saw.

"I'll be right back. I'm going for reinforcement," Simon told Felicia. He caught Stephen by the arm as he waited for them. The two joined Felicia and Harry. "Would you please tell Harry to stop being mule-headed and get in the car? He doesn't think it's safe," Simon told Stephen.

"Trust us when we say you're going to like riding in a car. This is an amazing modern machine. You can get to London in an hour or so." Stephen reached out and found Felicia's hand. She still had her arm looped through Harry's. "It was a three day journey in our time," he told her.

Harry let out a long sigh. "All right, I trust your word."

Felicia jerked on his arm. "Seriously? I said the

same thing. You believe them and not me?"

Was it not obvious? "They're men."

Simon and Stephen both sucked in a breath and retreated a step.

"They understand risk. Women have little head for properly evaluating danger," Harry explained.

"I wouldn't be so sure about the quality of men's ability to measure risk. You don't realize that lame belief could get you a bonk on the head. Maybe knock some sense in you," she added with a poke to his chest. "Medieval, misogynistic booby."

"What did you call me?" Harry asked suspicious she mocked his logic.

"Nothing." Felicia made a shooing motion for him to get in the car.

Harry turned to Simon and Stephen. "What did she call me?"

"A booby, just climb in the car," Simon told him and made the same shooing motion as Felicia.

The group loaded into the Rover. Stephen and Felicia put him in the middle. "Afraid I'll jump out?"

"It's a narrow road. Other vehicles going by appear closer than comfortable, especially for a first time ride," Felicia said.

Putting him in the middle had been a good idea. The moment Oliver started moving forward, Harry went stiff as a plank and pressed his back hard against the seat. He couldn't help it. He half expected for the carriage to take flight.

She laid her hand on his. "How are you doing?"

He kept his eyes on the road ahead. "All right." He had no fondness for the carriages facing past in the opposite direction.

A few minutes later, minutes that felt like a lifetime as they traveled at a horrible speed, the carriage came to a stop.

"We're here." Felicia gave his hand a light squeeze. "It wasn't so terrible, was it?"

"Not terrible but I still prefer my horse. Is it far to your house?"

"No."

"Good."

At Oliver's, Chloe rushed to Felicia fast as her stubby legs could go, her whole butt wriggling, tail wagging. Felicia picked her up. "My sweet pumpkin, I worried I'd never see you again." Chloe covered Felicia's face with dog kisses, little paws beating a tattoo on Felicia's shoulders.

"Here." Oliver handed Felicia a bag of small dog biscuits. "She loves these."

"I've never tried this kind. Thank you," Felicia said, taking the bag. "I realize you have a billion questions but Leland and Tony can answer most when they return. I'll meet up with you later this week to answer a few you have. Right now, I'd like to go home."

"The clothes from Alex are in this duffel bag," Oliver said. If you're ready we'll go." He gestured toward the door.

****

"Home at last," Felicia said and set Chloe down on the walkway to the front door. She used a key she'd hidden in a fake rock to unlock the door.

"May I see that rock?" Harry held his hand out. Felicia gave it to him. "Clever hiding spot," he said, examining the hollowed out bottom.

She went inside behind the sausage dog who'd dashed ahead. Oliver had dropped them off and asked if she needed anything or wanted him to stay. She told him they'd be fine and he'd left.

"Let me give Chloe a cookie and I'll show you around," Felicia said from the kitchen."

Harry remained on the walkway stunned by the reality of the house.

"Harry?" When he didn't answer, she went to the door. "Harry, what are you doing? Come inside."

"You do have a house in this spot." He eyed the house baffled by its existence as though she'd just conjured it up.

"I told you I did. Because it wasn't there for you to see when I originally showed you, didn't mean it didn't exist." She came back and took his hand. "You truly thought I'd made it up?"

"I knew what I saw with my eyes. There was no house. I never thought to question if you came from another time. Who would? You just sounded daft."

"Hmm. Well, come inside and I'll show you around. You're going to love the hot shower and running water and electricity and indoor plumbing. This is what we call a sitting room. I'll hold off a guess how you'll like television."

Inside, Harry paused at an archway between a kitchen to his right and the sitting room. The room had several pieces of furniture he recognized, pieces similar to the castle's reception room. What he saw of the kitchen had little he recognized. Several shiny metal doors covered various sized components. Later he'd ask her to show him what they did.

"Where do you want this?" he asked and nodded toward the duffel bag, hoping he'd recognize more in the other rooms.

"I'll take it. Follow me while I give you a short house tour. We'll start with the bedroom."

Harry followed, standing quietly as she removed the clothes from the bag and set them on the bed.

"As you can see, this is my bedroom or chamber as you'd call it. I won't venture a guess as to whether you like the decor or not. I'm not sure if you notice that sort of thing."

"No reason to when you live in a barracks. Those folks who live in the keep fill it with what they like. That's nothing to do with me."

"Which is what I've done, fill my home with my tastes. This room is what most people call eclectic but I love the furnishings. I swapped out the traditional furniture I had for years for this art deco style."

He didn't like or dislike what she'd chosen. In the sitting room, there were pieces that weren't very different from the castle's. If anything most looked more comfortable than in Elysian Fields. Her bed had a padded headboard in steel-grey satin which was the top half of a mahogany four-poster bed. All the chambers in the castle not used by servants had four-poster beds too. Hers had a black and grey counterpane that covered the bed. In the corner she'd placed a wine-colored velvet chair with a fat bottom and arms and with an ottoman.

"It's a pretty chair, isn't it? It lends a splash of color to the room."

"*Splash of color,* such funny English. But I know what you meant."

The three chests were strange. The larger one and small ones by the side of the bed were mirrored. Very unusual. He'd never seen anything fashioned in that manner. He knelt so the large chest was even with shoulders and then bent to look at his reflection on the face of the drawers.

"What a fine mirror. The images reflected are without flaw." Harry stood. "You must've hated the poor quality of our mirrors."

"Not the end of the world. A little blurry, a little rippled but I made do," she said and moved the clothes she had stored in one drawer to another. She laid the borrowed ones for Harry's use in tidy piles in the emptied drawer.

The knights each had one chest kept at the foot of their beds. Even the fine chambers in the castle only had one chest

"You have a lot of furniture. What are they filled with?" Harry asked, waving a hand at the dresser and nightstands.

"The chamber I had at the castle had a chest and table in addition to the bed too. I've just included two nightstands. They're all filled with different clothing items: lingerie, pajamas, casual sweaters, scarves, and gloves that sort of thing."

"Do women here not wear gowns, normal long dresses?"

"Yes, sometimes." She went to her walk-in closet and opened it. "I keep dresses, and skirts, and blouses in here."

All three sides of the closet were lined with clothes. "Why do you need so many garments? I doubt the queen has this much."

"I like nice clothes. I make a good living, why

shouldn't I buy what I want? I know how practical you are. You needn't waffle on about needing and wanting. We'll simply agree to have two different views of clothes. Let's move on to the bathroom.

"This is the shower I've raved about." She opened the glass door and turned a steel handle attached to a bronze and gold tiled wall. The tile pattern was familiar to a tapestry he'd seen while visiting court.

From above a metal disc with perforations rained down water. Harry started to reach in and put his hand under the spray.

"Not yet I'm letting it run until it's warm." After a moment she said, "Ready. Running hot and cold water, a luxury this time has given us. Stick your hand in there now and feel how pleasant it is."

He did as she said first with one hand then he stuck the other in. "This is a superior invention." He turned his hands over enjoying the heat.

"You mentioned your back aching on occasion. You can make the water hot as you like and let it beat on the areas that ache."

"I am excited to try that. Can you make the water hotter?"

"Sure can. Turn to the right for hotter water and the left for cooler. The dish on the shelf has a bar of soap. The bottle next to it is shampoo for washing your hair. Pour a dollop about this big." She made a circle on her palm. "Rub your hands together and it will lather up. Rub that through you hair and rinse all the lather out."

"At home I use the same soap for all my body including my hair."

"I know but bar soap isn't as good for your hair.

Shampoo makes your hair shine and smell nice."

"You know best in this matter. I assume lowering the handle shuts the water off?" He reached over pushed the handle down.

Closing the shower door, she then gestured to a white oval sitting on the floor. "Yes, this is—"

"The piss pot from the look of it." He tapped the top. "Ceramic?"

"Porcelain. Yes, it's piss pot and like the shower it has a control. Press this metal part and the contents disappear into a sewer system."

He grunted his approval.

"I show you around the sitting room now. We'll skip the kitchen today." She led him into the living area. "The two most important features you need to see are this switch and the television." She flipped the toggle on the wall switch up. "Lights on." She flipped the toggle again. "Lights off."

"Ingenious. Let me." He played with the switch, turning lights on and off and on. "How bright the room becomes. This is amazing. Do all the rooms have this ability?"

She nodded. "All."

He continued fiddling with the lights. "Do others know of this or is it rare to possess?"

Felicia clasped his hand and stopped him after he'd turned the lights on for the tenth time. "Most everyone has electricity. That's what runs the lights...generates the power to make them work. You can play with the switch later. Let me show you the television."

Using a black oblong device, she pointed it at a flat square hanging on the wall. The flat face lit up with an image of a powerful looking man with an enormous hammer chasing someone. The heavy pounding of drums accompanied his action.

Startled, Harry instinctively flinched but then moved to the front of the square. He ran his hand over the glass and poked at the man with the hammer fighting another man. How could these men be inside the box? Harry peered behind the box but it was how it looked from the other side—against the wall. He hadn't thought he'd find a different sight but he had to check. Coming round to the front again, he tilted his head to the side, studying the picture. "Who are these people? They appear real but that cannot be."

"They're both real and not real."

"I don't understand. How they can be both?"

"I'm not the best person to describe what's happening but I'll try. You are real—a flesh and blood man. You speak. You move. When you look in a mirror, the mirror reflects the real you but the reflection itself is not you, just an image. "Are you with me so far?"

"So far."

"Trust me. There's nothing bad about this. What you see here isn't a reflection but something similar. The images of those flesh and blood people and their actions are recorded by a camera, an invention I'll show you later. The recording, or illustration if you prefer, is then broadcast through the medium of television, which is what this is."

"How does the television capture the images from the camera you mention?"

"It involves satellites and cables and electricity. I can't really explain it well. Oliver will be able to give you the details."

The image men continued to fight. "This man in the strange looking armor and red cape, does he wear what most men do here? It's not at all like the way Oliver, Stephen, and Simon dressed. If so, I'd prefer to look the same as Stephen and the rest of my friends."

"No. Men don't dress like that in everyday life. That man is an actor pretending to be Thor, the Norse God."

"Interesting. According to this movie he is extremely powerful. You hear stories of how he invaded our island long ago. I used to wonder that they looked like."

"Norseman didn't look like him. It's a costume version of Thor. The man you see doesn't look like this in real life. The people who made the movie dressed him to make him more interesting as a god."

"The thing in your hand that looks like your cell phone, is it what makes the images come to life?"

She nodded and pointed to the television. "This black rectangle is called a remote and controls what you see and hear." She pressed a button and the sound grew louder. She pressed a different button and the image of one metal carriage pursuing another appeared. "Oh good, a Bond movie. They're exciting action movies. That's what we call these moving images after they are put together to make a story."

Harry watched for a long moment not saying anything. "God's teeth. These carriages are trying to ram each other and send the other off the road. Is that common?"

"Like I said, it's a movie, a make believe situation with actors portraying the heroes and the enemies. The man in the silver car is the hero named James Bond. He plays a spy for England. The dark-haired men want to kill him. Men try to kill him in every movie."

She gave Harry the remote and showed him how to change channels and adjust the sound. "Can you experiment with this on your own? I'm going to take a hot shower and get out of this nasty gown."

"There's not much to master. I'm interested in what is in the box and seeing other channels." He changed the channel showing a soccer game. "What's this then?"

"A football match. This is not a movie but an ongoing game. There are nets at each end of the field. Each team wants to send the ball into the opposition's net to score points."

"They must be soft in the head, the lot of them. No one has the ordinary sense to pick the ball up and run it in. Such dullards could never be knights."

"They can kick the ball or hit it with their heads but picking it up isn't allowed except by the man guarding the net. There are lots of different programs, not just Bond or Thor or football."

"I'll stay with this. I want to see how the teams do."

"Doesn't matter what timeframe the man is from, a man is a man, and for them sporting events on television are like catnip to cats," she muttered loud enough for him to hear.

"I'm nipping in to the bathroom now."

He set the remote down on the coffee table. "Before you leave, help with my fasteners. It will feel good to get this armor off."

She unbuckled the hard to reach fasteners in the back while he unbuckled the top ones on his shoulders. He propped the breastplate and backplate against the side of the sofa.

"Have fun. I'm going to call Tesco's and order a

delivery of groceries to tide us over until I do big shopping."

"But you'll be in the shower. What should I do when they come to the door?"

"I won't be long. I'll be done before they arrive. You can jump in when I finished. I'm dying to see you fall in love with hot running water."

Sinking into the sofa, he stretched his legs out, sighed and smiled up at her. "Me too. Afterward, I look forward to sitting quiet, having a hearty meal, and sleeping in a real bed."

"Sounds perfect to me." Felicia bent and kissed him and went into the kitchen. She opened a bottle of cabernet and poured him a glass. "I don't have any beer. I don't like it but I have wine." She handed him the glass. "The bottle's on the counter if you want more."

****

Felicia dried and pulled her hair into a simple ponytail. She didn't bother with makeup other than a little mascara and blush. She dressed in jeans, a short-sleeve white blouse and pristine white New Balance trainers. Clothes designed for the comfort medieval clothing didn't offer.

"Your turn," she said, coming into the sitting room. Harry was still watching soccer with Chloe curled up in his lap. "I see you've won Chloe's heart already."

"She's female. As you know, I've always been a favorite with the ladies," he said in a matter-of-fact tone.

"You are so full of yourself."

"Truth is truth. You're a perfect example." Winking he added, "You had a deep dislike for me in the beginning and now you love me."

He wasn't wrong. Annoyingly honest but not wrong. "I had cause. You weren't nice to me in the beginning. Go take your shower, Sir Conceited."

Harry gave her the remote. "I might be awhile if the hot water feels as good as you say."

"Take your time. Relax."

The grocery delivery came while he showered. He was in the shower sneaking up on twenty minutes. Felicia considered checking to see if he was okay. She'd never taken that much time. Generally, she was a get in, soap, rinse and get out person. Even today as excited as she was to finally take a hot shower and feel truly clean, she was finished in less than fifteen minutes.

She heard the water shut off. She stopped putting groceries away and hovered in the hall, expecting him to give her a shout to come show him how the zipper on Alex's borrowed clothes worked. Instead a few minutes later he came out of the bedroom fully dressed in a tee shirt and jeans and trainers.

He looked mighty fine in leather breeches and his tunic. But she'd fantasized how he'd look in tight jeans and a fit-to-his-broad-chest tee shirt. Her fantasy didn't do him justice. The cotton of the tee hugged his chest and showed off those sword-wielding biceps. The jeans hugged his muscled thighs and firm bum.

Felicia touched the tip of her finger to her tongue and then to his chest, hissing as she did. "Looks like everything fits you."

"I don't know why you hissed when you touched me but I take it from your grin it means something good."

"It means you're hot, which is really nice for me. Are you comfortable in these clothes?"

"Yes. Shoes are a little snug but not too painful. I like this metal closure." He pointed to the zipper. "Very convenient."

"You'll find we have many conveniences. Tomorrow I have to go into my office for a bit. I'm sure my receptionist has been going crazy wondering about my whereabouts. When I am done there, we'll shop for more clothes for you."

Harry looked her up and down. "Do all women here dress like the men? You're wearing the same clothes as me."

"We have similar clothing. These trousers we're wearing are called jeans and both sexes like them. The same with the shoes. They're comfortable. My blouse isn't exactly the same as your shirt. The blue flowers on the collar make it suitable for women. Most women dress like this. Do you hate how I look?"

He ran his hand over her bum, cupped her entire ass and pulled her to him. "No, the jeans make your butt look pert. I approve."

He had combed his wet hair back and shaved. She ran the back of her fingers over his smooth cheeks. He shaved everyday back in time but using water and his knife, he never got as close a shave as today. "How did you shave?"

"I invaded the drawers under your sink and found a palm-sized pink-handled appliance made of a strange material. I saw it held a thin blade and realized it was a razor. I used the soap from the shower to work up a decent lather. I feel nice, don't I?" He leaned in and offered his cheek for a feel.

"That you do. When we're out shopping, we'll buy proper shaving cream for you. It works better than soap." She kissed each cheek. He'd found the razor she used on her legs. For him a razor dulled by leg use was still better than the knife.

"I also used a tiny brush in a silver container on the counter. I noticed it next to a tube called mint toothpaste and also made of a strange material. I was curious and sniffed it. It smelled minty so I squeezed some of the tube's contents on a finger and tasted it. There was the hint of some kind of mint. I saw residue of paste on the brush. Since the tube said it was for teeth I smeared some on the brush and cleaned my teeth with it. The initial foaming of my mouth troubled me. I was reminded of a rabid dog. But after I rinsed, it left a fresh taste in my mouth. Better than the linen cloth and clove water I used in my time. I'd like to use it again. May I?"

He'd used her toothbrush, which was gross, but she had a new one from the dentist. He could keep on with her old one. "Absolutely."

"What is that delicious aroma?" Harry asked, following her into the kitchen.

"Sausage and cheese bake-at-home pizza. Here." She handed him another wine. She'd poured herself a glass while he showered and refilled his. "Once you've had a bite you'll understand why it's a favorite comfort food with Americans."

"What are Americans?"

How to describe Americans? "A couple hundred years after your time England established a colony in a land across the ocean. That worked for a while then the colonists got into a snit with us over the king's taxes. We went to war with them. They won and became independent. Relations between us were dicey for many years. We got over it. We're allies now."

She removed the pizza from the oven and cut it into slices. Harry reached for one. Understandable as both their stomachs growled incessantly during the baking. "It has to cool for a few minutes or you'll burn your mouth," she warned.

"Let's eat in front of the telly," she said, loading up two plates with pizza and grabbing several napkins.

"Is there more football on?"

"We're not watching football. I don't know what's on but football is not under consideration."

"Fine."

He wolfed the pizza slices. "That is the best food I've ever eaten. Do you mind I'd take more?"

"No, help yourself."

Midway through the third piece of pizza loving Chloe changed begging targets and moved to Harry's feet. She sat up, balancing well on her sausage dog bum and gave him her best *aren't I adorable* face.

"No pizza for you, little one. I'm keeping it all for myself," Harry told her but she didn't budge. "Oh, all right." He gave her a bite of crust. "One piece and then off with you."

Chloe promptly returned to Felicia and propped herself up on Felicia's calf with two paws, tail wagging like mad. Felicia tore a chunk of crust from her piece. "Here. Now that's it. No more begging."

Chloe jumped on the sofa and lay down between Felicia and Harry, resting her head on Felicia's thigh.

Neither Felicia nor Harry could stay awake that night past 8:00 and went to bed. "This is the nicest bed I've ever laid in, like pizza for the body." He said good night, patted her on the bum and then rolled over and immediately fell asleep. He wasn't inclined to spoon, which suited her. She didn't like the feel of being smothered.

There was no other way to describe the first few minutes when she crawled into bed other than delight. Stretching out, head on a pillow light years softer than at the castle. The castle pillows were either straw or feathers. The feather ones she could never mush into shape. The straw ones were better but not great. Felicia wallowed against the comfortable mattress, wriggling and rubbing her butt and heels and back on it.

She rolled over onto her side. Chloe liked to sleep plastered to Felicia. The little one didn't cuddle tonight. Felicia patted the space between her and Harry and by her feet. The doxie, like most of her breed, like to burrow under blankets. "Chloe, where are you?"

Before she resorted to searching the rest of the house, just for giggles, she peered over Harry's back. Chloe lay sound asleep plastered against him. "Goodnight my darlings," she whispered and rolled back onto her side.

Chapter Seventeen

Felicia slept like the dead well past nine in the morning. She woke to the sound of Harry brushing his teeth. He was already dressed in the same tee shirt and jeans from the evening before but barefoot.

She joined him in the bathroom to brush her teeth and hair. He stepped back from the sink when she did. "What is this you're wearing? Do not misunderstand. I very much approve. I've never seen anything like it."

Normally she wore loose fitting cotton pajama bottoms and a comfortable top to bed. Last night she broke out a pair of sapphire blue shorty pajamas by Natori. The camisole top had thin straps and delicate lace across the top with embroidered small, gold silk flowers scattered in the lace. The bottoms had a v-inset on the sides of the same embroidered flowers.

"Just simple pajamas," she said as though she commonly wore such cute nightwear and spun for him to admire her in them.

"Not simple but a lovely, lustful display of leg and bosom." He lifted her onto the edge of the sink counter and gave her a mad, head-spinning kiss.

He finished and helped her off the counter. Obviously, she didn't need help to slip down the short distance. But if it pleased him to do so, she was happy to let him lift her up and down like a feather.

Harry moved away, pausing in the doorway to ask, "I saw eggs and butter in the steel cold box in the kitchen and bread on the counter. Will you be preparing a meal? I'm famished."

"Me too. I'll fix breakfast as soon as I change." She dressed and made two eggs with bacon for herself and Harry a plate of four scrambled eggs with bacon and toast.

"When are we leaving for your office?" Harry asked as she set their plates on the table.

"As soon as we've finished breakfast. Are you excited to see how Stroud has changed?"

"Wouldn't you be?"

"Of course," she said.

Like her mother, she never left dirty dishes in the sink. Since there weren't enough to run the dishwasher, she hurried to do them by hand.

On the ride to Stroud, Harry was quiet. She thought he'd have a lot of questions. Instead, he watched the countryside but continued to flinch at fast traveling cars going the other way. Lorries because of their size, Felicia surmised, elicited a short grunt and flinch. She'd taken smaller roads and avoided the multi-lane carriageway. The smaller roads were also more scenic. Maybe if he saw the landscape had remained much the same as his time, he would feel more at ease.

Entering the town, they crossed the Thames-Severn canal. He finally spoke up. "The bridge is still here. I don't know why that surprises me as it was built well of local stone."

"A lot of stone bridges from your time and as far back as the Romans still exist. Some of the buildings too, York Minster, Westminster Abbey, and the Tower of

London are a few."

"Are they used by your people?"

The designation *your people* caught her off guard. He felt no affinity for this world yet, that was clear. "*My people* are *your people*," she reminded him. "We're just from a later time. Do you really feel we're that much different?"

"In ways." He turned his attention back to the activity around them. "I like that green area," he said, pointing to Stroud Park. "What is it now? I see benches and what you call walkways."

"A park. It's lovely and local folks flock to it."

"In my time, it was a farm. The town didn't cover so much area then, but you know that from the visit we made."

"Harry, does seeing Stroud so different from the town you knew trouble you? We don't have to spend much time here, if it does. I have to check in with my office. It shouldn't take long and we'll leave as soon as I talk to Roger."

"I am fine. I need to get used to the changes, that's all." The explanation was barely out of his mouth when he went ramrod stiff in the seat. "My Lord, what manner of town has Stroud become? In my day it was a market town." He pointed to a group of female pedestrians. "Mercy, there's so many harlots. The streets are awash in them."

"Those aren't harlots. I'm sure the town has a few but those women are normal every day women. What makes you think they're harlots?"

"Look at all the skin they show. Their legs and arms are naked."

"That's the fashion now. Women are allowed to

show their legs and arms. How much they show is up to the woman."

A smile crept across Harry's face as she explained. He watched several more women as they continued down the street. "Do they dress like this for free?"

"Almost all. Like I said, there are some harlots, as you call them, here who will dress any way you like. But yes, the everyday woman dresses this way for free. Do you disapprove?"

"Gracious sakes, no! Only a fool of a man would object to the sight of lovely feminine skin, I'm many things but not a fool."

She thought he'd get whiplash from watching women on both sides of the street.

Apparently, he had his fill and turned his observations back to the town. "I see the streets are as steep as in my day. I'd have thought that is something your people would've fixed."

"Perhaps the current powers that be..." She chose terminology she hoped would begin to reinforce that he and she were the same people. Centuries apart, but the same deep in their DNA. "The powers that be want to keep part of the past. They wish to show the connection we continue to have with our ancestors."

"Perhaps."

Felicia parked behind her office building. Every tenant had designated spaces for themselves, their employees, and clients. Shutting off the engine, she took a deep breath and mentally ran the lame excuse for her absence once more. Lame as it was, nothing she thought of seemed better.

"I take it this is where your office is?" Harry asked.

"Yes. You'll like my receptionist and nurse assistant, Prentice. I'd be lost without him."

Scowling, Harry took her hand. "We'll see."

****

Prentice stood when they entered the reception area of her office. "Where have you been? I've been beside myself with worry. A man named Oliver Gordon came the first day you weren't here and said you had a family emergency and would be incommunicado for a time. Incommunicado! Where in the world don't they have cell phones?" he said, coming over to her and Harry.

"It's a long story. I had to go somewhere and be alone to think."

Prentice listened to her with a quizzical expression. Exactly what she feared, the story sounded as feeble to him as it did when she dreamed it up.

"Oh? I was worried," Prentice said. "Mr. Gordon said he wasn't sure how long you'd be gone."

Ugh. What to say? She waved away the discrepancy and stammered, "It was both personal and a family matter. The important thing is I'm back at last. While I was away, I met someone who stole my heart." Felicia smiled up at Harry. "Prentice, this is Harry Quarles, heart stealer extraordinaire and all round chivalrous knight."

Harry extended his hand. "It's actually Sir Harold."

"Terribly sorry." Prentice withdrew his hand.

"You needn't apologize." He reached over and shook the assistant's hand. "In this time and place, Harry is acceptable. Nice meeting you."

"Fill me in on what happened while I was gone. I'm sure you took care of the patients scheduled. Did I lose any permanently?" Felicia asked.

"I was able to reschedule most. Dr. Gold took care of those I couldn't."

"Dr. Gold has his office across the hall. We fill in and take each other's patients when one of us is out of the office," she explained to Harry. "Start calling the patients who I missed seeing and make new appointments."

Prentice nodded. "Will do."

"Do you want to see my exam room and personal office?" she asked Harry.

"The exam room. I assume the office is similar to Richard's at Elysian Fields."

"Sort of." She led him into the room and closed the door.

The poster of the front and back views of the body with the parts numbered and the names for the numbers listed on the side immediately drew Harry's attention. "It's better to see the parts of the body this way than on the battlefield."

He moved to the counter and sink area. "I realize these are gloves but what is this material?" he asked, taking a rubber glove from the box. He held it up to the light and then worked to get the too small glove over his hand. He finally managed to get most of it over part of his palm and the back of his hand. He flexed and made a fist. "Is it supposed to be this tight?"

"No. You need a large and that's made to fit me. I'm a medium. It's called Nitrile and doctors often need to wear the gloves to prevent contagion between patients. For the same reason I rinsed my hands between treating the men at Waterloo."

He took a long Q-tip from the glass container. "And this?"

"I take swabs of infected areas or samples of body fluids, like saliva."

Harry set the Q-tip down and opened a drawer filled with hypodermic needles. He removed one. "May I?" Indicating he'd like to take it out of the protective wrapping.

"Feel free." She handed him scissors from another drawer.

He cut the package away, took the needle out. He studied it for a moment before working the plunger up and down and then tapped the sharp end with a fingertip. "I understand this is used as some kind of stabbing device but what is the attached cylinder for? If I discovered it hidden in a drawer at Elysian Fields, I'd suspect the purpose was to administer poison."

"Well, I'm sure it's been used like that by spies and such but we use them to inject medicine into a patient's system. I'll show you." She put her hand out for him to give her the needle. She took a small cup from the dispenser, filled it partway with water and withdrew the liquid using the hypodermic. She showed him the measurement markings on the side. "These tell me how much medicine I'm injecting the person with. I pierced the skin, or a vein, pretty simple really." Then she squirted a spurt of the liquid into the sink.

"It's so tiny. It doesn't look like the injection would hurt much. A kindness not pursued by doctors in my time."

"I try not to hurt my patients. I'm a needle-phobe myself, a whiny baby when it comes to shots. You'd think of all people a doctor would have more courage."

She took a bottle from the cupboard. "You know, I could vaccinate you, one to start for today. You said yourself how the needle wouldn't hurt."

"Vaccinate?"

"Against some diseases to prevent you catching them. Everyone gets vaccinated now."

He pulled back and shooed away the needle in her hand as she came closer. "No, thank you. I feel fine."

"It's a preventative. Because you feel fine now doesn't mean you won't get sick down the road with something we could prevent with a shot."

He waved her off again. "No. I think not. Perhaps another time. I thought we were going shopping for clothes."

"Later then." Smiling she threw the hypo into the bin for the disposal of used needles. "Ready to go shopping?"

"Sure."

****

They went to a nearby Selfridges department store. Felicia had checked the tag on a pair of the borrowed jeans for size before they left the house. Harry was an easy to remember 34 waist and 34 inseam. She tossed packages of underwear and socks in her basket then picked an array of tee shirts both white and colored, a variety of casual shirts, and two white dress shirts. Harry remained quiet as she gathered pairs of jeans and a few pairs casual slacks.

She piled that stack on the sales counter and went to the area of the men's department with business attire. "You should try these on just in case they need any tailoring," she told him, choosing a pair of black fine wool trousers from the rack along with a pair of grey trousers of the same material. "The fitting room is over there. Before you go, try these on first."

She'd chosen a navy blazer and tweed sport coat to go with the wool trousers. She held the blazer out. Instead of taking the jacket he asked, "Why do I need all these clothes?"

"It really isn't that much. You have a choice of casual clothes and a minimum of dressier choices if we go someplace that's required."

He eyed the stack of clothes she'd picked out for him on the counter and after a long moment he grabbed the blazer and put it on. Then tried the tweed jacket. Both fit. "Give me the trousers."

While he was inside the fitting room, she found two ties she liked that were electric blue silk and a lipstick red, bright without being too flashy.

He quickly returned, so quickly she wondered if he really tried on the slacks. They moved onto the men's shoe department. "I'll get a salesman to help. He'll have a way to measure your foot."

"The shoes you're wearing are called trainers. We need to get ones that fit better." She went to a rack of similar shoes. "Which trainers do you prefer and which dress shoes—more formal shoes do you prefer?" she asked, indicating the displays for each.

"Get what you like," he snapped.

Felicia couldn't tell if he was cranky because he hated shopping, which she had no way of knowing when she brought him to Selfridge's, or if he was angry with her for some other reason.

The salesman had Harry sit while he measured each foot. As he did, Felicia quickly picked out trainers that were identical to the ones Alex loaned him. She added them to the pile of clothing.

"Will that be all?" the salesman asked.

"No, there are two ties I want to add," Felicia told him and went to the counter with the tie displays.

Harry snatched the first from her hand when she pulled it from the table and threw it back on the display. "I don't want the ties."

"They're convenient to have to go with your dress shirts and trousers."

He bent down close. The overhead lights cast his face in a shadow that made his blue eyes look black. "I said, no!"

"Harry..."

"I'm done. I'll wait for you outside."

Felicia had the salesman stuff the clothes in as few bags as possible. When she met him outside, he took all of them from her.

"I'm sorry I was harsh with you," Harry said as they walked.

Obviously, his reaction to the ties didn't stem from tired-of-shopping crankiness. They reached the car as she broached the subject of what was the source. Being a stiff-upper-lipped knight, talking about his feelings might not suit him. She had to try. "You want to tell me what's wrong?"

He laid the bags in the trunk, closed the lid and stood over it without answering. She thought he was debating whether or not to answer.

He turned and leaned against the car. He took her hand, so she stood in front of him. "Felicia, everything I've ever owned I earned for myself. As a knight in service to Baron Guiscard, the Baron provided most necessities. I had sufficient garments to last me between visits from the castle laundress. I never needed this many clothes. Anything else I owned came from outside labors. When not campaigning, I participated in jousting tournaments from here to London. I'm an excellent jouster and won most competitions. My armor, my horse's armor, evenings with other knights at the village tavern came from those winnings. All these clothes you bought..." He shook his head. "You spent too much. What must that salesman think of me letting a woman provide for my needs?"

It was a lose-lose situation. Her paying for everything humiliated him. She got that. But she had to buy his clothes or he had to continue wearing the borrowed things. "I'm sure he thought we were a married couple. Like many couples, the wife goes with the husband to clothes shop. The woman often pays because she carries a handbag and it's easier for her to carry money."

"I suspect you're just saying that to ease my mind. If you aren't, then it seems a strange custom—a woman handling the family earnings."

"I'm saying it because it's true, ask Stephen. You wouldn't know that and I understand you were embarrassed. It never occurred to me to mention many women handle finances. Sorry. You did need the clothes or you'd have to keep wearing Alex's. I don't think you'd want that. I truly didn't spend that much. If it makes you feel better, we won't have to shop for anything but food for a long time."

"Food is a different story. Buy as much as you like. I do eat a lot. On that topic, I am hungry."

She'd planned on stopping at a restaurant she liked that was on the way home. Not a good idea now. She'd have to pay for the meal. In the mood he was in, his head might explode.

"Is there any pizza left?" he asked, opening the car door for her.

"No, you went through it last night."

"Pity. Can you make more?"

"Tomorrow. We'll shop for food then. I have other stuff for today."

Chapter Eighteen

The Next Afternoon

Felicia set her purse down on the sofa side table. When neither Harry nor Chloe greeted her, she went in search for them.

"Harry," she called out as she checked the bedrooms.

"Out here." He stood in the half-open side of her French doors to the patio. Chloe scooted past him, bottom wriggling, tail swishing like a weather vane in a wind storm, she ran to Felicia and rolled over for her expected belly rub hello.

Felicia complied. "You're the best baby girl," she said, giving the pink belly a vigorous rub.

"I've a bottle of wine and have a glass for you out here," Harry said. "I hope you don't mind I opened a bottle of Bordeaux. You said to make myself at home."

"I meant it. I'm more than ready for a glass of wine." She joined Harry at the outdoor table. He poured her a wine and refreshed his. "It's a lovely day. I couldn't bear to be inside. Chloe agreed. How was your first day back at the office?"

"Not bad. I reconnected with the patients and caught up on paperwork. What did you do all day?"

"I walked to Elysian Fields or rather what is left of

it. The ruin has changed even from when we hid there after Waterloo. More walls had tumbled down and broken up."

Natural curiosity to see how much it changed from 1815 would draw him. Without the distraction of providing safety for them and foraging for food of their post Waterloo time, the visit today must've stirred a hundred memories. Danger lay in how homesick those memories made him.

"Yes, the castle's ruin has worsened but two hundred years of exposure to the elements has to do a lot of damage. I thought one day soon, we'd borrow two of Alex's horses from his stable and ride over to the castle. I'm surprised you went today. That's a very long walk," Felicia said and took a sip of wine.

"I had time. It wasn't as though my day spilled over with burdensome chores."

"True. What else did you do?"

"I watched two discs from your stack on the machine you showed me how to work this morning."

"The DVD player. What movies did you watch?"

"One called *Gladiator*, which I liked very much. I liked him. He was an excellent strategist. The other was called *Henry V*. I had questions on that one."

"Like what?"

"This battle in the place called Agincourt, is it a pretend place based on Crecy or Poitiers? The action and surroundings appeared to be. Also, the armies were outfitted much like we were."

"No, Agincourt existed. The battle occurred in 1415 and it was similar to Crecy and Poitiers in that the English faced overwhelming French forces. The result was a great English victory."

He smiled. "I hoped that part was true. I can tell the

part where the king came to everyone's campfire to chat did not happen at Crecy. King Edward was there but he did not come to my campsite or to the tent of the other knight's I knew. He fought with us but at night he enjoyed the comfort of the Royal tent."

"What about the Black Prince at Poitiers?"

"I knew him, although not well enough to call him friend like the Baron. I knew him as a frequent guest of the Baron's. We spoke casually when he visited. I also knew him as a man I fought with and for. That told me more about him than a thousand conversations. I have the highest regard for his courage and honor. He was a fine man, which is rare among courtiers."

He picked at the wine bottle label with his fingernail. "Bordeaux was the Prince's favorite wine. It was the only province in France that we owned. The Prince enjoyed spending time there."

"What about you? Did you have a special place? You traveled around the southern shires on the tournament circuit and traveled around France on campaign."

"Elysian Fields. I am happiest there. It is the only place I think of as home."

The fact he spoke in the present tense troubled her. He'd only been away from his time a short while but his homesickness was palpable. Felicia figured the fastest and best way to help was commiserating with his friends. "Would you like me to drive you over to the Crippen's house tomorrow morning on my way to my office? You can visit with Simon and Emily. Emily might be able to take you both to see Stephen."

"I'd like that very much," Harry said, perking up.

As they talked, Chloe crisscrossed the yard at top

sausage dog speed terrorizing little birds who dared to land. If they sought shelter on tree branches, she wasn't deterred by the trunks. She leapt at them with great effort.

"She's a remarkable athlete considering her odd shape," Harry said.

"Odd shape, indeed."

"She's not shaped like any hound I've ever seen."

"That may be but she's cuter than any hound you've ever seen."

"True." He patted his leg and whistled. Chloe ran to him and he picked her up, setting her in his lap. He let her sniff his wine before he finished it. "You say Alex has a stable."

"He does."

"Do you have a way to contact him? I'd enjoy riding tomorrow and I'm sure Simon would too, if Alex would loan us two mounts."

"I'll call him."

****

Felicia dropped Harry off at the Crippen's early. She'd called Alex and he said the men could borrow any mount they liked. Owen the stable manager would assist them.

Harry wasn't home when she came home that afternoon. Chloe and her leash were missing as well. Clearly, Harry was growing smitten with the little dog.

Felicia changed clothes and put together a plate of appetizers to munch on before dinner while Harry and Chloe were out. If anyone else had taken Chloe out for a long walk, she'd have worried but Harry knew the woods better than she did. He'd ridden every inch of them over the years.

The French doors opened and Chloe came running

into the kitchen. She immediately sat at Felicia's feet waiting for her mom-is-home—now biscuit. Felicia doled out the treat and Chloe ran off to the drawing room with her treasure.

Harry wrapped his arms around Felicia and moving her ponytail out of the way, kissed the back and side of her neck.

"You smell wonderful," he said, running his nose along her neck from her ear to the curve of her shoulder.

"Thank you. I sprayed a small amount of perfume on all the places your lips should be tonight."

"I can fulfill that order and more." He turned her around and kissed her long and deep.

She broke off the kiss when she ran out of air. She was always the first one to run out of air.

Harry took her by the hand and started walking. "I want to show you a trick I've been working on with Chloe."

He made a kissing noise and the dog came over. "Sit."

Chloe sat on her hind end.

"She did that before," Felicia said, unimpressed.

"Just wait. Dance, little one." Harry made a circular motion with his finger and Chloe stood on her hind legs and turned in a circle, front paws patting the air. Graceful the dance was not. With Chloe's build, tricks closer to the ground would be more her forte.

Harry made a down stroke motion and Chloe went back on all fours. He gave her a treat he had in the pocket of his jeans. "Good girl."

"I can't believe you taught her that in one day," Felicia said, grinning and impressed in spite of the lack of finesse.

"One afternoon, actually. I went riding with Simon this morning. As you know, I came to the castle at a fairly young age. I used to watch the master of the hounds train the dogs. I thought Chloe a clever little dog. I can teach her using the master's methods."

She'd heard stories of trainers then and now using cruel methods on dogs in their care. Alarmed, she asked, "You didn't hit her did you?"

"No! How can you ask such a thing? I've never favored harsh methods on any animals. When she did what I asked, she received a treat reward."

"Thank you," Felicia said with a relieved sigh. "I didn't mean to insult you. She's my baby. I couldn't bear it if she was hit." She gave Chloe a well-earned belly rub. "What a talented girl you are." Then, kissing Harry on the cheek, she added, "You did a great job. I'll grab the appetizer plate if you'll bring the wine when you're done and we can sit on the patio. I want to hear about your ride."

She returned and set the plate down. Harry came a moment later with the glasses and the last bottle of Bordeaux from her rack. "Tell me, where did you and Simon go?" Felicia asked.

"We started at the castle ruin and then rode all the routes we used to when we went on patrols. We rode all morning, like before. At midday, we returned to the ruin and ate."

"You ate there?"

"Emily made what she called sandwiches of meat and cheese to take with us." Holding out his hand, fingers spread to show her how big the sandwiches were, he went on, "And these sandwiches were thick with meat and a slice of cheese thick as my thumb. She also put fruit in our sacks and sweets called cookies."

"Hmm...Emily's quite a treasure." Felicia nearly choked taking too big a swallow of wine.

Harry didn't notice her wincing and went blithely on, "She gave us a thermos of cider too. This thermos carrier—what a marvel. Do you happen to have one?"

"I do." He obviously had a good time. Spending the morning with Simon had helped with his homesickness. "Do you plan to ride tomorrow?"

"Yes."

"I'll make you a lunch with a big sandwich. I'll use two kinds of meat and include a thermos of cider."

"She gave us bananas. I'd never had one before. They were tasty. Do you have any of those?"

"No. I have oranges, which you like."

He sipped his wine as he nibbled cheese cubes and olives from the appetizer plate. Then, he popped a balsamic drenched cherry tomato with a mozzarella ball on a toothpick into his mouth. "This modern world has the best food. I am gobsmacked by all I've had."

"We've just scratched the surface of what's available. Did Simon say how Emily's medical treatments are going?"

"The doctors said they caught the disease in time. She'll still have to continue treatments for a while though."

"That's fabulous news."

"Simon said he's never been so scared. He thought he might lose her. With that worry out of the way, he's looking forward to returning home."

"Returning home? You can't mean Elysian Fields...1359 Elysian Fields? This is their home now."

Harry shook his head and said, "No. This *was*

Emily's home. Her home now is wherever Simon is."

"Why would he want to leave?"

"There's no purpose for him here."

Her heart dropped to her stomach and twisted hearing those words, that reasoning. "You don't feel that way do you?"

Harry popped an olive in his mouth and shrugged. "I miss my horse."

"Alex breeds Percherons. I'm sure he knows of other breeders."

"You don't understand. I miss Saragon. I trained him since he was a yearling. We are...were a team. I miss having something to do, a place to be during the day. You asked if I desired to return." He offered a half-hearted shrug like he had been mulling over the prospect. "I don't know yet. Ask me when I've been here longer."

Not the answer Felicia wanted to hear. She never thought for a minute, not in her wildest dreams, that he might not find this new world thrilling.

****

Harry and Chloe were in the yard when she came home the next day. Harry had a measuring tape and a pile of plastic poles about a meter long. Chloe stood at his feet and moved when he did. "Hello beautiful lady," he called out and dropped a metal disc at the spot he measured. "I'm almost done. Come, kiss me."

Not far from Felicia's first of three flower beds, he'd set up a short teeter-totter about twelve inches off the ground with a board two meters by twelve inches wide balanced on it. Several meters past the teeter-totter, curving to the left were two poles a meter apart with a cross beam ten centimeters high, the setup similar to a show jumping oxer, only much smaller.

"Are you setting up an obstacle course for Chloe?" Felicia asked after providing the demanded kiss and one more.

"I am. I told you she's a good little athlete, considering, her short legs and shape. I want to see how good she is after I work with her." He dropped another disc on the ground. "I'll put the tools away and join you in a moment."

"Since you mention them, where did you get the tools? I only have a hammer and a screwdriver. It took more than that to build these obstacles."

"Emily's father loaned me his tool belt."

Felicia wanted to pursue the question of Simon and his desire to return to the medieval world. She couldn't gauge what effect it had on Harry. She tried to keep a lid on her anxiety but it kept flaring up as she changed into jeans and a loose blouse.

She went into the kitchen and started preparing a shepherd's pie for dinner. In keeping with her limited culinary abilities, the pie was tasty and not hard to make. But how to approach the topic of Simon and their going home continued to dominate her thoughts as she worked.

"Shall I open some wine?" Harry asked.

She hadn't heard him come in the room, she was so absorbed in the Simon-Emily problem. "Please, I'd love a glass." She couldn't hold back any longer and had to see if Simon had said anymore on their ride today. Head down, she busied herself sautéing the meat so she didn't appear worried or overly concerned. "Did Simon talk about returning again today?"

"A bit. I told him before he does, he'd best come up

with a believable reason for his absence."

"True. Does Emily know he wants to go back?"

Harry handed her a glass of wine. "No. I asked and he said he doesn't want to discuss the matter until she's well again. He knows she'll be distressed about leaving her family."

He took the vegetable peeler from her and began peeling the potatoes. "Let me help. Why do you ask in that tone of voice about Emily? Do you think she'll refuse?"

"What tone of voice?"

He stopped peeling and gave her that *seriously, you have to ask* look. "You know her, do you believe she won't wish to go back?"

"I've known all the Crippen sisters since we were young. I know her older sister Electra the best. We were in classes together. I don't know Emily that well, certainly not well enough to speak for her on a situation like this."

"You use the phrase situation like this. Why is this a *situation?* Why would she hesitate to go where he goes?"

"I don't know that she would. Like I said, I can't answer for her."

From the look in his eyes, she knew the question on Harry's lips. *Please don't ask. Please don't ask. Please don't ask.*

Thankfully, he didn't. What he said was equally upsetting and cast the shadow of uncertainty on his desire to remain. "If she loves him, she will."

Chapter Nineteen

Three weeks later

Prentice stepped just inside the door to her office. She stopped recording her notes on the chart of the last patient. "What did you need?"

"That man, Oliver Gordon, is here. He says it is important he speak to you. Should I send him away or bring him to you?"

What could Oliver want? Probably to query her about her experience while back in time. She'd promised to talk with him but had kept putting it off. She didn't want to go through a litany of questions when there was little for her to add. He could find out whatever he needed to know from Leland and Tony.

"Show him in and bring us coffee, please." She minimized the chart report on her monitor and greeted Oliver. "Oliver how nice to see you. Please sit. If you're here because I've been lax about our meeting, I apologize. I have been busy catching up with patients and showing Harry the area and many of the good things in this modern world of ours."

"No, I want to talk to you about something else but it's related."

"Intriguing. Please have a seat."

Prentice returned and set the tray with coffee,

sugar, cream and a spoon on the side of Felicia's desk. She removed two mugs with pastoral Cotswold's scenes from the bottom drawer. "I took the liberty of having coffee brought but I can have Roger bring in tea if you prefer.

"Coffee is fine."

Felicia poured and handed him the cup to mix in the cream and sugar to his liking. The dark robust blend she liked turned almost white as he added cream. She drank her coffee black.

He finished and put the cup on her desk by the tray without taking a sip. The action of someone whose mind is elsewhere. She was regretting his visit already.

"What did you want to speak to me about?"

"Simon."

Definitely, not going to be a good conversation. If it was good, he'd be talking to Emily and the Crippens. "Why come to me? I don't know him well. I can't tell you much, if you're looking for information on him."

"Not information. I wanted to share information."

"Share? With me? Shouldn't you be talking to Emily?"

He shook his head. "Not yet. I want your opinion and any additional information you have, nothing more."

"Go on, ask. I'm still not sure I will be much help."

"Yesterday Simon came to me and asked how certain I was regarding the reliability of the lightning machine."

She'd swear her heart fluttered briefly and not in a good way. She had a bad feeling about the motivation for his interest but no need to panic yet she told herself. After all, the machine was remarkable by anyone's definition. Who wouldn't be curious about its capabilities? The little voice within all of us whispered, *you're grasping at straws.*

"Sounds like a natural question to me," she said, ignoring the little voice. "Perhaps he is curious about how much faith you had when you brought the family forward. Now that they're here, he feels it's safe to ask if you were confident or rolling the dice. Who knows?"

"I'd be hard pressed to think of a man I've seen more downcast. I don't believe he asked out of natural curiosity. I'm worried."

"Harry said Simon was going through a bad patch, feeling he had no purpose. This world is a huge change for them. He's probably still adjusting.

"No, Felicia. His attitude, his tone, suggested the man was well beyond having an adjustment problem."

"I'm sorry, Oliver but I'm confused. Why are you telling me all this?"

"Because Simon didn't come alone. He and Harry rode over together. Harry looked as interested in my answer as Simon. I thought Harry might've said something to you about Simon's intentions."

"I told you what Harry said, just that Simon's going through a rough patch." When Harry hadn't brought the topic of Simon's unhappiness up again after the first time, Felicia hoped the issue was settled and Simon had stopped thinking about returning. The fact he was curious and asked about the machine didn't mean he was serious about returning. *Again grasping at straws.*

"I think Emily should know how depressed Simon is and that returning has occurred to him. Maybe. I say maybe since he never said anything outright to that effect. I hoped you'd talk to her, forewarn her so she's not blindsided just in case."

"Oh no, no, no. I want no part of that sticky wicket. She's got enough on her plate trying to get healthy. It's not my place to meddle and repeat innuendo from a secondhand conversation. He hasn't said anything definite to you. Even if that is his plan, frankly, neither of us can say whether or not she'd be unhappy to go back. She may be fine with it."

A big decision like that was between husband and wife. At the moment, Felicia was far more concerned over Harry's intentions. A better person might suffer some guilt over selfishly fretting about her circumstance more than Emily's. She wasn't that better person, nor did guilt trouble her.

"Did Harry say anything at all while they were there?" she asked.

"Nothing, other than hello and goodbye. Do you think he might feel the same as Simon?"

"I don't know. I know he feels the strain of acclimating to a totally new world. When you went back to the Middle Ages, did you think: oh well, here I am seven hundred years in the past but it's all tickety-boo?"

"Not in the least."

She spread her hands out in a there you have it gesture. "I rest my case."

"You probably right. We shouldn't stir the pot and meddle."

Felicia stood when Oliver did and walked him to the door. "Thank you for listening to me," he said. Prentice went to remove the coffee tray from her office. Oliver took the opportunity to ask her, "Are you feeling all right? No physical after-transport issues?"

"I'm well and so is Harry. I was glad to hear Leland and Tony are back safe and I thought sound. Are they having problems?"

"No, but I had to ask. The fact they're well and healthy doesn't mean you are." He paused in the doorway. "At the end of the day, are you happy you went, even if it was unintended?"

"Yes and no, mostly no. I'm happy because I met Harry, who I love with all my heart. Excluding Harry, it isn't a time I care to experience again. Call me spoiled and shallow, but I couldn't abide the limitations on women for long. I'm also very attached to modern conveniences, hot and cold running water, electricity, central heat, and food from all over the world. If that makes me shallow, then so be it."

"But you managed without all of that."

"Think about my role as a doctor, Oliver. I'd have a devil of a time staying there. I'd have to stand by and watch people I know and care about die from illnesses that are curable now." Visions of bleeding, dying men flared. She waved her hands in a useless effort to wave away the memory. "I had a taste of how gut wrenching that is on the Waterloo battlefield. Thankfully, I had a romantic relationship, yes, but I won't romanticize the time."

"I appreciate your honesty. It helps me to know how each of you found the experience. Leland and Tony, in spite of Richard's demands, said they enjoyed themselves in the main. I need to present a fair case. If I can prove the machine absolutely reliable, this could be the greatest discovery of the century."

Felicia had thought about Oliver and his invention while at Elysian Fields. Harry's angry words in the kitchen in what seemed a lifetime ago lingered. When he learned the truth behind her and Leland's and Tony's arrival, his reaction cut to the core and she had no argument to offer.

"What a wicked, selfish lot all of you are. You treat the people here like landscape for your experiments. You disturb our lives. You tinkered and tampered, testing until you found a way to open a tear in time. Just leave us be."

He was right. They'd arrived and altered the natural order of things. For her, it turned out wonderful because she came away with Harry. The odds were she was an exception.

"Oliver, this is likely the greatest discovery of the last half century and a dangerous Pandora's Box. Do you really trust the world with the ability to move through time? Trust them not to save the wrong person from death or accidentally kill a person responsible for a great creation that affects our world? Frankly, I don't trust the world with that power."

"You would have me deny my life's work?"

"It's a matter of conscience. Would you be bringing the light of knowledge to the world, or the darkness of great evil?"

"My few successes with the machine are not enough to publish. Until that day, I don't have to decide." He turned and left.

If his success continued, asking him to keep secret what he'd worked toward for so many years would be a terrible sacrifice. Going public could be equally fateful. As he climbed in his car and drove away, she wondered how he planned to keep testing the machine. Who was going to volunteer for that?

"Please, not Harry. Please..." she said under her breath.

Chapter Twenty

Harry spread the metal hoops out farther and pressed them into the grass. He whistled and pointed and Chloe dashed over to the obstacle course's start. The little dog started up the board of the teeter-totter. He pointed to the starting spot again. "No. You go when I give you the word. Come back here."

Chloe hopped off the side of the board and stood at the beginning spot, ears up.

"Ready?" She gazed up at him, furry brows crinkled, and then turned her attention to the obstacle in front of her. "Go!"

Harry ran on the outside of the course, keeping pace with her. Chloe finished the teeter-totter in a blink and moved onto the hoops. When she first ran the "jump" obstacle, he'd surprised him with her speed. Those short legs hit the ground fast. He'd moved the hoops farther apart to give her a chancc to build up her speed.

"That's it." He clapped. "Well done. Wide strides, reach for the next jump as soon as you clear the last. Good girl," he encouraged as she went from one hoop to the next.

She hurried through the third challenge, the weave poles, hitting them all.

"Go, go, go." Coaching Chloe offered a welcome distraction from his thoughts of returning to Elysian Fields, back to his position as Captain of the Guard, or as Simon put it, *a place where he had purpose.*

Chloe pivoted to the tunnel he'd made with heavy wire and a tarp. "Almost home, little one."

He pulled a liver treat from his pocket to give her when she finished. "She's a clever one and swift," Harry said without looking behind him.

"How did you know I was here?" Felicia asked.

"I heard the car pull up." Chloe remained at his feet awaiting her treat, postponing her usual rush to greet Felicia.

"I can't believe you can hear anything over the music."

She'd shown him how to use the computer to play music outside but he disliked the machine. He preferred to play her CDs. "My CDs are music from my mother's youth. She played them all the time when I was growing up. I love it."

He had favorites he listened to repeatedly. A singer called David Bowie sang the three songs he never tired of: *Heroes*, *Space Oddity*, and *Fame*.

Felicia explained that *Space Oddity* was about an astronaut who dies on his journey into space. Harry didn't completely understand what an astronaut was even after she explained his purpose. He understood enough. "*He died in service to his country. He's a different kind of soldier than I am used to but his death is not unlike dying on the battlefield.*"

She'd asked, if Heroes made him think of the battles he fought in?

"*Yes and no. I fought with men I consider heroes but I'd never assign that honor to myself.*"

"*Why not? More than once you faced*

overwhelming odds in favor of the enemy. Your actions garnered the respect of all the knights at Elysian Fields."

"I fought well, yes. I have courage, yes, but I knew men who went beyond bravery. Sir Guy, my Baron, rode to the aid of his friend the Earl of Ashenwyck, knowing the number of enemy he'd have to fight through to succeed, knowing the chances of surviving were slim. I saw knights and foot soldiers fight through enormous chaos to save an injured friend."

"I think you underestimate your worth."

"I like the song very much and enjoy singing along. I'm fine with that. If I were to wear the mantle of arrogance, it would be the song, Fame. I had my share of fame on the jousting circuit. I was the English champion for several seasons."

"I see you've put out all the Beatles CDs and the Moody Blues. What do you like about them?"

"Their music is happy melodies. Cheery tunes."

"They are cheery and fun." Felicia turned the volume down and came over and kissed him. "Chloe is doing really well on your course."

He slid her over in front of him and wrapped his arms around her, pulling her to his chest. "She's a quick learner."

"Have you trained dogs before? I don't recall you working with the hounds at the castle."

"I am not a dog trainer like the Master of the Hounds. I just used the same method I did with Saragon."

"No one else assisted in his training?"

"No. He was my horse, a war horse. Our special bond, his trust of me had to be unquestionable"

She tipped her head to the side so she could see

him. "I understand. He was brilliant under saddle. I loved watching you work him out. But then I just love watching you, period." She snuggled harder against his chest. "So how was your day? What did you do?"

Grateful she changed subjects and he needn't dwell on the stallion he missed, he masked his feelings discussing the day. "I walked in the woods for a time. I wanted to see the area Simon and I patrolled most often. I was curious how much it might've changed."

"Had it?"

He shrugged. "Some, but less than I imagined."

"I'd think walking in that part of the woods or visiting Elysian Fields would stir memories for you that made you sad. I mean we had no choice but to hide at the castle ruin after we returned from Waterloo. That need is gone. Don't you feel a little sad seeing the old places?"

"Visiting stirs all manner of memories, not especially sad ones. Let's leave it at that. Afterward I returned and watched *Gladiator* again. I enjoy it the most of the movies I've seen so far."

"The arena Maximus fights in really exists. It's called the Coliseum, although it's mostly ruins, large sections of the stone have fallen down now."

"Another Old World ruin. That seems to be common to your time."

"Time marches on. Shall we go inside? I'm making spaghetti and we can have wine and nibblies while I see if I can make edible meatballs."

Harry opened a bottle of wine and poured while she changed clothes. He sat at the kitchen's island counter where he could watch while she prepared dinner. When she came in he gave her wine and she started laying out the ingredients for her meatballs.

"Tell me about your day? Sickness doesn't appear widespread here. How many people do you treat in a day?" Harry asked.

"We have sickness but it is generally not as deadly as in your time. Once a week Aaron Gold and I visit homes for the elderly. Aaron is the doctor who helped with my patients while I was away."

She added spices, onions, and an egg to the minced meat in the bowl.

"I remember you mentioning his name. Do a lot of old people require the two of you to help them?"

"Yes, the homes have vans to bring residents to their doctors but there's often a waiting list because of limited space for resident's special equipment."

She leaned over the counter and smiled a smile that would brighten the darkest night. "You should see their faces when we arrive. They perk up and laugh as they tell stories of their younger days."

"Doing this makes you happy. I can tell. Your face lit up as you talked about your patients there."

She nodded and went back to shaping the meatballs. "I do like visiting with the old ones even the ones who smell like mothballs. Many don't get any family or friends who visit. Aaron and I are surrogate family to them. I believe a few pretend to have physical symptoms as an excuse to come and talk with us."

"You're a good person and the kindest woman I know." What would she say if he asked her to leave? What in his world would bring such pleasure to her? Each day with her reaffirmed his worry that she needed more than love for him to find happiness there.

"Thank you." She dropped the balls into a combination of olive oil and butter she'd heated in a pan on the stove. While they cooked she filled a pan with salted water and began to heat it.

He picked up a few strips of stiff yellowish strands from the counter and broke one in two. "What are these?"

"Noodles, spaghetti noodles to be exact."

He took a bite of one of the broken pieces and spit it out into his palm. "God's teeth, that's nasty. Why are we eating these? A skinny twig tastes better."

"They will soften in the hot water and with the sauce and meatballs over them you'll see they taste nice."

"I doubt it." He joined her in the kitchen and prepared Chloe's dinner of kibble and a mystery mix of meat from a can. "If this spaghetti is nasty in spite of the sauce, I'll give mine to you," he whispered loudly to the dog.

"Trust me; you'll like spaghetti, even mine."

He stared at her profile for a long moment. "Look at me." When she turned, he cupped her face in his hands. The warmth of her cheeks heated his palms. He ran a thumb over her lips, relishing how both soft and firm they were. He committed the curve of her face to his memory, every angle, every smooth indent, in case the day came when he would leave without her.

She peered up at him through long lashes she darkened with a special wand. "What are you doing? You're staring at me."

"Appreciating how delicately beautiful you are to me."

"What a smoothie you are." She gave a finger on one hand a gentle bite and quick suck. "How about you set up a plate of cheese and crackers for us?"

"Does smoothie mean charming?"

"What do you think?"

He wrapped his arms around her, kissed her cheeks, then her nose and finally her mouth. "I think I am both."

****

The next afternoon Felicia surprised him and came home at midday. He'd just finished watching a movie called *King Arthur* and was putting the DVD in its box.

"Did you like the movie? As I recall it isn't set in your exact time in history but the setting is similar in a lot of ways," Felicia said.

"I liked it until the battle with the Saxons."

"Why didn't you like the battle?"

"War is chaos and battle is a reflection of that. But there is a strategy, a plan, and the men fight with skill. The swordsmen in the movie wielded their weapons in a topsy-turvy way bound to get them killed. Utter confusion."

"The director asked the actors to fight in a certain style to generate as much energy and excitement as possible. His goal is to entertain the audience. Historical accuracy is a victim of that desire."

"Balderdash. What a load of drivel. The battle can be performed correctly and remain exciting. By its very nature battle is exciting. The director needs a better person to instruct the actors."

"Most stunt coordinators don't possess your experience. The director shares his vision of the scene and the coordinator tries to recreate it. They're not trying to do things wrong."

He mulled the explanation over. Unconvinced he countered, "Why not learn to do the maneuvers right? As Captain of the Guard, I instructed the men in the lists as they practiced and corrected them when needed it so they honed their skills."

Harry slid a butcher knife from the wooden block. "Watch."

"Harry, don't!"

He stepped back and flipped the knife into a cutting board on the counter. It landed in the middle of the board, upright with tip sticking in the wood. "Don't what?"

"For heaven's sake, I know you're proficient without you tossing knives around in the kitchen. What if you missed and you hit Chloe?"

"Your tiny baby is eating her dinner the opposite direction of where I threw. If I'd missed, which I wouldn't, the knife would probably hit the fancy tile on the wall and bounce. I'd never put my furry little athlete at risk."

He retrieved a bowl from the cupboard and the lettuce and salad makings from the refrigerator. "Do you trust me to chop the greens? I will be wielding a knife."

"Don't be a smarty boots. Of course you can cut all the salad veggies." Felicia put a jar of her homemade dressing by the cutting board. "Since you have trained men at Elysian Fields, and Saragon, and now Chloe, which do you prefer, working with men or animals?"

An interesting question he'd never been asked before. The skilled results of both men and animals he trained were a source of pride. If he had to choose between them, he'd pick animals. "Animals but the choice is close."

"Why?"

"With the men I enjoyed seeing the knights and those in training to be knights gain a skill I helped them perfect. It's rewarding to see how different men grow."

The question awakened a flurry of memories, like

the anticipation the first time he mounted Saragon.

"That said, to develop the trust in me and the courage for battle in an animal like Saragon, gives one the feel of great accomplishment. As a prey animal it is against a horse's nature to allow a man on their back the way a predator attacks. Every cell is driven by survival instinct. Trust has to be greater than instinct to bolt or rear. Once I have that, my ability to teach them not to panic at the din of battle and the clash of steel all about them, is a talent. I know that sounds conceited but I am being honest."

"You're not being conceited. It does take a special ability to achieve that in an animal, any animal, without resorting to brutal methods. Your ability is worth bragging about. Now kiss me, my equine Lord."

****

Harry spent the morning walking to Elysian Fields. He cut through the ruin's grounds toward the river. What had been the castle vegetable and fruit garden was completely overgrown now. When he and Felicia hid there after Waterloo, some of the trees still bore a small amount of fruit. They occasionally found a bit of veggie on the vine on dying plants. Today the garden was a mass of ragged growth, trees that looked as though they hadn't born fruit in centuries, and twisted vines choking in weeds.

The long walk from the house to the ruin never bothered him. He welcomed passing the time even if it was only a simple walk. He had nothing else to do.

At the river he stripped down and swam naked in the cool water. He'd built up a sweat on the walk and the refreshing water felt good. Some things hadn't changed with time. The river flowed south from the Cambrian Mountains in Wales through the Midland shires before reaching

Chris Karlsen

Gloucester. No matter how hot the summer sun, the river never warmed much. She held onto her crisp mountain origins.

Harry swam until he tired and then lay on the shore for a while letting the sun warm him. On the walk home, he passed through the castle ruin and paused at the cornerstone of what had been the stable. The talk the night before of horses and the memories of Saragon had stayed with him all morning. Like the rest of the castle, Elysian Fields had a great stable in his time. He'd asked Felicia early on what had caused so much destruction that nothing of the buildings but broken stones from the walls and foundations remained. She said the castle had been brought down by Cromwell's cannons and fire from his army. She said there had been a vicious civil war centuries back. The Guiscard family stayed loyal and supported the king, not Cromwell. As a result, Cromwell destroyed Elysian Fields and slaughtered many of the people living there.

He knew nothing of Cromwell other than what Felicia had told him. From the little he did know, Harry thought the man should've faced the ax for his traitorous actions.

Harry had just finished showering and getting dressed when Felicia came home midday. "You're home early."

"I have a surprise for you. If you're ready, I can show you now."

"Sure. Show away."

****

Felicia drove to Alex Lancaster's stable. "Are we going riding?"

"Not exactly." She hopped out of the car and went

320

straight for the paddock.

Harry followed.

They were met my Alex and another man. "This is Bertie," Alex said and introduced Felicia and Harry. "Bertie has   a Shire and Friesian farm down the road."

Out of force of habit, Harry eyed the stallions with an evaluating eye. "They're handsome horses."

"Please, check out the conformation of each," Bertie told him.

"Why?" Harry asked uncertain of Bertie's motivation.

"I know your expertise with horses. I'd like another opinion," Alex interjected.

Harry gravitated to the Shire horse, the bigger of the two horses. He stepped up and ran his hand along the shire's topline and wide shoulders. He worked his way down from the neck to the animal's medium height wither's and then along the back. Good withers of medium height help keeping the saddle in place. A strong back can determine the length of stride and the horse's balance. From the hips, Harry felt down the shire's legs to the feathery hocks. The Shire was well-muscled with good angles.

"Can I get a pick?" Harry asked, lifting a front leg and swinging around to hold it between his knees like a farrier.

Alex pulled a hoof pick from his pocket and handed it to Harry. Harry ran the pick over the indented sides of the frog and then examined the hoof walls. He examined all four hooves in the same way. When he finished, he looked into the horse's mouth, lifting the lips to see not only the condition of the teeth but to get an idea of the animal's age.

The horse had lost a lot of baby teeth, replaced with adult molars. But he still had numerous milk teeth, which hadn't been lost to maturation.

"How old is this horse?" Harry finished checking the upper and lower teeth. "I'm guessing two."

"Just under two-and-a-half. He's had a bit of training. He's good on a lunge line and has been saddled but not had a rider on him. He also is learning to respond to vocal cues," Bertie said.

"What's his name?" Harry anticipated a grand name to match the huge horse in size.

"Blackie," Bertie said.

Harry hid his disappointment and turned to Alex. "His confirmation is excellent and his dental and hooves are in good shape. Is that what you wanted to know? He's a majestic animal. He'd have made a fine warhorse."

"What about the Friesian? He's magnificent too," Felicia said.

As he and Felicia moved to the Friesian Harry bent and whispered, "Blackie, ugh. What a dull name."

"What would you call him?"

"Maximus."

Harry repeated the examination on the Friesian. "He's another elegant and strong stallion. Hard to say one is better than the other. Is that what you wanted to know?" he asked, turning to Alex. "I thought Percherons were your breed of choice."

"They are. If you'd rather consider the chestnut you've been riding, I can bring him out."

"What do you mean, if I'd rather the chestnut?" Harry looked from Alex to Felicia. "You cannot be thinking to buy one of these for me?"

"The way you spoke of training Saragon last night, you beamed with pleasure just talking about him. I know you're bored during the day. Why not work with a young horse? We can go riding together, eventually. I'd love that. Wouldn't you?"

Harry grasped her by the elbow and pulled her to the side. "You will not do this. I do not want you to buy me a horse. I don't want you spending more money on me. You shame me in front of my friend and a stranger."

"I never meant to embarrass you. I was trying to do something nice for both of us."

Harry released her arm and went over to Alex. "Did you know what she planned, that she intended on buying me a horse?"

Alex nodded. "Yes."

"You should've known better. My lack of funds to purchase the animal myself is a humiliation. I deserve better from you."

"I am sorry, Harry. I thought this was discussed with you and you approved." Alex shot a heated glare Felicia's direction.

"It's not his fault, Harry. I didn't tell him. I wanted to surprise you," Felicia explained.

"I don't like surprises. I have never liked them and this is no exception. I'm sorry you wasted your time," Harry said to Bertie. He turned to her, his jaw tight, a small muscle in his cheek flexed. "I'm done here, Felicia. I'm going to the car."

Chris Karlsen

Chapter Twenty-One

Felicia set her purse and car keys on the hall table. Chloe rushed over, which meant Harry busied himself with other activities. Since no movie noise came from the other room, she thought he was likely on the patio.

She found him in the sitting room's large overstuffed chair nursing a scotch. A bottle of Johnnie Walker Black was on the table beside the chair. From the level of scotch left in the bottle, he'd nursed more than a few. To her knowledge this was the first time he'd tried the whiskey. She kept it on a wine table with a variety of other liquors. The scotch was her drink of choice but the rest were for guests who preferred something else.

"How do you find the scotch?" she asked and poured one for herself.

"I like this." He raised the glass as though to toast her but immediately lowered it and threw back the remaining three fingers. "The label says it is from Scotland. Aren't they the crafty ones, keeping it secret from us? I suppose it's retaliation for the trouncing Edward's grandfather gave Wallace ages ago."

"I don't think it's retaliation. As I recall, they didn't develop the means to brew it until the 1400s, some decades after your time." Felicia sat on the end of the sofa nearest to the chair. "Are you all right? You've had a substantial amount of scotch. Do you feel light-headed or foggy?"

He shook his head. "I'm none the worse for having downed half of your scotch. I'm very resilient as you, of all people, should know. I suppose I should apologize for drinking so much of your drink but it would be insincere."

"No apology necessary. Speaking of apologies, you've been awfully quiet the last two days. I realize you're still upset. I don't know how many more times I need to say I'm sorry about the horse issue. I feel like you don't believe me, but I truly did not mean to embarrass you."

"I know. Please, no more sorrys." Here set his drink on the end table. "Come sit next to me. "Aren't we supposed to kiss when one or the other has been away, even for a short duration?"

"Yes! How remiss of me."

He held out his hand. "My lap is empty, plenty of room to mess about," he suggested with a wiggle of his brows. "Hand me your drink." He set it on the table too.

She sat in his lap ready for a deep and delightful smooch. He didn't disappoint. "I missed you today," he said but his tone lost the brightness of a moment earlier and a ghost of a smile touched his lips. "I miss you more than you know and more often than I should."

She combed his hair back from his face with her fingers. "I'm not blind. Something is troubling you. If it isn't the horse business, then I wish you'd tell me what."

Harry's bright green eyes dulled. He shifted her from his lap to next to him, close so their thighs touched. He poured another three fingers of scotch and replenished what she'd sipped of hers without asking. "I had an interesting talk with Oliver today."

How'd he get to Oliver's? "You didn't walk to Oliver's did you? That's quite a hike."

"Simon and I had planned on riding. Emily came to pick me up. Instead I asked if she'd take me to Oliver's. She dropped both Simon and me off."

Oliver had warned her about Simon's interest in returning to the middle ages and how he might not be alone in that desire. To Oliver's face, she rejected the possibility Harry shared Simon's feelings—then.

Now, a terrible sense of foreboding filled Felicia. That weird sixth-sense warning that whatever comes next, she'll wish she didn't know it. She ruthlessly tamped down her fear.

"What did you talk about?" she asked in as light and lilting a tone as she could muster. Perhaps she was being silly and worrying for nothing. Perhaps.

"I'm not good with words or know how to spout flowery drivel like some courtiers. I can only tell you that I love you more than I know how to express. I hope you know my heart is yours."

There it was, the caveat said to soften what comes next. "I do."

"I've never been in love before. There is only you and will only ever be you."

Will only ever be you. She realized the declaration for the goodbye line it was. She'd slipped on ice or sidewalk debris a handful of times. In those few seconds of freefall, she was keenly aware of the ground coming at her and the inevitable pain it brings. In this moment, Harry was the ground.

"I cannot stay. There's no place for me here. I have earned my keep since I was a lad first arrived at Elysian Fields. It shames me to live off your charity—"

"Harry—"

"Allow me to finish. I love you too much to plead with you to join me not when this world, your world, is filled with wonders I never imagined. Your carriages that travel at astounding speed and even more amazing are your steel vehicles that fly. The simple pleasure of a hot shower is worthy of angels flying down from heaven to enjoy."

"Harry—"

He held his hand up for her to let him finish. "Worse than losing those wonders would be what you'd have to give up that's far more personal. You could never be a doctor. Oh, you might save a life here and there, but you'd never be more than the Captain of the Guard's talented healer-wife. It would crush your soul to silently stand back while a male physician bumbled about with our rudimentary medical abilities and potions."

He was right of course. True she was loath to give up modern conveniences. But what doctor could remain quiet while a well-intentioned medieval doctor bled a sick person in the ignorant belief blood-letting would heal them? The Hippocratic Oath all medical doctors take carries the promise of "first do no harm." She'd have to speak up. In that time and place, her interference would carry a price.

"If I hated it, would you reconsider returning to this time?" She knew the odds were slim but she had to ask.

"Probably not. If you still wish to consider coming with me, I'd be extraordinarily happy. That said, we must factor in other scenarios with due caution.

"Even though we are holding the French king for ransom, the war goes on. As a soldier, I may be sent to France on campaign. I fear for your safety if I am killed. A woman in my time without a protector is at risk."

"Even if I am a resident of Elysian Fields?" she

asked, wanting to make an informed decision. *If* she did decide to go back, she needed to know all the pros and cons.

"Not everyone there is honorable, most are, but not all. It only takes one wicked man to cause you great harm. You wouldn't be able to simply leave. The ability to return was one of the questions I had for Oliver in case you couldn't bear spending the rest of your life there."

"And?"

"No, we cannot return," he said with a small shake of his head.

"Why not?"

"Oliver fears permanent physical damage. The most anyone has gone through is twice. Although no one has observed a negative side-effect, his words not mine, he can't say they won't. He brought up Shakira Lancaster as an example."

She didn't know Shakira well but Electra's husband worked for Stephen and Alex. If there were something seriously wrong with Shakira, Electra would've said. "Did he say what worried him?"

"Apparently, she miscarried her first child. The doctors weren't sure why. Oliver is afraid it's due to her coming through the tear while she was pregnant."

"Well, he can't say for sure. Many women have miscarriages during their first trimester. If, and I'm just saying if, we were to come back here, I'd make certain I wasn't pregnant."

"Oliver was adamant. He will not risk a third transport, not until he's had time to experiment with the machine to the point where he is confident it is safe."

Felicia hadn't given the after effects much thought. She'd been too grateful to be home. She hated to admit it but

Chris Karlsen

Oliver's concern was justified. Who knows what happens to all the cells in the human body during the process of moving through centuries of time? A little damage here, a little damage there, when does the damage become irreparable?

She sipped her scotch, the amber liquor warming her throat as it went down. The deep, rich liquid tinged with what some said tasted like iodine should've been a burst of flavor. But grief stole the flavor from her. She tasted nothing when she wanted to feel nothing. Heartbreak never works out that way.

Harry put his glass on the table and did the same with hers. He took her hands in his. "You know how much I love you. Love me enough to be honest."

Freefall again. Sick to her stomach, freefall. *You must choose. Lose him or lose yourself.*

"I see the torment in your eyes." Harry brushed the hair back from her face with his fingers. He cupped her cheek and kissed her softly on the lips. "You needn't answer right now. Oliver said he won't be ready for several days. This is the most difficult decision you'll ever make. Think hard on it. Don't answer with your heart. Answer with the truth that lives within your soul."

Lose myself or lose him. The horrible choice kept her awake all night as it circled her mind again and again. Tears flowed. They rolled down her cheeks and onto her pillow. She didn't blubber but quietly wiped them away but Harry knew. "Sorry to make you cry." He grabbed his pillow and slept on the sofa.

****

The next morning Felicia told Prentice to reschedule the morning patients for that day. She'd called Emily while Harry showered and verified Emily was home and available to go to breakfast. Felicia drove to the Crippen's house and picked Emily up so they could talk in private. The last thing she wanted or needed was to have Simon enter the conversation. It was important for her to hear Emily's perspective on everyday life there over a long period of time. Felicia had a brief taste of the lifestyle but she was treated differently, like a visitor, where Emily was accepted as one of the castle folk.

Felicia chose a village restaurant frequented by locals where they'd have no problem finding a table. They sat at the far corner away from the other patrons. Emily ordered a standard English breakfast of eggs, sausage, beans, grilled tomatoes, and toast. Felicia had no appetite and settled for black coffee.

"I have a suspicion why we're here but I'll wait for you to confirm it," Emily said and squeezed lemon into her tea.

"I want to know about your life at Elysian Fields. Were you truly happy? Would you wish to stay there if Simon weren't around?"

"Ah, it is as I suspected. Simon mentioned Harry had talked about returning. He's in love with you. Obviously, he's asked you to go back with him."

Felicia nodded. "Not completely. He's given me a choice."

"I'm not sure what more I can add. You were there for a while, long enough for you and Harry to fall in love. You already have knowledge of daily life."

"The devil take me as the expression goes, we fell in love in spite of ourselves. I got a glimpse of life. You have a much better window on daily life." In spite of her lack of appetite, her stomach growled loudly watching Emily soak up runny yolk with her toast

"I see. Let me try to offer a fair assessment. It's the same for people then as now, in that it isn't all one thing or another. There are many good things about the time. But bear in mind my view is skewed by the fact I lived in an insulated environment. Living at Elysian Fields I wasn't subjected to many of the struggles of people outside the confines of the castle."

"Understood. If I hadn't been brought to the castle, I don't think I'd have survived on my own."

Emily nodded in agreement. "A woman alone is easy prey."

She was echoing what Harry had said.

Emily went on, "One thing that I hadn't expected was the pace of life. The world is far less frantic. Lord knows in this time, I loved my cell phone and didn't go anywhere without it. When put in a situation without it, I quickly found I didn't miss it as much as I thought. It's nice to walk around looking people you pass in the face. I like that they aren't obsessed with devices, staring down at phones or iPads at whatever app has them transfixed. They talk to you with words, not their thumbs.

"I can't speak for life at court. I never accompanied Simon and Richard when they went. I've heard it's a treacherous place, a place where new faces like you and I would need to go out of our way to not attract attention. Conversely, life at Elysian Fields is the opposite. The people love celebrations. You weren't there for Christmas or village fair or a visit from the young Baron. It's mad fun."

Felicia hadn't even had the opportunity to see a joust when she was at the castle. She'd love to have seen Harry compete.

"Take Christmas, for instance," Emily said. They don't fret over what gifts to give or the quality of those they receive. They're happy to enjoy a special meal, hear traveling minstrels, and just laugh along with everyone as the knights and ladies share funny stories."

Emily had put a pretty spin on life there. But in fairness, Felicia had to admit it wasn't all spin. She'd seen some of what Emily spoke of.

"I'd be lying if I didn't say I miss modern plumbing of all kinds," Emily continued with a smile. "I'm sure you did too."

"Oh yeah."

"Lordy, I wish everyone's hygiene was better. The potent odor of the unwashed can get overpowering especially in the winter when the castle's more closed. I miss books. I love to read and hate, hate, hate to needlepoint. Some days all I want to do is sit with a good book, which reminds me of how I missed television. I used to hate it!

"Harry's not alone in his unhappiness. Simon grows more depressed with each passing day. You've no idea how much the rides with Harry raise his spirits. I've tried. Nothing I say or do helps. At home he spends hours playing *Xbox History Great Medieval Battles* and *Assassin's Creed*."

Felicia thought he should be commended for venturing into the video world. She doubted Harry would bother to try it.

"Simon would go back in a heartbeat," Emily said. "I feel so guilty. Only my health keeps us here."

Felicia didn't let on she knew how deep Simon's desire was to return. "Would you really want to return if your health allowed or do you really want to stay?"

Emily nibbled on her sausages as she thought about the prospect. "I don't know," she said at last. "Coming home has rekindled my attachment to this time. The answer is yes and no. I'd go with Simon and I'd be fine. We have a pleasant enough life there. If I could lift Simon's spirits, we'd have a good life here. Good surpasses pleasant."

"At least you know Simon wouldn't be asked to go on campaign again. I don't know what I'd do if Harry were killed in battle. The thought terrifies me. I am afraid of being without him."

"You of all people should know people die from all sorts of causes. Harry could break his neck falling off his horse at any time in history. Any number of diseases can take him wherever he is in time. That fear can't be your make or break factor."

"Yes, there's no guarantee he won't keel over tomorrow from an aneurism or get hit by a car or some such thing. The difference is the safety net of support I have here."

"I have no sage advice or brilliant insight to offer you. I wish I did." She didn't touch the beans and pushed the plate to the side.

"Harry doesn't dislike life here but he feels there's no place for him. He feels lost and without purpose. He wants to contribute but can't see how."

"Simon has expressed the same. I'm desperate to help him. I have a shot-in-the-dark idea I've been pondering. Want to hear? I'd like to bounce it off you. See if you think it has legs. See if you're interested in conspiring with me."

Felicia gestured open-handed over the table. "Desperate, table for two. I'm open to any ideas."

"I'm going to talk to Esme and tell her what's

happening with Simon and Harry. Stephen and Alex gave Electra's husband a job. I'll ask Esme to talk to Alex. He has a ton of connections. Maybe he can generate jobs Simon and Harry are suited for and would like."

Felicia's instinct was to jump on the opportunity. But after Harry's reaction to her attempt to help by acquiring the horses, she wasn't sure how he'd be about her interfering again. If she didn't do something though, Harry would leave with or without her. Maybe if she didn't spring it on him. If Alex came up with a job or jobs, she'd let Harry know. He could decide if he wanted to hear the options or not.

"Well, are you in or out?" Emily asked.

"In for a penny, in for a pound. I say let's go for it. Do you want me to come with you when you talk to Esme?"

"Nah. But call Oliver and tell him to stall Harry. Oliver can use the machine as an excuse and say he's having trouble with it."

"Good idea."

By the time Felicia dropped Emily home, she felt like the weight of the world had been lifted from her. The plan might work. She had to try any and all means to keep Harry here.

Chris Karlsen

Chapter Twenty-two

The call from Emily finally came a week later. Felicia had just about given up hope. Oliver advised her he didn't know how much longer he could put Harry off. All week long Harry's mood had remained somber.

After she hung up, Felicia closed her eyes and said a silent thank you to the heavens. Alex wanted the four of them, Emily and Simon, Felicia and Harry at his house tonight for cocktails. He told Emily he had good news, if the men were interested.

Felicia joined Harry in the backyard where he was playing with Chloe. He'd become her new favorite human. Felicia was reminded of how flirtatious the women at Elysian Fields were around Harry. Apparently, females of all species adored him.

"Harry..." She took his hand and led him to the patio table. "Let's talk."

"Should I be worried? You look like a woman gathering the courage to remove a still wriggling mouse from the trap."

"I am uncertain about the news I have."

"You can tell me anything. People who love each do that or so I've been given to understand," he added with a smile.

"Straight off, let me say, I am not trying to upset

you or do anything that wounds your pride. I did something in hopes of finding a solution to the problem of staying or returning that suits both of us. So, don't get mad."

His genial smile faded. "I was at ease until you said the last. Now I'm concerned. Do go on."

"If you were offered a job that held your interest, would you be willing to stay here?"

"I suppose. Much depends on how this job was obtained for me. I've no wish to be deeply beholden to another. Being a knight in service to the Baron, is not the same as being obligated for a favor rendered that steals my dignity from me."

It was definitely a favor rendered but Felicia doubted Alex would offer anything that wounded Simon or Harry's pride. He shared their history and understood them. "The employment offered came from Alex. I don't know what it is yet, but he has positions for you and Simon. Emily sought his help. Simon, as you must know, suffers from lack of purpose-same as you. She asked if I'd like for her to speak to Alex for you as well. I took the liberty of saying yes. Stephen's career is because of Alex. I figure if Stephen could accept Alex's help, maybe you would, too."

"I make no promises but I'll listen to the offer." He drew her into his arms and kissed her on the forehead. Still holding her close he said with a long sigh, "When do we meet with Alex?"

"We're invited to cocktails this evening, along with Simon and Emily. Just hear him out. That's all I ask."

****

Alex answered the door and led Felicia and Harry to the drawing room. To Felicia's surprise, beside Emily and Simon, who she knew had been invited; Ian and his wife

Miranda were there along with Esme and Stephen. Hopefully they were there to act as reinforcements for Alex's plan.

As Felicia sat next to Emily, she took a moment to appreciate the room. Not being close friends with either Alex or Shakira, Felicia had never been inside the Lancaster's home. The drawing room was nothing like what she expected. As wealthy as the Lancasters were, she assumed Shakira had the best London interior decorators furnish the home. But the room didn't have the look of a designer's staging. Warm shades wine, green, burnished copper, and gold were throughout, none of the cold, neutral colors fashionable with designers. It radiated comfort with thick pillowed chairs and two sofas. The lighting was recessed, hidden in a trayed ceiling with an occasional porcelain lamp on tables here and there in the room.

"If I stay, I'd like to redo my plaster ceilings like this with recessed lighting as well," Felicia whispered to Emily.

"It is lovely," Emily whispered back. "Well, decorating was a nice distraction for about 30 seconds. Are you nervous? I am a wreck inside."

Felicia nodded. "I obsessed over the issue all the way here."

"Me too." She gave Felicia's hand a squeeze.

"I'm taking cocktail orders," Alex said and made each request accordingly except Harry's.

When Harry asked for a Johnnie Walker Black, Alex suggested he try the Blue Label. "It has a darker, smokier flavor. I think you might like."

"I'm game," Harry said and added, "no mixer please. I'd like it straight."

"Only way to drink it or with an ice cube or two,"

Ian said. He reached over and extended his hand to Harry. "Let me introduce myself, I'm Ian Cherlein and this is my wife, Miranda."

Harry shook hands, eyeing Ian hard. "You remind me of a man I knew long ago, the Earl of Ashenwyck. We fought together at Crecy and Poitiers."

"I knew him well too." Ian smiled. "I see the confusion in your eyes. One day I'll explain my resemblance."

One tray of appetizers sat on the large coffee table between the two sofas. Shakira came in with another tray and set it down on the same table.

"Let's bypass small talk for now and get to the heart of the matter and why we're all here," Alex said, sitting on the arm of the chair where Shakira sat.

Harry groaned softly but didn't complain aloud. He leaned into the sofa back and at least appeared willing to hear Alex out.

"Emily came to me and said you..." He looked at Simon. "And you..." He turned to Harry. "Are in need of professions that served your interest and skills in this modern time."

Neither Harry nor Simon spoke to confirm or deny the statement.

"Ian and I believe we have a solution. I'll go first. Simon, I realize you know nothing of the music industry. I am a successful music producer, that's enough to know for the time being. Stephen is one of my clients. He's a popular singer who tours the world, playing to large audiences. Right now, Electra's husband, Roger, serves as Stephen's driver and security guard. I need what we call an advance man. I'd like for you to consider filling that spot."

Emily squeezed her husband's thigh and nodded, smiling her approval of the opportunity.

"What does an advance man do?" Simon asked.

"Stephen plays large venues. You would meet with the operators of those venues ahead of his appearance and work out the details. You'd discuss location security, props, and the placement of audience members depending on the location's setup. Think of it as battle strategy without weapons."

"Say yes. It will be the two of us working side by side again, sort of," Stephen said.

Simon gestured to his blade leg. "You trust me to assist with security with my disability?"

"You're one of the most capable men I know. If you can lead men as Captain of the Guard with only a crutch, I trust you'll do just fine with your blade leg," Alex said.

Sipping his scotch, Alex shot a glance Emily's way. "Does the offer meet your criteria?" he asked Simon.

"I won't be dropped into a situation cold. You'll train me, won't you?"

"Yes, Roger and I will both work with you."

Simon turned to Emily. "What do you think?"

She stroked his hair and said, "I want you to be happy. This sounds like a wonderful opportunity."

"I'll do it," he told Alex. "Thank you for this chance."

"We'll start this coming Monday."

"Your offer doesn't sound like a two-man job," Harry said with resignation. "I don't know why I'm here."

With a sweeping motion of his hand, Alex said to Ian, "You're on."

"Now for the visual part of our program," Ian said,

playfully. A sixty-five inch television sat on a rolling stand. It had been positioned so no matter where you sat in the room you could see the screen. "Let me give you the setup first. Do you know what I do for a living?"

Harry said, "Yes. Felicia mentioned it once while we watched a History Channel program. You recreate famous battles for the station and also act as a historical advisor on movies occasionally."

"That's right. With the popularity of television series like, *Game of Thrones*, *Vikings*, and *Knightfall*, battle scenes using medieval weapons and tactics are in high demand. The reenactments are done by people called stuntmen in addition to the lead players. They rely on stunt coordinators to show them how to use the weapons and to establish the setting in a realistic way. Let me play some of the scenes for you so you have an idea what I'm talking about."

Ian played a cut from all three shows where a battle was involved. As the scenes played, he continued. "You can see, the programs need men on foot and fighting on horseback. Because of the high demand, stunt coordinators are engaged for months ahead. The man I used the most, Terry Gatcombe, is pretty good but he's difficult to schedule."

"He's a wanker. No loss if you never use him again," Miranda interjected.

Ian winked at his wife and then told Harry, "Miranda can't stand the man, as you can tell. He is a wanker but also good at stunts."

He moved to another scene. "There are also times when tactics are needed for defense of a castle or in this next case the walls of a city. This is from *Kingdom of Heaven.*

The lead knight is trying to defend Jerusalem against Saladin's Saracen army."

A scowl crept across Harry's face as he watched. A couple moments into the scene he stood and went to the television. "May I touch the screen?"

"Feel free," Ian said.

"This is where the lead knight—" He pointed to Orlando Bloom. "Has deployed his men poorly." He pointed to a part of the city walls. "Here is the weakness in the walls. This is the focal point of Saladin's trebuchets. That is where they'll breech the wall. The knight needs to redeploy his men sooner to contain the attackers."

Felicia saw Ian and Alex exchange a knowing smile. "This is why I would like your expertise," Ian told Harry.

When Ian's scenes finished and he shut the television off, Harry looked from the screen to Ian. "Are you asking me to be a stunt coordinator?"

"I am."

"You've never seen me use a sword or fight on horseback or defend castle walls. I was merely voicing my opinion on the knight's tactics. How do you know I'll be capable?"

Ian smiled again. "Oh but I have. I'll explain one day. For now let me say I trust in your skill by virtue of the fact you replaced Simon as Captain of the Guard. You wouldn't be put in that position if you weren't excellent in all manner of fighting."

He raised his glass for Alex to refill it. "What do you say, Harry?"

Felicia sent more silent pleadings to any god or angel listening: *Please, please, please let him see this is a great opportunity and not charity.*

Harry paused before answering. Felicia suspected he was formulating questions that made him hesitate. "Is this just one job or will there be more, enough for a man to make a living?"

"Absolutely."

"And the pay?"

"Excellent, you'll be pleasantly surprised."

Felicia wanted desperately to put her two pence in but didn't dare. As it was, all eyes were on Harry. This had to be his decision alone. If he truly wanted to remain here and only desired a purpose he could be proud to serve, then he'd say yes.

"I know what you wish for me," Harry said to her.

"I'd be lying if I denied that I prefer you to stay."

"I notice you said, 'you' not us. Your heart is here."

"My heart is with you, but my desire is for us to lead the best life has to offer here," Felicia admitted.

"If it makes a difference, I forgot to mention, you won't be demonstrating only weaponry," Ian added. "You'll be showing men how to joust too."

Harry perked up. "Jousting too? I was a champion."

"I know," Ian said.

"I like this profession you're offering—very much." Harry hugged Felicia close and bent her just enough to kiss her. "Looks like you're stuck with me. I never truly wanted to leave. I believe you're right. We can live the best of lives here."

He eased his hold around her shoulders. "I'd be proud to serve you, Ian."

"We need to toast. I'm refreshing everyone's drink," Alex gathered glasses. "How do you like that Blue,

Harry?"

    "I like everything about tonight."

Chris Karlsen

Epilogue

Harry came home with his arms full of flowers. He'd been at the new job for two weeks and thoroughly enjoying himself. He hadn't had to go on a location shoot yet but that was scheduled in the near future. In the meantime, Ian had him at the studio discussing what was needed for the upcoming episode. Every night Harry returned with a report on what they'd done that day. Felicia hadn't seen him so happy and excited since they arrived back in the modern world.

"Did Ian give *you* the flowers or are those stunning stems for me?" she asked.

"Silly lady. Flowers for me? Please. These are all for you. Why do you wonder?" He didn't give Felicia a chance to respond. "When need to celebrate the surprise I have for you. Put these in water and then grab your purse. Your surprise awaits us."

"Where am I taking us?" Felicia asked and started the car.

"To Alex's stable."

Would Harry have purchased the Shire and Friesian? How? He was paid a good salary but hadn't made enough money yet to buy expensive horses.

When they arrived the Shire and Friesian were tacked up and tied to the rail outside the stable's barn. Owen the stable manager and Bertie the horse's owner standing nearby.

"You can't have bought these horses," Felicia said, exiting the car.

He ignored her statement. "We're going to ride them around the arena and test their gaits. I already long-lined them in the round pen. They looked smooth at all three gaits and transitioning. But, best to ride to know for sure."

"Hello Owen, Bertie," Felicia said. "I understand you'll let us try the boys out."

Bertie patted the Shire on the rump. "I expected no less. I've never sold a horse yet that wasn't ridden beforehand. This Friesian isn't the one you saw the other week. This one's a gelding. He's displayed a kinder nature than the stallion. He'll be easier to work with."

Felicia poked Harry in the ribs. "You should've told me. I'd have changed into my riding boots and jodhpurs."

"It's only a test ride. You'll be fine in your trainers. Do you want a leg up?" Harry asked.

"No." Felicia had been riding since childhood. She untied the gelding and quietly spoke to him as she stroked his cheek, then his neck and along his back. The horse showed no sign of fear or distrust and she mounted him with ease. "What's his name?"

"His papers say Charlemagne but we call him Charlie at the farm," Bertie said.

"Let's see if we suit each other, shall we Charlie?"

Harry had mounted Blackie. The stallion hadn't shown any aggression toward Charlie, so Harry followed him into the arena.

Charlie and Blackie proved to be excellent mounts. At Felicia's light cue, Charlie transitioned like a horse riding on silky sand. Even with Blackie's limited training, Harry appeared to have no issues getting him to respond.

Felicia caught up with Harry and trotted next to him. "I'm happy with Charlie. I don't need to ride him longer. I'm getting off."

She left the arena with Harry right behind. After dismounting, Felicia took Harry by the arm and pulled him aside out of Bertie's hearing. "They're beautiful animals, both of them. But how do you intend to pay for them. I'm not trying to be a wet blanket but you can't have made enough money yet."

"Bertie has agreed to let me make payments, which is good. Alex is letting us board them here for free and I've already had a brass plate made for the stall with the name Maximus. I have another surprise for you at home, if you're ready to go."

"I'm ready. I'm very curious about this next surprise, how about a hint?" She asked as she climbed into the car.

"No hints. You'll know soon enough."

When they reached home Felicia practically leapt from the car. She blocked his path as he started up the walkway. "One hint, just one. Is it animal, mineral or vegetable?"

"What?"

"Never mind. Just tell me this, is it in the house?"

"You'll see. Open the door, please."

She did and he stepped inside. Immediately taking her hand he led her to the sitting room. Chloe went into her typical happy you're home mad dash and spin, her prelude for a welcome home treat.

"Not now Chloe," Harry said and she miraculously obeyed.

"Stand here." Harry maneuvered Felicia so she faced him. Then he knelt the way medieval heroes do in paintings when they're being knighted, one knee touching the floor, one leg bent at the knee. He reached into his pocket and removed a small velvet box and extended his hand. "Would you honor this old-world man by becoming my wife? And unless you object, I'd like you to consider Charlie an engagement gift."

"I'd love to be the wife of a chivalrous, old world gentleman like yourself."

"Once a knight always a knight," he said with a wink. "Do I have your permission to rise milady?"

"Of course, how else can you kiss me, milord? So get up and kiss me." He gave her a long lingering kiss, a kiss no other man could hope to master. She was sure of it.

When she could breathe again, she opened the box. The ring inside was a wide band of gold filigree. "It's beautiful, Harry."

She slipped it on her finger and hugged Harry tight, then kissed him again. They'd pretended to be husband and wife all their time traveling from Waterloo back to Gloucester. Now, there was no need for pretense. She was living the fantasy of marrying a knight in shining armor. In his time, she'd be Lady Felicia. In this time, she was over-the-moon happy to be Mrs. Harold Quarles.

"I'll get you a nicer ring for our wedding," Harry said, kissing the back of her fingers.

"Harry, I love you so much. I'd be happy with a cigar band."

"Cigar band? Will I ever understand all your strange language?"

"We have a lifetime for you to learn."

About the Author

Chris Karlsen

I was born and raised in Chicago. My father was a history professor and my mother was, and is, a voracious reader. I grew up with a love of history and books.

My parents also love traveling, a passion they passed onto me. I wanted to see the places I read about, see the land and monuments from the time periods that fascinated me. I've had the good fortune to travel extensively throughout Europe, the Near East, and North Africa.

I am a retired police detective. I spent twenty-five years in law enforcement with two different agencies. My desire to write came in my early teens. After I retired, I decided to pursue that dream. I write three different series. My paranormal romance series is called, Knights in Time. My romantic thriller series is Dangerous Waters. The newest is The Bloodstone Series. Each series has a different setting and some cross time periods, which I find fun to write.

I currently live in the Pacific Northwest with my husband and four wild and crazy rescue dogs.

Knights in Time

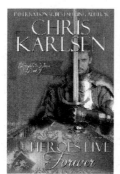 

Heroes Live Forever, Journey in Time, and Knight Blindness are three romances that take the reader into a world filled with heart-warming heroes and heroines. Theirs are stories where heartbreak and danger is faced with courage. They're stories of how love is stronger than any challenge. Each mixes history and the modern world where the settings are brought vividly to life.

You can find more stories such as this at www.bookstogonow.com

If you enjoy this Books to Go Now story please leave a review for the author on Amazon, Goodreads or the site which you purchased the eBook. Thanks!

We pride ourselves with representing great stories at low prices. We want to take you into the digital age offering a market that will allow you to grow along with us in our journey through the new frontier of digital publishing.
Some of our favorite award-winning authors have now joined us. We welcome readers and writers into our community.

We want to make sure that as a reader you are supplied with never-ending great stories. As a company, Books to Go Now, wants its readers and writers supplied with positive experience and encouragement so they will return again and again.

We want to hear from you. Our readers and writers are the cornerstone of our company. If there is something you would like to say or a genre that you would like to see, please email us at inquiry@bookstogonow.com

Made in the USA
San Bernardino, CA
24 October 2018